# Murder in the Fast Lane

## A Jason Hunter Thriller

## Natasha Orme

To Fanny
I hope you enjoy it!
Natasha

First edition 2023

ISBN 978-1-7394505-1-9 (paperback)

ISBN 978-1-7394505-0-2 (ebook)

# CONTENTS

To Lee, for all your love and support.

# THE GUNMAN

## HUNGARIAN GRAND PRIX

*Sunday 26th July*

He watched Stacey James as she stepped onto the podium, adjusting his position while peering down the scope of his L115A3 sniper rifle. Stacey had finished a mere 2.86 seconds behind the winner, and was smiling about it. She stood with the first and third position winners, waving to the adoring fans. A sense of satisfaction slowly spread through his body; a feeling he would only allow himself to savour in these few moments - a selfish indulgence.

He let out a slow breath and examined the track. Heat waves rose from the tarmac. A bead of sweat trickled down his face and his shirt felt sticky. A slow, calm inhale caused the shirt to tug against his damp skin. The barrel of the rifle moved ever so slightly to refocus on his target.

It was all about timing.

The race winner was handed a magnum of Champagne by a race official. He shook it hard and then popped the cork, sending a spray of bubbles over all of them. Stacey's squeal could be heard even from this distance.

He let out a long exhale through pursed lips.

Thick strands of blonde hair were now plastered to Stacey's face by the sticky champagne as she desperately tried to make herself presentable for the photographers. Her innocence and naivety only sweetened the deal. Alongside the £2.5 million currently sitting in his bank account. Once the job was done, all he had to do was text the burner number to claim the rest.

He watched the celebrations. A crowd of microphone-wielding reporters clambered forward like hungry jackals, all wanting to cover this story, to have their own moment of glory. They would definitely get more than they bargained for. He almost smiled. The crosshairs followed Stacey's every move as she laughed and soaked up the moment.

He didn't care for Formula One and so he was oblivious to the fact that this was the tipping point in Stacey's career. This was the moment where she became a real threat to those at the top.

He inhaled once again, held his breath, then lightly squeezed the trigger until he could feel the spring begin to protest - the final moment before things would change. He gently pulled the trigger the rest of the way as his body tensed and braced against the sharp recoil. The rifle slammed into his shoulder but the adrenaline coursing through his system held it steady, guaranteeing a clear shot through Stacey's skull.

Stacey's head snapped back as the bullet slammed into her forehead. Brain matter and blood sprayed across the wall as her body crumpled into a heap on the podium. Her head twisted at an awkward angle on one of the steps, facing the crowd. The reaction was instant. Spectators screamed. They tried to push themselves away from the podium, trampling anyone in their way. The other drivers stood motionless, staring in horror. Paramedics and police, with weapons drawn, swarmed the scene.

He exhaled but didn't move. Instead, he watched as all hell broke loose.

After a few moments, he placed the rifle on the ground next to him, exchanging it for the high-powered binoculars. Peering down at Stacey's body, he smiled. Lifeless blue eyes stared up from either side of a neat, circular bullet hole in her head.

# Chapter 1

## JASON HUNTER

### LONDON OFFICE

*Sunday 26th July*

"Is this supposed to be a fucking joke?"

The tall blonde with waist-length hair stormed through the double swing doors into the open-plan office. Two thick-set, intimidating men followed her, both wearing suits and struggling to keep up. "I fucking told him. I did. Did he listen? No! I swear to God when I get my hands on him..." The bodyguards didn't answer.

Trailing somewhere behind the bodyguards was a smaller woman carrying a clipboard, her shuffling steps doing little to keep up with the long, elegant strides of the woman in front of her. I almost laughed as they approached, except I was pretty sure a whirlwind was about to hit me at full force.

Simon, a small and bespectacled man always wearing a wrinkled suit, graciously tried to step in before her, but was shoved aside. I don't know why he even bothered. It wasn't like he was going to be able to help. Or maybe he just wanted to act as a buffer. Stacey was my client, after all. My responsibility.

This wasn't something I wanted to deal with; not now, not ever. I adjusted the silver-plated photo frame on my desk, carefully arranged my pens in the desk tidy that Lily had made me for my birthday, and then took a deep breath.

The blonde didn't wait for the courtesy of one of her guards, instead she yanked open my door herself and made a beeline for me, jabbing a finger in the air. "You had one fucking job!"

The two bodyguards and the podgy little PA followed. The large office suddenly felt unusually cramped and claustrophobic. I tried to smile, and looked pleadingly at the two oversized pieces of muscle flanking the PA. They exchanged a glance over the top of the woman's head before looking apologetically back at me.

I gave a slight nod before returning my attention to the full five foot ten, lean, athletic build of Stacey James across my desk. She was dressed in faded blue, skin-tight jeans, a leather bomber jacket and black, heeled boots.

"Stacey," I said, desperately trying to calm the storm. "Stacey." I could see the PA wince in sympathy out of the corner of my eye.

"Don't fuck with me, Jason. I drove in the most important race of my career today, hopped on a plane like some dog with its tail between its legs, then I switched on the fucking news. Gemma is dead, Jason! What the fuck happened?!" Her voice was increasing in pitch, but I could still hear the dangerous edge in her tone, warning me to tread carefully.

I kneaded the bridge of my nose to try and ease the migraine building behind my eyes. "Stacey, please." Everything went silent. I looked up in surprise. She stood with her arms crossed, glaring at me. I cringed. "What do you want me to do? Gemma knew what she was doing. As long as you're alive, that means we're doing our job and, ultimately, that's the most important thing." My voice was emotionless, but it was too late to correct it.

Stacey's jaw physically dropped. "That's what's important? That's what's important?! You heartless –"

The door to my office opened again, and Adam walked in. "Stacey," he said, authority ringing in his tone. I rolled my eyes. "Why don't you come into *my* office so we can discuss this further?" His voice had that diplomatic edge that he used exclusively for fixing things. He held the door open and gestured for Stacey to leave. He was smiling but his eyes were deadly. Man, I was in trouble. Stacey shot one last look at me before storming out of the room. My boss turned and pointed a finger at me. "This isn't over, do you hear me?" I nodded but he'd already left, the two bodyguards and the PA trailing slowly behind.

Adam wasn't my favourite person. We disagreed on just about everything. He had a business to run and I had a job to do. Unfortunately, that meant we were often stepping on each other's toes. It didn't help that Adam was one of the most territorial men I had ever met. The guy was just such a *cock*.

I turned away from my desk and looked out of the floor to ceiling windows. The sun was just setting across London, peeking out from behind the tall and irregular shapes that now defined the city's skyline. I walked up to the window and looked down onto the street below. There was the usual hustle and bustle of commuters, tourists and Londoners.

A red double-decker pulled away from the pavement, leaving a collection of wide-eyed people glancing around, trying to work out where they needed to go. Those familiar with the city pushed through them impatiently.

Nestled in the back doorway of an office block next to the bus stop was a homeless man. He sat huddled in his sleeping bag with an old, dirty cap on the floor in front of him.

"Jason," Lucy said, jolting me from my thoughts. I turned around, startled to see her peering around my office door. "The boss wants –" she stopped, frowning at me. "You okay?"

"Yeah, yeah," I said, gathering myself together. I wiped a hand over my face. "What did you say?"

"The boss wants to see you."

"Great," I muttered, glancing down at the homeless man again before leaving. The office was almost empty. I glanced at my watch, surprised to see that it was past 6pm. There was normally a low humming of machinery that filled the room, but instead it was blanketed in silence.

I knocked on the door and entered. Adam was sitting behind his Apple Mac, frowning. He moved the mouse frantically, relentlessly clicking.

"Come in," he said without even looking up. I stepped forward and closed the door. Adam looked up at the projection board on the far wall. I followed his gaze and saw that he'd brought up Stacey's file. "Sit down, Jason," he said, picking up his clicker. He pointed it at the projection board. "What do you see there?" he asked.

"Money," I sighed. I knew what was going to come next.

He waved a hand towards the door. "We're done here. I can't have you on the team anymore."

"What?" I looked at Adam, shocked, but his attention was back on his Mac. This new tactic worried me. "Is that it?"

Adam looked up at me with a strange expression that I couldn't read. "Gemma died today, Jason. You need to face the consequences."

He held my gaze and a heavy weight settled on my chest. I suddenly couldn't breathe. I nodded with a swift jerk and turned to leave.

"Wait," I said, something on the board catching my eye. I walked over to it. "Who's that?" I asked, pointing to a mugshot of a man. He had a wide angular jaw, dark brown eyes and short hair cropped close to his skull. Adam looked up, interlocked his fingers and rested his hands on the desk.

"That is Captain B.A. Cooper. Served four years, did a tour in Afghanistan and Iraq. Was diagnosed with severe PTSD. Spent 18 months in an institute receiving therapy. Was released into the world six months ago." Adam fired this information at me as if he was being tested.

"So where does he fit in all this?"

"He's Stacey's ex."

"What?" I turned and looked at Adam, the shock clear on my face. "And you never thought to tell me this?" I could feel the anger bubbling inside of me. All I could think of was Gemma. I would never have put her on the podium if I had known this.

*Was this even my fault?*

"It was in the file." I could see his eyes become unfocused, as if he was looking right through me. It was the same reaction he always had when someone became confrontational.

"Don't you *dare* fob me off. I read that file the moment it was in the system and there was no fucking PTSD ex-boyfriend!"

*Shit. Was Adam responsible? Had he deliberately not told me?*

"Jesus Christ, Jason! Don't make this about you," he said dismissively.

I couldn't take my eyes off him as I felt the heat rising up my neck. How could I possibly make it about me? This whole fucking catastrophe was about Gemma. I clenched my jaw so hard my muscles began to ache. I opened my mouth to retaliate but I just didn't trust myself, so I left.

Back in my office, I brought up Stacey's file and went through the details. Adam had been right. The section on Cooper was definitely there.

*Why had Adam signed off on Gemma being a body double if he knew about Cooper? How could he have given the go-ahead?*

*More importantly...how had I missed this?*

Questions crowded into my skull as I tried to think back to the day he'd signed the paperwork.

He had been a bit hesitant and had quizzed me about the whole operation. *Fuck.* I looked back at the file on my screen. Adam had covered pretty much all the basics about this Captain Cooper but he had left out the finer points; born in Sheffield, graduated Cardiff University with a 2:1 in engineering, considered an excellent marksman and had a passion for sports.

I stopped and went back over what I had just read. An excellent marksman. Alarm bells were beginning to ring in my head. He'd won trophies and everything. This guy could be a serious threat. Hell, this guy could have killed Gemma. *Fucking hell, why hadn't I seen this before?* I studied the mugshot again, committing his face to memory. Every line, every detail. Now that I really looked at him, something was familiar.

I scanned the initial application form. Stacey had requested personal protection after she'd become adamant she wasn't doing public appearances again. Several threats had been made to her via creepy phone calls, emails and letters. She'd been constantly looking over her shoulder, scanning the faces in every crowd, looking for whoever was targeting her. In the end, her PA had suggested personal protection as a precaution, with the hope that we could put a stop to the torment. I leaned back in my chair, let out a deep sigh and stared out the window.

I watched the slow rotating wheel of the London Eye, letting it lull me into a daze.

The phone on my desk buzzed, bringing me sharply back to reality. I pressed the answer button.

"I have a potential client on the line," said Lucy's tinny voice through the speaker. "He says he'd like to talk to you about some personal protection. Asked for you specifically. Shall I bring put him through?"

"No, not today. Schedule him for an appointment tomorrow. I'm going home."

"Consider it done."

"Oh and Lucy, once you've done that, I want you to go home too." I could hear the smile in her voice as she said her goodbye.

# Chapter 2

## DIANE PARSONS

### SOMEWHERE IN LONDON

*Sunday 26th July*

Diane fidgeted. The noise was unbearably loud and her stomach was twisting itself into such tight knots she thought she was going to be sick.

The bouncers on the door to the club had let her in without even taking her name. This went beyond an exclusive guest list. She scanned the crowd of faces, desperately looking for Volkov but the strobe lighting made it almost impossible to make out anyone's features.

A large hulking figure appeared at her side, grabbed her elbow and steered her away from the dance floor and into a back room. She felt small and insignificant next to him, his hulking frame dwarfing her.

He left the room, holding the door for Volkov to walk through.

"Dima," she breathed desperately. "What have you done?"

"Done? I did what you asked." His voice was thick with his Russian accent. He smoothed his hair back and stared blankly at her.

"I didn't ask you for anything." Her voice cracked and she could feel the panic bubbling over inside her.

"Sssh." He approached her and embraced her. She clung to him and gasped for air.

Another figure appeared in the room. This man was shorter than Volkov and looked stocky compared to his lithe frame.

"Allow me to introduce Mr Gromov," said Volkov, pulling away from the hug and gesturing towards the other man. "He is my patron, my investor. He has been like a father to me."

"I...I remember Mr Gromov."

Diane could feel her knees trembling. She felt like she was falling into a bottomless pit, and she would never be able to climb out. The music from the dance floor reverberated in the walls, making the space feel claustrophobic. She couldn't breathe.

"I need-"

Her knees gave way.

Volkov dashed forwards and caught Diane before she hit the ground. He guided her across the room and lowered her into a chair.

Gromov also crossed the room and seated himself on a nearby plush sofa that she hadn't noticed until now. The stress had made her blind to her surroundings and now she looked around at the elaborately decorated room. Dark, plush purple velvet was everywhere. Cushioned sofas lined the walls, with a few armchairs scattered in the middle, one of which she sat in now.

"I...I'm sorry," she stammered. "I believe there's been a misunderstanding."

Gromov frowned. Volkov glanced anxiously in his patron's direction.

"Please, continue," said Gromov.

"I...I...I didn't." She swallowed. "I didn't want you to kill her," she whispered, her eyes darting around the room and toward the door.

"What is she talking about?" asked Gromov.

Volkov ignored the older man, as understanding dawned on him.

"You asked me for help?" he said.

"No, no," croaked Diane. "I didn't ask for anything. I was drunk. I was just...she can be a bitch to work for sometimes. I just wanted to offload."

Volkov slowly shook his head. "You don't remember, do you?"

Diane didn't respond. She was afraid of the answer, of what she was about to be told.

"You were complaining. I offered you help. You said you wished that life was easier, that she wouldn't be so hard on you. I asked if you wanted me to have a word with her."

Diane swallowed hard, unable to remember what she had said, but knowing from the sick feeling in her gut that what he said was true.

"You asked me if I could get rid of her," Dima continued quietly.

Diane shook her head, unwilling to believe it.

"I asked if you were sure. I asked if killing her would really be the answer." Volkov paused. "You said yes." Volkov looked towards Gromov.

He spoke in quick Russian.

Diane's eyes flicked between the two men as she tried to understand what was going on.

Volkov shrugged. Gromov got up from his seat and began pacing.

He spoke again in Russian and then switched back to English, "We now have an issue."

Diane blinked.

"This miscommunication has cost us. You see, Dima here did not phrase himself correctly when he spoke to me. He did not make me aware that this was on behalf of a...friend. He did not explain the situation to me as he should have done, and therefore there has been this miscommunication.

"However, a man has done his job as instructed. He has been paid the money he was owed, and that now leaves me out of pocket."

Diane nodded, unsure of where this was going.

"You are indebted to me. And you will have to work hard to pay off this debt."

"How...how much?"

"£5 million."

"Million?" Diane's mouth gaped open. She tried to process what he was saying but it was just too much. How could this have happened?

"Yes, million. Taking a life is a costly business." Gromov stopped pacing as he continued to think. "I want you to go home. The time will come when we will require your services, and you will be contacted."

With that, Gromov left.

Volkov slumped onto one of the plush sofas and covered his face with his hands.

"How...how...?" he looked up at Diane, who still sat motionless. "After everything I've ever done for you, this is how you repay me?" The bitterness in his voice made Diane flinch. She tried to reach out and touch her friend's arm but he yanked it back.

"You asked me," he said. "You asked me to deal with her."

"I didn't mean...I don't know what I was saying," she stammered helplessly.

"Fucking hell, Diane. You asked me!"

"I can't remember." The seriousness of the situation hit her and she burst into tears. "I don't know what happened. I was so drunk. I was high. I can't even remember getting home, being here. I don't know where I was or what happened."

"Shit." Volkov stood up and aimed a kick at one of the chairs, narrowly missing. "Shit, shit, shit!"

"I'm sorry."

"Sorry? This is my career on the line. Do you know what he'll do to me if I fuck it up now? If I fuck it up because of you?"

Diane shook her head.

"He'll kill me. I'm a dead man."

"I-"

"Just get out," said Volkov with a resigned sigh.

Diane didn't move.

"You better think of a way to come up with £5 million, otherwise you're screwed." He didn't even look at her as he spoke, his voice a flat monotone.

Her journey home was uneventful. She tried thinking back to last week; she remembered arriving at Volkov's place with the party already in full swing. She'd said hi to those she knew and had helped herself to a drink at the bar.

They'd left for the nightclub at some point, but she couldn't remember if that had been before or after the cocaine. Stacey had been a real bitch that morning, had belittled her in front of everyone at the press meeting, had yelled at her after lunch and then thrown a vase halfway across her apartment when Diane had told her one of the sponsorships was considering pulling out.

It had been a hell of a day. Stacey's behaviour was getting out of hand. Sure, she'd probably bitched and whined about how much of a pain in the ass Stacey was, but ask someone to kill her? No. Surely not?

She might have asked for Volkov's help, but she wouldn't have asked him to kill her, at least not outright. But she must have said something for him to interpret it that way.

Her mind flitted back to the conversation just half an hour earlier. If Gromov was going to hold her accountable, she was in a lot of trouble.

# Chapter 3

## Jason Hunter

### Home

*Sunday 26th July*

I sat on my sofa in the dark. I didn't have the heart to turn the lights on - that seemed too cheerful. Instead, I nursed my beer and propped my legs up on the coffee table.

As my eyes adjusted to the dark, I was confronted with familiar surroundings. The usually teal walls had turned to a dark and oppressive green. Framed photographs scattered the opposite wall. Even from here I could make out Max and Lily's smiles. Further along the wall was my old, antique bookshelf. I'd found it at a car boot and instantly fell in love. It had all the character and worn edges of a lifelong partner and it carried my most prized possessions; a collection of signed novels, first editions, limited editions. Every one of them had been read at least five times. I looked over at the large flat-screen TV that stood on the glossy black and white unit and considered turning it on.

This morning's newspaper lay discarded on the coffee table and I willed myself to pick it up, leaf through the pages, even attempt the crossword, but my heart wasn't in it.

Gemma's face came to the front of my mind. I fought back tears. She'd been so young. 6 months after she'd graduated from the University of Winchester with a first in Criminology, I approached her, asking if she would be a body double for Stacey. She was over the moon; she said it was like being James Bond. She'd spent a week training with Sam before I'd allowed her out on her first assignment – a trip down the red carpet.

She'd loved every second, and it was then I realised there was no one better for the job. I'd been considering offering her full-time work once Stacey no longer needed her.

The first time she came into the office, she'd made me laugh. Came through the door all smiles and sweetness, dressed in skin-tight jeans and a chequered shirt. Her dark brown hair was pulled into a ponytail and she was chewing gum, almost obnoxiously. But there was something in her mannerisms that just made her seem...at home. His thoughts wandered back to their last encounter.

*"How do I look?" Gemma asked.*

*"Like Stacey James." I smiled like a proud father.*

*Gemma was dressed in Stacey's overalls. Her hair had already been dyed blonde and extensions had been added. Stacey had helped where she could to make Gemma look as much like her as possible. She'd even asked her makeup artist to step in. It had taken a while. Putty had been moulded to her cheekbones and jaw to make them more prominent, more like Stacey's.*

*After the success of the red carpet event, and several other public appearances, it was time for Gemma to step up and do what she was paid to do. For the last few months, Stacey had vehemently refused to get on the podium after a race. Her team manager at Red Bull had stepped in and excused her, but it was starting to look bad. Today though, would be the first time 'Stacey' was back in the public eye.*

*Stacey kissed Gemma on the cheek and then left through the back door where there was a car waiting to take her to the airport. I would follow her in a matter of minutes but I wanted to have a few last words with Gemma. The next time I'd see her would be on English soil. She spat out her gum and slipped on her boots.*

*"Am I a good enough match?" she asked a little nervously.*

*"You know you don't have to do this if you don't want to," I said quietly.*

*"Oh, give over, that's not what I meant. I just don't want people getting suspicious."*

*"Yes, you look fine."*

*She nodded. "Good. Now, piss off. I'll see you in the office tomorrow."*

*I clapped her on the shoulder. "Remember to test your earpiece before you go out there."*

*"I think I'm getting the hang of this, you know?" she smirked.*

*"Go on," I nodded towards the door. "See you tomorrow."*

*"See ya, boss," she said over her shoulder, already walking away from me.*

The image that stuck in my mind was of her walking out with the red and white helmet tucked under her arm. Gemma's own mother would have hardly recognised her.

My heart sank. Gemma's mother would never see her again. I'd overheard Adam on the phone in his office just before I left for the day. The police had already informed Gemma's parents but they needed someone to blame. And that someone was probably going to be him or, more specifically, me.

About an hour before Stacey had stormed into the office, Lucy had popped her head around my office door.

"I think you want to turn the news on," she said. I didn't really register the look on her face and I didn't remember her coming all the way in but the next thing I knew, I was looking at the latest headlines and Lucy was squeezing my hand.

A news anchor, sitting behind a desk, announced the death of Stacey James to the world, running through a list of her accomplishments and offering his condolences to her family. I was one of the few people who knew it wasn't Stacey, and mourned the death of the real girl.

The phone rang and I jolted, pulled from my thoughts. The screen on my mobile had lit up and it was vibrating on the coffee table, making an awful sound on the wood veneer. I picked it up without even checking the caller ID.

"Well, you're certainly not easy to get hold of, are you? I've called and called today but that snotty-nosed assistant – Lana, or whatever her name is – kept blowing me off, saying you were busy or something. I bet she was just trying to get rid of me, I swear she just wants you all to herself. One of these days she'll come right out and ask you for sex..."

I took a deep breath, closed my eyes and rubbed my forehead before I interrupted the ramblings of my ex-wife.

"What do you want, Adrianna?"

"Charming, aren't you? God knows what I saw in you. Sometimes I wonder and wonder and I just can't remember. I mean, there must have been something there to start with, surely, otherwise I wouldn't have gone through it all but now you're just like a different person, someone –"

"Adrianna! What do you want?"

"There's no need to be rude. I wanted to know whether you were still having your children tomorrow. I have plans."

The frostiness in her voice almost made me feel guilty, but I'd put up with enough of her shit over the years.

"Yes, I'll come pick them up around nine."

"I'm sorry, that's not early enough. You'll have to be here before eight."

"Fine."

"And you need to remember to –"

I hung up.

# Chapter 4

## JASON HUNTER

### HOME

*Monday 27th July*

A heavy pounding brought me to my senses. I opened my eyes and squinted at the ceiling. My tongue felt like sandpaper stuck to the roof of my mouth and my throat had never felt so dry. The thought of sitting up made my stomach queasy.

Boy, I did not feel good. My head was all over the place and felt like it was being pricked by a million tiny needles.

The noise that had woken me sounded again, and this time I realised what it was. A fist banging on my front door.

"Jason?!" came the shrill voice of Adrianna. I groaned as I painfully dragged my body from my bed. I was unsteady on my feet as I descended the stairs and the memories of last night came rushing back. Stacey's file sat untouched on the kitchen counter as I'd drank one beer after another in the hope of forgetting Gemma's face. But it hadn't worked. I'd been desperate. Once the beer was gone, I'd moved onto the vodka.

Stumbling into the kitchen, I was confronted with the sight of cans everywhere. They littered the kitchen counter and lay scattered on the floor. I peered into the living room, confirming my suspicions that it would be just as bad.

"Jason!" Adrianna pounded relentlessly on the door again. My head felt like it was going to explode. I scrunched up my eyes and held my head with my hands.

"Alright, alright!" I shouted. I didn't have time to clear up so I made my way into the hallway, trying not to trip over the obstacles on the floor.

I yanked the door open to see Adrianna dressed up; strappy high heels, tight jeans, a top that revealed far too much cleavage, and a Gucci handbag sitting in the crook of her arm whilst she held out a meticulously manicured hand decorated with diamond encrusted rings. She was pouting at me with that stern look I knew too well.

"I have been standing here for what feels like a century, Mister! When I said eight o'clock, I meant eight o'clock. I don't have time to be running all over the place dropping them off because you can't be bothered to get out of bed. And it's nearly nine by the time you finally drag your half-dressed self down here to answer the door. I mean, seriously, Jason?"

"Oh, leave it alone, Adrianna. There's more to life than pretty nails and shoes –"

"Are you hungover?" She leaned in close to my face and sniffed. "My God, your breath stinks. What the hell? You're a mess. I'll take the children to my sister's -"

"No! I'm fine, Adrianna. Honestly. I just need a shower."

She paused and looked at me sceptically. "And brush your teeth."

I nodded.

"Daddy!"

I looked past Adrianna to see Lily and Max running up the pavement toward me with huge smiles on their faces.

"Hey guys," I said, holding out my arms. They ran into me and I hugged them tight.

"Right, give mummy kisses," said Adrianna. She bent down and tapped her cheek. Lily and Max let go of me to kiss their mother. "They're going to stay the night, okay?" She indicated a small holdall down by her feet.

"Of course. Party!" I said and began to dance. The kids cheered.

"No, no, no!" said Adrianna, almost shouting. "No mucking about. I don't want them full of sugar with no sleep. They've got a date with my mother tomorrow."

"Great," I muttered, grabbing the holdall and closing the door on her pouting face.

Max went straight into the living room and switched on the TV whilst Lily disappeared upstairs. I dropped the bag next to the sideboard and quickly began clearing the cans from the coffee table, dumping them on the kitchen counter as the familiar voices of Leonard and Sheldon from *The Big Bang Theory* came from the living room.

"Since when did you like this?" I asked, appearing in the doorway.

"I absolutely love it, Dad."

"Really? My favourite is Leonard."

"No way do you watch this!" Max said, shocked.

"Yes way," I said, scrunching my face up. "Your Dad is definitely down with the kids." I ruffled his mop of dark brown hair and he laughed.

"I don't think you are!"

"Why you cheeky -" I dropped onto the sofa and tickled him. He had always been ticklish but it was right under the armpits that got him best. I watched his skinny little body squirm as he squealed and tried to get away from me.

"Dad!" He screamed. "Dad," he shouted, more seriously. He coughed and arranged his features into a scowl as I relented. "Don't do that."

"Oh, I forgot, I'm sorry." I held my hands up in defeat. "You're a big boy now. Like what, 10 and a half?"

"Almost eleven," he grumbled and turned his face away from me. I studied him for a few seconds and his face began to crack. Little creases began to appear in his cheeks and before he could control himself, the unmistakable Hunter dimple appeared.

"What do you think you're doing?"

We both turned around to see Lily stood in the doorway with her hands on her hips. She had adopted the bossy authority of her mother. I tried very hard to look serious and sorry for our loud noises but the determination on her face was adorable.

"What are you talking about?" asked Max. I glanced sideways to see he'd adopted the same approach and was fully intending to honour his sister's grown up attitude.

"I'm sorry, sugar puff. We were just having a tickle war."

"Don't you 'sugar puff' me." Her stern expression coupled with her rosy cheeks and blonde pigtails were too much for me. I burst out laughing and she stormed back up the stairs. Max had joined in the laughter and we rolled around on the sofa.

Eventually the laughter subsided and we went back to watching *The Big Bang Theory*.

"Sheldon is definitely my favourite," said Max.

"Yeah? You gonna be a brainbox then?"

"Didn't Mum tell you? I got all A's this term. My teacher thinks I should be moved up a year."

"A whole year group? Wow, you must be some sort of genius then. Max the genius," I said, waving my arm through the air like I could see his name in lights. Max laughed. "Right, I'm going to get dressed buddy, okay?"

Max nodded. I rumpled his hair again and then went upstairs. The moment I left the room, my hangover came back in full force. I got to the top of the stairs and peaked into Lily's room to see her lying on the floor with her favourite stuffed teddies. It looked like a town meeting with Mr Giraffe very sternly telling everyone how to behave. I couldn't help but smile. "Hey, sugar, how're you doing?" I said gently, pushing the door all the way open.

Lily looked up and smiled.

"Have you forgiven us for being loud?"

Lily nodded and went back to her stuffed animal meeting. I lingered for a moment, wishing that both my kids would stay this way forever.

# Chapter 5

## STACEY JAMES

### HOME

*Monday 27th July*

Stacey padded around her apartment as she made breakfast, singing along to the radio. The shock of Gemma's death was at the forefront of her mind and no matter what she did, she couldn't shake the guilt she felt.

The thought of singing along to some upbeat music seemed like a great idea to get out of the funk she was in, but she couldn't get into it. It felt so false, so forced. She let the lyrics trail off.

Technically, it wasn't her fault, she knew that. But that didn't mean it was any less gruesome and devastating. Her thoughts flicked back through the last few weeks.

She glanced at the pile of letters on the corner of her kitchen counter, the letters that had started all this. She almost reached out a hand to pick one up, but held herself back. She didn't need to read them again; the words were already etched into her mind.

Having finished making her coffee, she made her way over to the sofa where Sam was already sitting, flicking through the channels on the TV.

His company was oddly reassuring. Which was silly, considering the whole reason he was there was to reassure her of her safety. He was a quiet individual, only speaking when spoken to, but the silences weren't awkward.

She glanced down at the Rolex on her wrist and noted that it was quarter past ten. Sam would have been here for three hours already. Sam and his team rotated shifts from 7am to 10pm every day, sometimes arriving earlier or leaving later depending on her schedule.

As she sat down, he handed her the remote. He might be bored out of his brains, but she was the boss after all. The thought made her smile.

Without the control of the remote, Sam picked up the newspaper next to him and began flicking through the pages. The routine was comforting. Stacey knew that in approximately fifteen minutes, he would have flicked through all the news articles and come to the puzzles page where he enjoyed completing the sudoku.

It was interesting, she mused, how she spent so much time in the company of this man, felt completely safe with him, and yet she knew nothing about him.

She flicked through the channels, and stopped when she came across an old rerun of *Frasier*. It was a bit rubbish watching it these days, but she enjoyed the humour nonetheless. It was easy watching, and that's all she wanted right now.

Easy.

Her thoughts went back to Gemma and she tried not to choke up.

Life wasn't easy. In fact, it had just got more complicated.

Her landline phone rang, interrupting her thoughts. She glanced anxiously at Sam, who calmly put down the paper and crossed the room to answer it without even looking in her direction. She watched patiently as he listened for a moment or two before replacing the phone in its cradle, ending the call.

"Who was it?" she asked, even though she already knew. Even though she dreaded the answer.

Sam looked at her. It seemed like he was debating whether or not to tell her the truth.

She knew it.

It was *him.*

"Your friend," said Sam simply.

Stacey closed her eyes briefly before opening them again. Sam had covered the distance between him and the sofa and was now sitting doing the sudoku again.

She tried to concentrate on the TV, but her mind was all over the place.

Moments later, her phone vibrated in her pyjama pocket. The number was unrecognised, her iPhone pinning the location down to London.

She looked up at Sam who was eyeing her warily. After a deep breath, she slid the phone icon across and answered, pressing it to her ear.

"It's very inconvenient when your manservant answers the phone. It's you I want to talk to, not him," said the male voice on the other end.

Her hand began to shake but before she could respond, Sam had swiped the phone from her and hung up.

The resolve she had been so carefully holding together broke and she started to cry.

Unsure how to react, Sam put his large arms round her, engulfing her in an awkward hug.

After a few moments, Stacey was able to compose herself again and she made a decision; "I'm going to get dressed and then we're going to go see Jason."

Sam nodded. "Yes, boss."

# Chapter 6

## JASON HUNTER

### HOME

*Monday 27th July*

I stepped out of the shower and wrapped a towel around my waist. Wiping away the steam on the mirror, I examined my face. There were unmistakable crows feet around my eyes and a few grey streaks in my stubble. My headache had reached a steady dull throb that was definitely more manageable. My mobile rang. I padded into the bedroom and scooped it off the bed.

"Jason Hunter," I said.

"Mr Hunter. This is Detective Inspector Hayley Irons from CID. I'm investigating the murder of Gemma Brown."

"I thought the investigation was being handled by the Hungarian police?"

"It is, but considering Ms Brown was a British Citizen, I will be assisting with their investigation. I'd like to ask you a few questions, are you at home?"

"Yes, yes I'm at home."

"Excellent. I'll be over shortly."

I gave her my address and hung up. Something was making me feel uneasy. Why was she coming here? Surely she should be speaking to

Adam? He normally dealt with this kind of thing. Or maybe that was the point?

I thought back to the blank expression on Adam's face and how out of character he'd been. Had he thrown me to the wolves?

"Daddy?"

I looked up to see Lily standing in the doorway, staring at me.

"What is it, sugar?" I asked. She shuffled over and I picked her up.

"Have you got to go to work?"

"No, but a police lady is coming to visit us in a little while, so we've got to tidy up and make the house nice and neat," I said. "Can you help me do that?" Lily nodded eagerly. She jumped down and ran downstairs. I could already hear her bossing Max around. *That's my girl*, I thought with a smile before getting dressed.

I towel-dried my hair and then looked in the mirror again. I looked scruffy and the bags under my eyes were unmistakable. I slipped on a t-shirt and pulled myself into a pair of jeans. It always felt strange when I dressed in casual clothes. I walked around the room for a few seconds, getting myself comfortable and then dug around in a drawer for a pair of socks without holes.

I wandered downstairs to find Lily, as expected, tidying up. Although I wasn't too sure she was actually being helpful. She was collecting the beer cans I'd missed in my first scout round and was piling them up as neatly as her five-year-old sense of order would allow. Max was still watching TV. *The Big Bang Theory* was still on and this time Sheldon was lecturing Leonard on something, causing Max to laugh out loud.

I walked into the kitchen and began making myself some breakfast.

"Are you kids hungry?" I called. I walked out with a bowl of cereal.

"No," said Lily. Max was shaking his head, unable to take his eyes away from the screen. I stood watching them as I ate. Lily stood back from her work, brushed her hands and placed them on her hips. She gave one single nod of satisfaction and then began to remove the cushions from the armchair. She plumped them up one by one and then carefully replaced them. Once this had been done, she looked around herself before abandoning her cleaning and joining her brother on the sofa.

"Why don't you bring your colouring down?" I said.

Lily hopped up almost instantly and disappeared upstairs. I spent five minutes putting all the remaining beer cans in the recycling and making the place look at least presentable before opening the cupboard underneath the TV and pulling out two PlayStation controllers. I threw one on the sofa next to Max. He didn't hesitate snatching it up.

"Stick the Formula One in, Dad," he said.

"It's already in," I answered, joining him on the sofa.

"You been practising after I whooped your ass last time?"

"Language," I scolded. "And no, but I'm gonna give you a good run for your money, champ."

"As if!"

Lily came back in with her colouring stuff and moved the coffee table so she had her own workstation in front of the armchair.

I chose Aldric St Pierre as my driver and Max chose Dima Volkov.

"Are you going to get the new version?" asked Max.

"I don't know," I answered. "Probably not, why?"

"Because the technology in the cars gets better every year and you get new drivers. Apparently, you can be Stacey James in the next one."

"Really?"

"Yeah, don't you think she's super cool? She's definitely going to win this year."

"Is she?"

"Yeah, it's a sure thing."

I smiled to myself and made a mental note to ask Stacey for her autograph.

Max paused and I could sense he wanted to ask me something, so I patiently waited as we went through track selection.

"Is she safe now, Dad?"

"Stacey?"

He nodded.

"She's safe now, buddy."

"Good. I don't like what happened in Budapest."

"Me neither."

Our conversation dissipated and was replaced by hard concentration. We'd both managed to pull ahead of the other drivers but we were constantly fighting each other for pole position.

"Yes!" roared Max, as he crossed the finish line 0.08 seconds ahead of me. He jumped off the sofa and did his victory dance. I laughed.

Half-way through the second race around the Japanese track, there was a knock at the door. I paused the game to answer it.

Assuming it was DI Irons, I was surprised when I opened the door and saw the swishing of blonde hair as my house guest turned to face me.

"Stacey?" I said in disbelief.

She looked almost as surprised as I felt.

"Hi, Jason," she said with an apologetic smile.

"Who is it, Daddy?" asked Lily, peering out from the living room. Stacey looked from Lily to the PlayStation controller still in my hand.

"Oh, you're busy," she said. "I'll come back later."

"It's okay," said Lily, before I could answer. "We've tidied up and I'm colouring." She edged forwards but hid behind my legs.

"Are you?" asked Stacey, bending down to Lily's height. Lily nodded.

"Do you want to see?" she asked.

"Only if that's okay with your Daddy," said Stacey.

"Of course it is," I smiled. "Come on in." I stepped aside and Lily took her to the living room. I caught sight of Sam sitting in the front passenger seat of Stacey's Land Rover Discovery and waved before closing the door. I walked back into the living room as Max unpaused the game, not noticing our guest and giving me barely enough time to get back to the sofa.

"You snooze, you lose, Dad," he said, laughing.

"Go on, play solo." I dropped the spare controller on the sofa. Max didn't look up. "Can I get you a drink?" I asked Stacey.

She smiled. "A coffee would be great."

We walked into the kitchen and she sat down at the island whilst I made our drinks.

"They seem like sweet kids," she said.

"Thanks."

There was a moment's silence punctuated only by Max's shouts of frustration.

"I never pictured you as a Dad."

"It's the shirt and tie," I said with a smile.

"I must admit, it did shock me a little when you opened the door," she said, looking at my jeans and t-shirt.

I laughed, setting a mug down for her. "So what brings you to my neck of the woods?"

"Well I, erm, I thought." She paused. "Let's face it, company does me good." She laughed nervously and avoided my eyes. I could see what she meant; her usual confident and charming manner seemed to have been replaced by a more anxious Stacey.

"You're always more than welcome here," I said. "You can see Lily loves making friends. Max spends a lot of time in his own little world."

Stacey laughed.

"We were actually talking about you earlier," I said.

"Oh yeah?"

"Yeah, apparently you're going to be in the new Formula One game."

"Yep, that's right," she said and laughed again.

"I don't think he's noticed you yet," I said, nodding towards Max.

"Shall I go say hi?"

"If you want, but you could end up regretting it."

"Watch this," she said with a wink. She walked into the living room. "I'll give you a game," she said to Max.

"Okay," he said, handing her the second controller. He didn't even look up at her as she sat next to him. "But I'm pretty good," said Max. "Dad can't even beat me." I had to try very hard not to laugh, but I couldn't help smirking. Lily had looked up at Stacey and then me. She could sense something was going on but wasn't quite sure what. I brought the two coffees to the coffee table and sat in the armchair behind Lily.

It was a good race but it was obvious that Stacey was going to win. She was, after all, a good driver. Her judgement of speed in relation to the map of the road was near perfection.

"Wow, you're pretty good," said Max when she won. "Now you have to do your victory dance." I expected her to look at me for help but instead she jumped to her feet and did the robot. We were all laughing. Max was now looking at Stacey with an odd expression and I could see the cogs turning in his brain.

"Oh my God. You're Stacey James," he whispered.

"I sure am," she winked.

I half expected Max to scream or something, but he just stared at her.

"What are you doing here?" he asked.

"I needed to talk some work stuff with your dad," she said with a smile.

"About Budapest?" he asked.

She hesitated then nodded. "You gonna be alright on your own?"

Max nodded.

"Don't worry, I'll give you another game before I leave," she added.

Lily continued colouring, oblivious to our celebrity guest.

Stacey followed me into the kitchen and this time I closed the door.

"What's on your mind?" I asked.

She looked at me hesitantly before saying, "Gemma."

I nodded.

"I feel like this is all my fault," she said. "I didn't think it would go this far..."

I reached for her hand and squeezed it. "You are *not* to blame," I said. "The person to blame is the psychopath that did this." We both went quiet.

"And, there's something else."

I raised an eyebrow as I took a sip of coffee.

"I...I had a call earlier."

"Like before?"

She nodded. "But this time was different."

"Different, how?"

"Sam answered the phone, like last time. But then he called my mobile. The sick bastard called my mobile." She shivered. I glanced towards the living room door.

"What happened? What did he say?"

"Just that when he called, he wanted to speak to me. Not my 'manservant'."

"Then what?"

"Sam took the phone and hung up. But it really creeped me out."

"I'm not surprised. And you still don't have any idea who it could be?"

Stacey shook her head. Her forehead creased and she looked away from me. I put my mug down on the counter.

"Do you want to talk it out again?"

"No. I've already done that, Jason. With you, with the police, hell I've gone over it a million times in my head." Tears spilled over and streamed down her cheeks.

"Hey, hey," I said gently, leaning forwards. I didn't know what to do and so I settled for holding her hand between both of mine. She abruptly angled her body away from me, trying to hide the tears. Looking around me, I spotted the kitchen roll, grabbed it and pulled a few sheets off.

"Thanks," she whispered as I handed them to her.

We were silent for a few moments.

"I was planning on going through your file again anyway, we could do it together. I know it feels like we're covering old ground, but this time might be different."

She shrugged.

"Let me grab it," I said. I remembered it being on the kitchen counter the night before, but I couldn't see it. A quick glance in the living room told me it wasn't on the coffee table either. "Lily? Where did you put the folder that was on the kitchen side?"

"I moved it into a drawer in the kitchen, Daddy," she said without looking up.

I rummaged in the drawer behind me and then triumphantly held up the folder in question. Dropping it on the counter, I pulled out the papers, the photographs, the maps, the transcripts and everything else related to her case. I pulled myself onto one of the breakfast stools next to her.

"There was a phone call," I began.

Stacey nodded. "Di answered. On the publicity phone, that is."

"Can you remember what the caller said?"

"No, not really, she just ignored it. She didn't want to waste my time with it. I think she said it was a man."

I leafed through the papers and pulled out an interview with Stacey's PA; Diane Armstrong. A photo of Diane was stapled to the top left corner and the typescript of the interview followed.

"Diane described the voice as almost charming. He seemed to want to know about your engagements for the week," I said, scanning down the page. I didn't really need to read the document to know its essence, I'd read it a hundred times already and was starting to feel Stacey's frustration.

I passed the document across the table. Stacey glanced through it and nodded.

"Then it was a couple of weeks before anything else happened, right?"

Stacey nodded. "It was an email. The police tried to trace it but they said something about a VPN?"

I nodded. "They'd used a VPN server to hide the IP address."

"Right."

I pulled out a copy of the email and glanced over it.

*Hello Stacey,* it read. *I tried calling, but your PA wouldn't let me speak to you. Why would she stand in our way like that? I wanted to share something with you but it will have to wait. It needs to be the right time and I'm starting to get the impression that you're not that interested in me.*

*I need you, Stacey. I need you to understand that we're supposed to be together. This is about you and me. The world can stand in our way now but the day will come when we'll be together. It might not be in this lifetime, but I won't rest until it happens.*

*Until next time.*

"Do you know what he's referring to here?" I asked, pointing to the first paragraph.

"No, I mean the whole email took me by surprise. Not many people have my private email. The police thought it might have been a subtle death threat. The whole 'it might not be in this lifetime' thing. They think it's just some crazed fan."

I nodded. "So, you came to me."

"Well, yeah. I had that consultation," she said. "It was a week or so later that he phoned my house-"

"And then you became a paying client," I finished. "We went over all that with a fine tooth comb, didn't we?"

She nodded.

"Nothing since then?"

"Nothing until this," she said, dropping her head into her hands.

"Who knew you'd be in Hungary and who knew you'd be on that podium?" I asked.

"Well, everyone knew I'd be out there, but even I didn't know if I'd get a place on the podium."

"True, so whoever shot Gemma would have had to have faith that you'd win."

"Doesn't that make them a twisted psycho?"

"Yes," I answered simply. "They wanted to cut you down the moment you succeeded."

"Oh God."

"But that does tell us something."

"What?"

"This could have something to do with your career."

"How do you mean?"

"If you hadn't won, who would they have killed? No one."

"So it is my fault?" she gasped, emotion causing her to choke on the words.

"No, that's not what I'm saying."

"What if they're not the same person?" she asked.

Before I could answer there was a knock at the door. I could already hear the door opening and Lily's voice travelling down the hall.

"Hi, can I help you?" she said sweetly.

# Chapter 7

## JASON HUNTER

### HOME

*Monday 27<sup>th</sup> July*

"Is your Dad home?" asked a female voice.

I appeared in the hallway to see a delicate-looking brunette with large brown eyes dressed in jeans, converse and a chequered shirt with the sleeves rolled up.

"Hi, Mr Hunter. I'm Detective Inspector Irons," she said.

I gently manoeuvred Lily out of the way and stepped forward to shake the outstretched hand. "Please, call me Jason." I looked down to see Lily had attached herself to my leg and was peering curiously at the stranger on our doorstep. Two unknown women in an hour must have been sending her little brain into overdrive.

"Lily, would you like to invite our guest in?"

She looked up before politely asking DI Irons if she would like to come in for a coffee. I had to hold back the laugh.

I walked DI Irons through the living room and into the kitchen, whilst Lily went back to her colouring.

"Sorry about that, Detective Inspector."

Stacey looked up from her file when I spoke and recognition flashed across her face.

"Hayley," she said, smiling.

DI Irons walked around the island and they hugged.

"Would you like a drink? Tea? Coffee?" I offered.

"A coffee would be perfect," Irons answered.

I nodded.

DI Irons sat herself on the bar stool next to Stacey, both of them chatting happily.

I made the coffee, going through the motions automatically whilst trying to comprehend the easy chatter of the women in front of me. By the time I'd finished making the coffee, they were quiet and looking at me.

"What?" I asked, slightly self-conscious under their scrutiny.

"Nothing," smiled Stacey.

"Are you going to explain this?" I asked, waving a hand in their direction.

"We went to the same school," she said simply.

"Ah." I nodded, taking it in. "Isn't that like, against the rules or something?" I asked.

"Not really. I'm investigating Gemma's murder. Which means I'm going to need to know the whereabouts of you and all your staff between 4 and 5pm, local time," replied DI Irons, suddenly back to business.

"Sure, but didn't you speak to Adam about this?"

DI Irons smiled at me sweetly. "Mr Edwards was unavailable and the message with his assistant said to contact you."

I frowned.

"Your staff?" DI Irons prompted when I didn't answer.

"Er, sure. What do you need?"

"The whereabouts of your team between 4 and 5pm yesterday."

"I was in the office. I'd left Hungary that morning - it wasn't necessary for me to be there. Sam would have been on the plane with Stacey, and he would have had a couple of guys with him – I'll need to double check the names. Then there would have been two guys with Gemma. And then the rest of the team would have either been back here or would have gone home. Like I said, I'd need to double check."

"Sure, if you could. It would be very helpful." She sipped her coffee. "Of course."

"We'll need to verify flights as well."

"Sure, I can give you details for that now, if that's any help?"

DI Irons nodded.

I jotted the flight time and the flight number down onto a piece of paper and handed it over. "I'll get the flight details for the others."

There was a silence as we all drank from our mugs.

"I know you're likely to want to conduct your own investigation into what happened,"said Hayley, fixing me with a stern look. "After all, Stacey is a client and Gemma was an employee, but I would highly recommend you don't. The last thing we need is an amateur investigator getting in the way. We're talking about murder here, not some local hooligans being loud at night. I don't want any more casualties."

I nodded, not really sure how to reply.

"When you do have that list of your employees' whereabouts, please bring it to the station where you can make your formal statement. In the next 24 hours would be best." There was a pause as she drank the rest of her coffee. "I believe that's everything for now. It was great to see you," she said to Stacey, placing a hand on the other woman's arm and giving it a gentle squeeze. "I'll see myself out."

# Chapter 8

## DIANE PARSONS

### STACEY'S APARTMENT

*Tuesday 28th July*

Links of London had asked Stacey to do a photoshoot with some select pieces of jewellery, and if they were to be on time, they needed to leave now.

Diane looked down at her watch. The watch that had been a gift from her Grandmother and something she knew she would need to sell in light of the fiasco with the Russians.

Her stomach churned horribly at the thought. Her chest felt heavy and she was struggling to breathe. Ever since her conversation with Gromov, she'd been struggling to work it all out in her head. *How could this have happened?*

The memories of the party were still hazy, but she did remember complaining about work. She tried to banish the thoughts from her head, but it was impossible. They were leading her down a dark path.

Footsteps on the glass staircase interrupted her thoughts and she looked up to see Stacey shrugging into a leather jacket.

Stacey took one look at Diane and frowned. Diane swallowed and felt suddenly queasy; there was a hard knot in her stomach.

"You're going to wear that?" Stacey asked.

"Yes," muttered Diane.

"No, no, no. Go change. There's an outfit in my spare room."

"You got me an outfit?" She looked at her, shocked. "Why-?"

"Chop, chop. We haven't got all day," said Stacey, clapping her hands together impatiently.

Diane glanced down at her watch. She needed to be quick.

Running up the stairs, she reached the guest room and found a simple black dress laid out on the bed, along with some plain black court shoes.

Wrinkling her nose in disgust, she felt angry. The anger washed through her as she balled up her fists. *Why was she such a control freak?* Glancing down at the outfit she currently wore, Diane could see nothing wrong with the black trousers and white shirt. In fact, it wasn't all that different in design from the dress on the bed.

"Hurry up!" Stacey shouted up the stairs.

Diane stripped down to her underwear, leaving her clothes in a pile on the floor, and ripped the tags off the new dress before slipping it over her head.

She barely had time to check herself over in the mirror before Stacey came through the door.

"Come on, will you? It's on, it fits, excellent. Let's go, go, go."

The anger that she'd felt before came surging back. "Stacey-"

"Not now. Come on."

Stacey stormed out the room, leaving Diane to trail behind. She pushed her anger down, taking a few calming breaths to prepare herself for the day.

# Chapter 9

## THE STALKER

### COVENT GARDENS

*Tuesday 28th July*

He weaved between the people and sat down at a small table with his coffee. He opened his newspaper, drank his coffee and blended in, just another regular son-of-a-bitch taking some time for himself. He was pretending, of course.

The sun was warm, but there was a slight breeze and it ruffled the paper. Currently open on page 5, there was a story about escalating gang warfare in London. Some crazy bastard was going around shooting people, all in honour of defending his turf. Not that he could concentrate on what he was reading. He was looking over the top of it, towards Links of London, the jewellery shop. He knew she would appear any second.

The pavement outside the shop was already swarming with journalists and paparazzi; it was her first public appearance in weeks. Stacey had become the new hottest thing in a matter of days, and everyone wanted a piece of her. Security guards worked hard to keep the reporters back as they pushed against the barrier between them and their big fat paycheck; Stacey James.

He glanced down at his watch and then across the street. She was running late. Stacey appeared, trying to walk through the gaggle of reporters, photographers and fans. Everything suddenly got louder as more people joined the throng. She signed whatever was handed to her in an attempt to get rid of them.

He scowled. The smug bitch just wouldn't listen. Why would she pay attention to them, but he couldn't even get one phone call with her? Was that too much to ask? He just wanted to talk, to make her see that they were meant to be together. Admittedly, the email might have been a little too much, but...

Stacey disappeared into the shop. He looked down at the notebook in front of him. It was positioned perfectly on the table next to the coffee. It had all the details of her day mapped out. Lunch with a friend, a session with her physiotherapist, an appointment with the hairdresser and a session with her personal trainer. She lived an easy life, almost completely oblivious to his existence.

He scanned the faces in the crowd of unknown people who, moments ago, had been clawing at Stacey's fame.

Getting up from the rickety table, he handed the nearest waitress a £5 note. She smiled at him but he didn't care.

He made his way across the street and silently slipped into Links of London just as Jason's boys closed it off to the public. A gaggle of reporters and photographers pressed themselves against the glass.

Glancing around the shop, his eyes came to rest on Stacey.

There she was, in all her beauty, bending over a glass casement where she studied a diamond bracelet that had caught her eye.

How he wanted to touch her. To reach out, sweep her hair back from her beautiful face and caress her cheek. To tell her he loved her and that she was the most stunning creature he'd ever laid eyes on.

He could feel himself getting hard at the thought.

He counted the others in the store; the PA anxiously hovering at Stacey's elbow, the store manager loitering just behind her, two store assistants floating around near the till, a photographer clicking away with his camera, two protection officers near the door and Sam discreetly tucked away in the corner.

He wandered over to the other side of the store and slipped out his mobile. It was tricky work, but he just about managed to take a photo as Stacey lifted her head to speak to the store manager.

# Chapter 10

## JASON HUNTER

### LONDON OFFICE

*Tuesday 28th July*

"Hi, Detective Inspector Irons–" I balanced the receiver between my neck and my shoulder as I leaned back.

"Jason? What a surprise."

"I'm just putting together that information you asked for. Do you mind if I come over and talk through Stacey's case with you?"

"You mean Gemma's case? Please do come to the station, we still need to formally take your statement. As for discussing the case, you know I can't do that."

"I might be able to help?"

"If you have any information you'd like to share, that would be helpful. But I can't provide you with any details of an ongoing investigation."

I sighed. "I'll be there in an hour."

The conversation ended and I hung up just as Lucy popped her head round the door.

"Jason?"

"Yes?"

"Mr Gromov is here to see–"

"You're going to have to reschedule. I'm going to see Detective Inspector Irons."

"But Jason-"

"Just do it, please, Lucy."

# Chapter 11

## JASON HUNTER

### HAMMERSMITH POLICE STATION

*Tuesday 28th July*

I placed a styrofoam coffee cup amongst the stacks of paperwork on the desk in front of Detective Inspector Irons along with a paper bag from Costa.

"I wasn't sure what you liked so I got a selection," I said. DI Irons looked up from her computer and smiled.

"How are the kids?"

"Good, thanks. They're back with their mother now."

She smiled and turned back to the computer.

I sat down in the seat opposite the desk and took a moment to look around the room. The walls were a pale blue and unnaturally clean. There was a filing cabinet in one corner, a potted plant in the other. There was a framed certificate on one wall alongside a graduation photo.

I took a sip of my own coffee and looked back at DI Irons. She was dressed casually in a pale pink shirt. Her sleeves were rolled up again and her collar was open. A simple silver bracelet dangled from her wrist and her hair was pulled back in a ponytail. She finished typing and then leaned back in her chair, taking a tentative sip of her coffee.

"Did you give your statement?" she asked.

"Yes. I just wanted to go through the case. You know, talk it over with you," I answered, beginning to feel a bit foolish.

"I've already explained that I can't discuss the case with you," she said, and took another sip.

"Well, let me just talk then," I said, desperate for a way in.

"Fine," she sighed.

I took a deep breath. "So I'm guessing that Gemma wasn't the target." I ticked off my first finger. "They've had weapons training." I ticked off the second. "Which makes me suspect a military background." I ticked off a third and stopped.

DI Irons' expression was impassive, but I'd noticed her body tense as I spoke.

"My immediate reaction was to suspect the ex-boyfriend," I said slowly.

She didn't respond.

"Have you spoken with him?"

"Not yet –"

"Why not?"

"I can't say."

"Detective Inspector-"

She held up a hand, stopping me mid-sentence.

"Look, I can't divulge anything about our investigations. My job would be on the line if I did."

"The thing is, Detective Inspector, I'm not asking you to. By all means, keep the details close to your chest. I'm asking out of the interest of my client. The same client you went to school with, remember? She's scared out of her wits and I can't do my job protecting her if I don't know who or what I'm protecting her from. Job on the line or not, I'm not going to go running to the press. God, I hate those guys more than most."

"Hayley."

"Sorry?"

"Call me Hayley." I saw a small smile tug at the corner of her mouth.

"Do we have a deal?"

"Did you bring the information that I asked for?" she asked, ignoring my question.

I handed over a small brown file that contained all the details of where my team were throughout the day, with evidence where possible.

"He's off the radar."

"Who is?" I asked.

"Her ex."

"How can he be off the radar? For how long?"

"There's no record of him since he was discharged from hospital."

"How is that possible?" I said.

"I don't know. The best person to ask is probably Stacey. I wouldn't be surprised if he's contacted her since their breakup."

"Possibly, but what if he's behind all this?"

Hayley didn't answer straight away. Her brown eyes searched mine and I knew she was choosing her words carefully. "That's something we have to take into consideration." She looked away. I knew what that meant.

"You need my resources, don't you?" I said, the pieces finally falling into place.

"I don't need your resources," she snapped.

"Then why are you here behind your desk instead of finding the fucker who did this?" My voice was louder than I intended and I tried desperately to regain control. Hayley didn't look at me. I leaned back in my chair and exhaled. "Christ," I muttered.

"Jason –" she said but faltered. I studied her for a few moments.

"What do you need me to do?"

She smiled suddenly, catching me off guard. I could feel the dumb grin that automatically spread across my face in return and cursed myself.

She leaned forwards, eager. "The crime was in Hungary, not here. It's not in our jurisdiction. I can't just fly out there and hassle the Hungarian police, it would be too unprofessional. And right now there's a dangerous person out there and nothing to stop him from attempting another attack on Stacey."

"There's me," I said.

# Chapter 12

## STACEY JAMES

### OXFORD STREET

*Wednesday 29th July*

Stacey walked back onto the high street. Reporters and fans pounced the moment she appeared. Microphones, camera phones, and dictaphones were all shoved in her face as people shouted their questions. It was utter chaos. All she could see was a wall of faces, pressed together and blocking her path. There was a hunger in their eyes for a story that no-one else could have, a hunger for the sliver of fame that came with breaking news. She felt sick. And claustrophobic. The air felt thin and she struggled to breath. Her bodyguards, four of them today, muscled their way in front and carved a path for her.

She tried to remember their names. Was this one here John? No. Ben? No. Was one of them a Charlie? Liam. She was sure one of them was called Liam. In fact, she wasn't even sure they'd told her. She knew Sam, he barely left her side these days, but as for the other three, Jason kept them on an ever-changing rota.

After the call to her mobile, he'd insisted on the extra protection. Was that only two days ago? Time seemed to run together and get muddled at the moment.

One of the bodyguards opened the limousine door for her and she climbed in. It was unlike her to be travelling in such extravagance. Most of the time she'd prefer to get in her beaten-up Land Rover Discovery and be done with it, but Diane had pointed out that it wasn't very elegant.

Once in the car, the noise outside was drowned out by the hum of the engine. The constant and ferocious clicking of cameras was almost inaudible. Almost. Two of the bodyguards climbed into the front, one behind the wheel and another in the passenger seat. She glanced at Sam as he and the fourth bodyguard piled in next to her. There was plenty of room, but somehow these burly men made the space feel small.

She thought of Jason, of his kids and his easy way with her. He always knew what to say. Come to think of it, she quite liked Jason. He was funny, calm, collected, in control, and he made her feel safe. Jason was a good one, she decided. Someone worth keeping close. She thought back to how he'd held her hand, touched her just to reassure her everything was okay. The way he'd squared up to her when she was angry about Gemma's death. *Shit.* She *liked* him. Oh fuck. That was not—

There was a commotion outside. The car had barely moved five feet when it stalled. The bodyguard in the passenger seat muttered something to the driver as he tried to turn the engine on again.

Stacey was still conscious of the bodies pressing tightly against the outside of the car. Where were the police when you needed them? The windows were blacked-out but that didn't stop their faces from getting as close to the glass as possible in an attempt to catch a glimpse of her.

The driver tried to start the engine again but it just turned over, making a loud whining sound. Slamming his foot down on the accelerator, the driver swore.

"What-" began Stacey when an almighty bang erupted from the car.

Instinctively Sam threw himself on top of Stacey, shielding her from whatever had just happened. After that, everything felt like it was in slow motion. There were shouts and screams from outside, instructions being shouted inside. Chaos surrounded her and Stacey still didn't know what was happening.

Sam's voice penetrated her confusion. "Are you two alright?" he shouted. The bodyguard in the passenger seat waved a hand.

"Fine."

"What happened?"

The driver turned. "No idea. Engine's stalled. Tried revving it a few times to help it along and then, bang. Everything looks fine up here, boss."

"Okay. Liam?" Sam looked at the bodyguard on the other side of Stacey as he sat up, releasing her from his protection. "Watch her, you hear me?" He pointed to Stacey. "I'm going to find out what the fuck is going on."

Sirens wailed in the background as Sam opened the car door and climbed out. The crowd outside seemed to have lost interest in Stacey now and were cautiously backing away from the car. Liam glanced at Stacey before turning and winding down one of the windows a few inches.

He peered out, looking one way and then the other. "There's no fire. Not that I can see, anyway." Pulling his head back in, he turned to Stacey. "Don't move." And then moved down the car toward the driver. Winding down her own window, Stacey cautiously looked down the street.

There was no sign of Sam, but everyone was keeping a respectable distance from the car. She tried to lean out further but Sam appeared, blocking her view.

"In," he snapped, opening the door and forcefully shoving her along the seat. "Nobody leaves the car."

"What's going on?" she asked, taken aback by his abruptness.

"We need to wait for the police."

"Sam, what's happened?"

It was then that she noticed it. The brown envelope on the seat, underneath the still open window opposite. She didn't move, just stared at it, unsure of how it got there.

Sam noticed her stillness and followed her gaze.

"What-?" He snatched the envelope off the seat just as Stacey reached for it. Without waiting for instructions, he tore it open and peered inside. "Oh, shit."

Stacey was sitting unnaturally close to Sam now and her body stiffened at his tone. He pulled several sheets of stiff, glossy paper from the envelope, allowing her to reach out and take them.

It was a stack of photos. Stacey felt a chill tiptoe down her spine. The first three photos were of her; shopping, meeting friends, walking down the street. The fourth was a picture of her in Links of London. She went cold.

# Chapter 13

## JASON HUNTER

### THE GYM

*Wednesday 29th July*

My phone was buzzing frantically on the bench.

"Hello?" I answered as I desperately tried to fix my tie. I'd spent the morning tied up in meetings and decided to swing by the office gym during my lunch hour. Now I was running late.

"Boss, you need to get to Oxford Street. We have a... situation."

"What's happened?"

"Stacey's fine. There's been an issue with the car, a bit of a scare and some photos that I think you're gonna want to look at."

"I'm on my way."

In the car, I tried hard not to break any speed limits between the office and Oxford Street. I used as many shortcuts as I could to avoid the city's congestion but it made no difference. I was sitting behind a Mini Cooper and could feel the frustration building. No-one was moving. I slammed a fist against the steering wheel.

"Dammit!" I shouted. "Fuck this." I drove the car up onto the curb and along the pavement. Adam was going to have a field day with this one but my impatience had got the better of me. Cars beeped their horns at me as I cut in. A couple of drivers gave me the finger, but I didn't care.

I heard sirens from behind and slowed the car, expecting to be pulled over.

"Fuck!"

They drove past and carved the perfect path through the sea of vehicles. I followed closely behind, hoping they could keep this up all the way to Oxford Street. The police disappeared at Hyde Park Corner and once again I was on my own and battling my way through the traffic.

Park Lane was clear so I pushed the accelerator down and pushed in front of the cars turning right onto Upper Brook Street. I could immediately tell something was wrong. Oxford Street had been closed. Double-decker buses lined the street as they found their usual routes blocked. I sounded my horn a few times before abandoning my BMW at Hanover Square.

I ran past the Police Officers keeping the public at bay, flashing my ID as I went.

"Hey, you can't come through here," shouted one of them.

Another officer blocked my path. "Authorised personnel only."

"Yeah, I am authorised." I showed them my ID.

"No, you're not. Police only."

"Look, pal," I said, trying to get past. He squared up to me and I couldn't help but be a little impressed. I was quite a big bloke and this guy had nothing on me, but that didn't seem to deter him.

"My client is on the other side of you and I need to get to her, right now."

"Hey!" called a woman. The policeman turned around to see DI Irons coming towards us. "He's with me," she said.

"Yes, Detective Inspector," he said and gave me a cold look.

"What's happened?" I asked, jogging over to Hayley. We began walking towards the hub of chaos as she filled me in.

"They've cleared the area and evacuated everyone. Stacey's over there. She's fine, just being kept here as part of protocol." I nodded as we walked. The street looked fine to me. A few police cars were parked up on the side of the road, and a cordon was holding back the general public.

"Someone heard gunshots. So they said. Looks like the limo was sabotaged. Just a harmless prank. Someone put some devil bangers in the exhaust which caused the car to stall and set the firecrackers off. People panicked."

"Fuck."

"Exactly."

People were leaning over the police tape, snapping pictures and filming videos on their mobiles.

I approached Stacey. "Are you ok?" She looked fine, but I wanted to make sure.

"Can you please tell these knuckleheads that I need to leave?" she said.

"Detective Inspector?" said Liam, one of the bodyguards, as he appeared at Hayley's side. "An Officer is asking for you," he said and then stepped back. Hayley nodded and left.

I pulled out my mobile. There was already a voicemail flashing on my phone. I groaned.

"What?"

"Nothing."

We stood in silence for a few seconds.

"What's going on?" she asked me, cautiously. I looked at her. She seemed fine but there was something off that I couldn't put my finger on.

"I don't know," I sighed.

We were silent again.

"You ready to go home?" I asked.

She nodded.

"Boss?" Sam handed me a brown envelope and I noticed he was already wearing the classic latex gloves that told me this was evidence. Stacey seemed to twitch involuntarily next to me as she saw the envelope. I looked up to see the colour had drained from her face. My stomach filled with a sense of dread.

I carefully peeled back the sticky seal flap using the end of my tie as a cover for my fingers to avoid contaminating any DNA evidence someone might have been stupid enough to leave on the seal and pulled out the photographs.

"Fucking hell," I muttered. I carefully flicked through the pictures again, noticing that Stacey had a bodyguard in each one. I didn't know if that was a comfort or not.

"Can you remember when these pictures were taken?" I asked Stacey.

Sam took the photos back from me and methodically went through them. Stacey carefully looked at each one in turn. "This was yesterday," she said. "This was last week before I went to Hungary but these ones must have been a couple of weeks ago."

I frowned.

Hayley reappeared. "You're free to go," she said to Stacey. "What's wrong?" Sam handed the photos over.

I watched Hayley's reaction to the images. She looked disgusted. The burden on my shoulders seemed to have increased tenfold and I suddenly couldn't breathe. The first picture was taken yesterday, which meant there was a forty-eight-hour window where the stalker had travelled back to the UK.

Hayley was still flicking through the photos with her white-gloved hands, but it seemed she'd had a similar thought to me. "We'll need a list of everyone who flew out of Hungary in the last three days. Everything from after the race, to yesterday afternoon." She looked up from the pictures and at Stacey. "I'm going to need you to make a statement about these, and..." she trailed off.

"What?" The look on Stacey's face told me she dreaded the answer.

"I don't think it's a good idea for you to be on your own just now."

"Why?"

"This is serious, Stacey. We don't know what this guy might do next. I'll pass these along to whoever's managing your stalker case but I don't think you should go back to your flat."

"I can't-" began Stacey.

"Great idea. You'll stay at mine."

Both women looked at me.

I shrugged my shoulders. "My job is to protect you. Remember?"

"Fine," sighed Stacey. Hayley nodded her approval.

"That's settled then. You two go on home. I need to finish up here," Hayley said with a small smile.

"Whisk me away, Mr Hunter," said Stacey sarcastically.

"My car is at Hanover Square." I turned to the bodyguards. "Boys? We've had a change of plan."

# Chapter 14

## JASON HUNTER

### HOME

*Wednesday 29th July*

The security detail followed us back to mine. I approached the limousine parked outside my house as Sam rolled down the window of the driver's seat.

"Will you need me as sentry, boss?" he asked.

"Yes," I said. "Drop these guys back at the office, change vehicles."

Sam nodded.

I watched the car drive away as I locked the front door and set the alarm system.

"Am I on the sofa?" asked Stacey from the living room. I paused. I hadn't really thought that far ahead.

"No," I called. "I'll have the sofa. You can have my room." I joined her in the living room.

"Are you sure?"

I nodded. "Unless you want some fairies or footballers on the wall, although Lily might beat your ass if she knew."

Stacey laughed. "Your room it is then."

I took her upstairs, gave her some spare towels and a spare pair of old pyjama bottoms.

"Erm, Jason?" said Stacey.

"What?" I turned to see her holding up the pyjama bottoms.

"I'm gonna need the other half."

I laughed and tossed her an old t-shirt. "I'll send Sam to get some of your stuff later."

"It can wait until tomorrow. In fact, might as well send Diane. She has a key."

"Sure, but I wouldn't want her going on her own. I'll get Sam to go with her."

Stacey nodded before going into the bathroom to change whilst I gathered the few things I'd need. Then I pulled out my phone and hit play on my voicemail. It was Lucy, checking in with me. I hit delete. Lucy could wait until tomorrow.

Stacey re-entered the bedroom and brushed past me. She pulled back the duvet, climbed into bed and sat with her legs crossed, watching me.

"How do you manage to always look so fresh and stylish?"

Stacey laughed. "What are you talking about?"

"You're in a pair of old PJs that don't come close to fitting you and yet..."

"And yet what?"

"You look ready for the day all over again."

"Well that's a load of rubbish," she said, shaking her head.

"Have you got everything you need?" I asked.

"I think so," she said.

"Okay, well, I'll be downstairs." I turned to leave.

"Jason?"

"Yeah?" I stopped, turning back to look at her.

"I can't get Gemma out of my head."

"I know." I knew the feeling all too well. Gemma had been plaguing my thoughts too.

"I just can't understand why someone would do that."

I sat down on the edge of the bed and looked at her.

"That's mine and Hayley's job to work out," I said. "There's someone out there who isn't right in the head, for whatever reason. And I will make sure nothing happens to you. Today was just a prank, nobody got hurt."

She nodded, unconvinced. Lying down, she pulled the duvet up to her chin, reminding me of a small child waiting to be tucked in.

Before I could get up to leave, she reached out and took hold of my hand. "Thanks, Jason." My heart jumped in my chest and suddenly I felt warm.

I gave her a small smile and squeezed her hand before leaving.

# Chapter 15

## DIANE PARSONS

### STACEY'S APARTMENT

*Thursday 30<sup>th</sup> July*

"What else do you need?" asked Diane, cradling the phone between her cheek and her shoulder. "Yeah, I've got that." She listened to a seemingly never ending list of requirements. "I still don't understand why you can't get it yourself?"

The wave of abuse that came down the phone made her sigh.

"Yes, of course. Sure, that's fine." She hung up.

Sam stood by the door, patiently waiting for Diane to finish.

She scanned the room before making a quick dash up the stairs for one last glimpse around. Satisfied she'd got everything Stacey had requested, she went back down the stairs and handed the two duffel bags to Sam.

"I'm just going to grab the mail."

He nodded but didn't move.

She collected the mail from the kitchen counter without even looking and led the way out of the apartment, setting the alarm and locking the door behind her.

"You don't talk much, do you?" she asked.

Sam didn't respond.

"Sure, I get that," she muttered, unsure on what to say to this imposing, silent figure.

They got into the lift and descended in silence. Once in the garage, Diane and Sam climbed into the sleek black Mercedes.

It took them about twenty minutes to navigate the London streets to Jason's house.

When they arrived, Diane climbed out of the car, leaving Sam behind the wheel and proceeded to struggle with getting the duffel bags out and carrying them to the front door. Sam didn't get out to help.

The door was answered on the first knock by Stacey, who practically yanked the duffels out of her hands.

"You're welcome," she muttered under her breath.

"You remembered to pack everything, right?"

"Yes."

"You didn't forget anything, did you?"

"No, Stacey. I was on the phone to you as I was packing."

"Good." Stacey gave her a radiant smile. "Do you, er, want to come in?"

"Yes, I need to talk to you about publicity for the next month."

Stacey opened the door wider to let Diane through before answering, "I'm not doing any."

"I'm sorry, what?"

Stacey led the way into the kitchen and began to make a coffee.

"I can't do it, Di. I can't go into the public eye and feel safe at the moment. First Gemma, the phone calls, now the photos? Did I tell you he called my mobile?"

Diane nodded.

"So you're not going to do any publicity at all?"

Jason appeared in the doorway, finishing the buttons on his shirt.

"I'm afraid not," he said. "If this gets any more serious, we may have to pull her out of the next race."

Diane didn't respond, simply looked from one to the other. "So, what am I supposed to do?"

"You'll get paid, don't worry," tutted Stacey, coffee forgotten on the counter.

"It's not about that-"

"What's it about then?" She folded her arms across her chest.

Diane fumbled for something to say. "Nothing. I'll cancel all your appearances."

"Thank you," said Jason as he began to fasten his tie.

Just as she was about to leave, Diane remembered the mail on the kitchen counter.

"Before I forget, I got your mail. Looks like the maid's cleaned." She handed over the wad of envelopes. "I haven't looked through them."

Stacey nodded and took the bundle.

"You checked out the maids, didn't you?" asked Diane, looking at Jason.

Jason nodded.

Stacey briefly flicked through the letters before coming to a stop on one that was handwritten. She frowned, turned it over and opened it.

Out came a single, handwritten sheet of paper folded in half and a photo. Diane tried to glance at the photo, but Stacey passed it to Jason.

She watched as Stacey's eyes scanned across the letter before she passed that to Jason too. Stacey was frozen in place, her hands clasped tightly in front of her. Jason read the letter in record speed and looked up.

"Where was this?" he asked.

"On the counter," said Diane. "With the other mail."

Jason looked back down at the letter, frowning.

"Why? What's wrong?"

He handed the paper to her and showed her the photo.

A shiver ran down her spine as Diane began to read;

*Dear Stacey,*

*I hope this letter finds you well.*

*I've been trying to reach out to you lately, but nothing seems to work. If I call you, you hang up. Why do you insist on punishing me this way? You know that we are meant to be together. Unless this is all part of a game? Is this a game, Stacey?*

*By now I'm sure you've seen the photos. I just wanted you to know that I'm always here for you. I will always be here, even when you don't think I am. I will be your rock, your support through these hard times. What happened to Gemma is terrible, and I want to make sure that I am here to protect you.*

*Yours Always.*

She finished the letter, glanced at the photo of Stacey on Oxford Street, and handed them both back to Jason.

She felt sick and bile rose in her throat.

How could this happen? Who-?

"Do you know-?"

"Do I look like I know?" snapped Stacey.

# Chapter 16

## JASON HUNTER

### LONDON OFFICE

*Thursday 30th July*

"How was Stacey last night?" asked Hayley.

"What do you mean?" I said, sitting up and grabbing the phone from the cradle, instantly regretting putting the call on loudspeaker.

"Was she okay? She didn't have a breakdown or anything? She was always pretty dramatic when we were at school."

"Oh, I see." I relaxed back into my chair. "Yeah, she was fine." I shifted the phone so it was cradled between my ear and my shoulder as I flicked through the paperwork on my desk.

"That's good. We cleared the scene yesterday after you left. The roadblock was just a precaution anyway. Spoke to some potential witnesses, but nobody saw anything, just heard the loud bangs. I've had to refer it to the officer in charge of Stacey's case. I can only deal with what's related to Gemma, but I'll obviously pitch in where necessary, it looks like the two could be related."

"Related but not the same?"

"I don't think so. The incidents with Stacey's stalker seem to be mild in comparison."

"Speaking of which, I have something for you. Or should I give it to the guy dealing with the stalker case?"

"What is it?"

"Stacey's received a letter. It came in the mail. And came with another photo," I said, pulling it out from the pile of paperwork.

"Really? Saying what?"

"It might just be easier if I show you?"

"Sure, bring it into the station."

I leaned back in my chair and looked at the projection board opposite my desk. I had all our notes up on display, including the photographs of Stacey.

"Have you checked the airlines?" I asked.

"Yes. And we've managed to verify the whereabouts of you and your team."

"Well, that's a relief."

Hayley didn't respond.

"Have you had any luck finding Cooper?"

"No. This guy is a professional at not being found."

"I know," I sighed. "His fingerprints have got to be in the system somewhere, right? Have you contacted the family?"

"I have an officer trying to track them down."

"Okay, well, I'll pop by in a little while," I said and hung up.

I sat in silence for a few minutes, flicking through the photographs again, hoping something new would jump out at me. All the images were very different; in public, in private, there was definitely a message here. No. These photos were a warning. Or were they? Were they just the affections of some crazed maniac?

The telephone on my desk buzzed. "Adam wants to see you ASAP," came Lucy's voice.

I pressed the button. "Yeah, I'll be there in a minute." I sighed. Two summonings in one week, this was definitely not good.

I left my office and headed towards Adam's. Lucy gave me a pained look and shook her head which meant Adam wasn't in a good mood - great. I knocked on the door and then entered.

Adam was typing on his Apple Mac and had the phone cradled between his ear and his shoulder. He waved a hand towards one of the chairs facing his desk. I sat down and tried not to look nervous.

"Yeah, yeah. Okay. Right. And that gives us exclusive access? Yeah, okay, sure. Okay. I'm going to have to call you back but I definitely want to continue this conversation. Sure, okay. I'll speak to you later." Adam hung up the phone and looked across the room at me.

"Do you like your job, Jason?" he asked.

*Shit.* I swallowed hard. "Yea –"

"Then why the *fuck* are you behaving like a tool?"

"I, erm –"

"Shut up." The room fell silent. "First Gemma," he continued. "But then I get a phone call informing me that you think you're above the law. You're making me look like a fucking idiot!" He glared at me across the room.

After a few moments, I tried to explain. "It was an emergency."

Adam didn't answer. We sat in silence for a few more minutes.

"I heard about what happened," he said quietly. I nodded. "Traffic cameras have a record of you curbing your car."

"Um –"

"Don't do it again," he said.

I nodded again, unsure of myself and then got up to leave.

"How is she?" Adam asked as I reached the door.

"Stacey? She's fine. I've assigned her extra protection and all public appearances have been postponed."

"And the police?"

"I'm working with Detective Irons to get to the bottom of all this."

"Good. Don't cock it up."

I left the office and saw Lucy anxiously glance in my direction.

"Is he okay?" I asked her, indicating Adam's office.

She shrugged. "Who knows?"

I walked back into my office to see some emails had come through whilst I'd been out. The little icon in the left-hand corner was blinking furiously. Hayley had kindly forwarded me the list of passengers that had been on a direct flight to and from Hungary within the same 5-day window the photos could have been taken.

I opened the document and was immediately overwhelmed by the amount of information. I hadn't considered just how many Formula One enthusiasts would have followed the race to Hungary. This was going to take hours to sort through and there was still the possibility of connecting flights. I was starting to think it would be impossible to find Gemma's killer. Whoever was cold-blooded enough to have done this had made sure that it would be incredibly difficult to find them. I almost envied their skill. Captain Cooper came to mind again.

Without the information from the Hungarian airports, I wasn't going to be able to narrow down the search area. The shooter might have nothing to do with the photos. What did that mean? A shooter *and* a stalker? I exhaled and dropped my head into my hands. What were the chances of that? I looked again at the photos. How the hell was I going to solve this?

If Stacey was accurate with her estimations, the shooter was only in the country for a few days; they could have gone at any point after the first few pictures were taken but was back in the UK in time to take the last one on Tuesday. Everything was coming across as far too personal. Was a duo responsible or were they two unrelated incidents?

If we go with the theory of this being two different people, the question I kept coming back to was *why*? Why kill Gemma? Why take the photos? What did it achieve?

I hit the print button on the list of passenger names and listened to page after page being ejected from the printer. I opened the next email, hoping for better news. It was a copy of the official report from Captain Zsaldos with a note that asked me to phone him as soon as I'd read it.

I dialled the number for the Hungarian Captain. He picked up on the third ring.

"Százados Zsaldos."

"Captain. Jason Hunter."

"Ahh, Mr Hunter."

"You wanted to discuss the Gemma Brown case?"

"Yes, of course. You've read the file?"

"I'm sorry?" I said, struggling to understand his Hungarian accent.

"The file. You've read it?" he asked more slowly.

"Yes."

"Good. You know we have the crime scene."

"Yes." I scrabbled for a pen and held it poised, ready.

"It's not good."

"What? Why?"

"We have the murder weapon."

I flinched at the word 'murder'. "Surely that's a good thing?"

"Normally. But this was a professional. No fingerprints. The weapon is a popular one. You can buy it easily."

"A professional?" I let out a sigh. "Fuck," I whispered.

"Forensics are still checking the scene."

"Okay. So where does that put us now?"

"We don't have much."

"Would you mind if I came over?" I asked, already looking up the flight timetable to Hungary on Google.

There was a chuckle from the end of the line. "That's why I wanted to talk."

"I totally understand," I said. "Captain Cooper is still a prime suspect from this end. Detective Inspector Irons is trying to track him down but he's gone AWOL."

"AWOL?" he asked, confused.

"He's disappeared."

"Ah."

"But he's our best lead at the moment."

"I see. She hasn't called me."

"I'll speak to her. Let me clear these flights with my boss and I'll send you the details."

"Thank you, Mr Hunter."

"Call me Jason."

I hung up the phone and printed the flight schedule. I walked out of my office and down the corridor. For the second time that day, I knocked on Adam's door.

"Yes?"

"Hi," I said, walking in. He looked up from his Mac, surprised.

"What do you want, Jason?"

"I've just been on the phone with the Hungarian Captain in charge of Gemma's case. Considering Stacey's safety and the current situation –"

"Get to the point, please," he said.

"I want to fly out there. Tomorrow, if possible."

"What?"

"To help with the case."

Adam sighed, let his head fall into his hands and began massaging the bridge of his nose.

"Why the hell do *you* need to go to Hungary?"

"The police need help. Detective Inspector Irons can't go and I'm the next best thing."

"Did it not occur to you that we might be busy here? How many clients have you rescheduled in the last week?"

"I –"

"You need to do your job, Jason. Leave the crime solving to the police. It's their problem."

"But –"

"Enough. Stacey's protection is obviously paramount but there are other people out there. We're a security firm, not a travel agent."

# Chapter 17

## DIANE PARSONS

### SELFRIDGES

*Thursday 30<sup>th</sup> July*

"But Stacey-"

"No 'buts', Diane. Now hurry up."

Diane glanced down at the outfit laid out by the Selfridge's personal shopper. Between the edge of the curtain and the wall, she could see Stacey's reflection in the mirror as she sat on the plush taupe sofa and sipped her champagne.

Feeling disgruntled, Diane began to change.

"Why do I have to wear this?"

"Because I said so. We have an important appointment this afternoon and I need you looking your best."

"What was wrong with what I was wearing before?"

"Your, er, coordination skills need a little work."

Diane could hardly believe what she was hearing. She pulled the Ted Baker dress over her head and attempted to do the zip at the back before yanking the curtain back.

"I can't believe you would say such a thing. After everything I do for you-"

"Well, that looks wonderful," replied Stacey, getting to her feet and ignoring Diane's protests.

Still frowning, Diane turned to the mirror and was surprised to see that the elegantly cut black dress actually looked flattering on her.

The personal shopper still hovering to one side quickly rushed forward to help adjust the dress and finish the zip at the back before once again blending into the furniture.

"See. Doesn't that look better?"

Speechless, Diane merely nodded.

"Excellent. Now, chop, chop. We have a busy afternoon ahead of us."

She turned to look at Stacey. "Where are we going? All of your public appearances are cancelled."

"Well, I fancied doing a little sightseeing."

"What about..." Diane nodded towards the two bodyguards positioned ominously outside the suite.

"It's fine," said Stacey with a dismissive wave of her hand.

"Stacey, I don't think it's a good idea."

"Of course it is. We'll do a bit of shopping, have a bite to eat. The boys will be with us so we'll be fine."

"Stacey, I *don't think it's a good idea*," replied Diane through gritted teeth. "Your car was sabotaged just yesterday, how can you even-"

"I know," hissed Stacey, forcefully grabbing hold of Diane's arm. "But I won't let the little fucker get the better of me. I'm not going to hide away like some coward, okay? Now be a good girl, put on the nice shoes the lady has picked out for you and quit your whining." She released Diane's arm and stepped away, waving at the personal shopper to bring forward the shoes.

Rubbing her arm gingerly, Diane frowned. She had a bad feeling about this.

# Chapter 18

## DIANE PARSONS

### HARRODS

*Thursday 30th July*

As Stacey weaved her way between the luxurious furniture, Diane struggled to keep up. The shoes she'd been forced to wear were definitely too high for her and so her usual shuffle had been reduced with an awkward teetering that couldn't keep pace with Stacey's elegant strides.

Once again, Diane was left feeling frumpy, unattractive and downright miserable. She thought back to her conversation with Volkov and his uncle and shuddered. She needed to control herself. It was these feelings that had got her into this mess in the first place.

Conscious of the two bodyguards behind her impatiently wanting to catch up to Stacey, Diane tried to increase her pace but tripped, pitching forward. A steady hand caught her arm. Diane looked up to see Sam had rushed forward and caught her. She blushed.

Sam released Diane's arm without a word and fell back into step with the other bodyguard – Liam, was it? Flustered, Diane tried to compose herself.

Stacey had paused to look at a dining room table made entirely of glass and was already being accosted by one of the many store assistants. By the time Diane had caught up, Stacey was being guided over to one of the consultation desks. This didn't bode well and Diane inwardly groaned. Experience had taught her that when Stacey stopped to talk, she would ask a million and one questions before spending an obscene amount of money on whatever had caught her fancy. This process could take well over an hour.

Just as Stacey took a seat, Diane attempted to intercept in a bid to excuse herself.

"I'm just going to-"

"No, you're not," interrupted Stacey, without evening glancing in Diane's direction. "I need you here."

The sales assistant awkwardly looked from one to the other before Diane finally relented and sat in the empty seat next to Stacey whilst the two bodyguards positioned themselves behind the chairs.

She really didn't know why she put up with all this. Well, actually, she did. The money was amazing. Much higher than anything she would get elsewhere. But was it really worth this abuse? She was less of a PA and more of a personal lackey. A manservant to suit Stacey's every whim. Or should that be woman-servant? Either way, it was downright depressing.

Diane sighed and let her mind wander back to that night in the club with Volkov. She could vaguely remember complaining about her life but the combination of alcohol and his undivided attention was intoxicating, and she'd lost herself to it. They may have been friends for years, but it had never gone further than that. The word 'crush' didn't even cover it, she was in love with him. Head over heels. But he was just too blind, or too famous, to notice.

She knew she could give him everything he wanted and more, if only he would give her the chance. That night she thought she'd come so close. They'd been cosied up in a booth together. The music was so loud that he had to put his lips right against her ear. Remembering how close he had been made her shiver. The yearning in her chest was almost unbearable.

Although she remembered being close to him, she couldn't remember what they'd spoken about. She remembered laughing, and casually placing her hand on his leg. She remembered him looking down and instead of removing her hand, he placed his own on top. Just thinking about it made her heart beat faster and her chest feel tight. If only she could remember the conversation.

"Diane? Hello?"

Diane blinked, coming back to reality to see Stacey and the sales assistant both looking at her impatiently.

"What is going on with you, girl? I've been talking to you for the past two minutes."

"Sorry," she mumbled.

"Penelope here," she waved a hand towards the sales assistant, "has been telling me about the gorgeous Porada dining table over there. Isn't it just charming?"

Diane bit back her retort and instead smiled gracefully and nodded. Satisfied, Stacey continued to talk details with Penelope. Diane listened to the conversation for less than a minute before drifting away with her thoughts again.

By the time the sale had concluded, Stacey's account had been charged and the delivery details ironed out, Stacey declared it was time to eat. Rather than venturing outside, they skipped the queue and found a table at The Georgian on the fourth floor.

"Why do you put it on?" asked Diane as she perused the menu, unable to help herself.

"What? Put what on?"

"To most people, you're down to earth and *normal*. But then when you talk to me, or as soon as you come here – or anywhere else fancy – you become 'Stacey James'; posh and upper class... And mean."

Expecting a harsh reply, she was surprised when Stacey paused to think.

"I didn't even realise I was doing it."

Diane nodded, spurred on by her own confidence. "It's like you become this whole other person. Trying to be someone who needs designer furniture and a *Made in Chelsea* accent in order to fit in."

Stacey didn't look up from the menu and didn't respond.

# Chapter 19

## JASON HUNTER

### LONDON OFFICE

*Thursday 30th July*

I stopped by Lucy's desk on the way back to my office.

"Oh dear," she said. "You don't look very happy."

I sighed. "When's my next appointment?"

She scanned her finger along the open diary next to her and said, "You wanted me to reschedule Mr Gromov's appointment –"

"Don't. Tell him I'll see him as soon as he wants but I need you to make sure my weekend is as wide open as possible. Try and keep tomorrow afternoon free as well, if you can."

"Got something planned?"

"Not quite, but I'm thinking it's time for a holiday."

"Oh?"

"Message me when Mr Gromov arrives."

She nodded and turned back to her computer, tapping away on her keyboard.

I closed the door to my office and dialled Stacey's number on my mobile.

"Do you fancy a weekend away?" I asked when she answered.

"How very forward of you, Mr Hunter."

I blushed at her insinuation but ignored it. "This weekend?"

"I guess I could do that. Where are you whisking me away to?"

"How does Hungary sound?"

"Hmmm, I'm not sure. Last time I was there it didn't end well."

"They found the gun, Stacey."

"They what?"

"Yeah, exactly. But they need my help. Hayley can't get out there."

"Oh, I see. And I'm assuming Adam has said no to you doing this on company time, right?"

"Am I really that transparent?" I asked with a smile.

"A little, yeah. So I'll get on and book these flights, shall I? That is why you've called me, isn't it?"

"How could you possibly think such a thing? Maybe I just like your company."

"Uh-huh, sure."

I hung up.

The next number I dialled was Hayley's.

"They found the weapon," I told her when she picked up on the third ring.

There was a brief silence. "This changes things," she said matter-of-factly.

I told her that me and Stacey would be flying out as soon as possible. I expected her to protest, to remind me I wasn't police, but instead she said, "Don't get into trouble."

"I'll try not to. Any news on Cooper?"

"You know I can't tell you that during an ongoing investigation," she sighed.

"Hayley," I implored. "It's important I know for the safety of my client. We've been over this."

There was a pause and then she lowered her voice, "Nothing yet. The last anyone heard, he was hiring out his talents."

"You mean he's a gun for hire? An assassin?"

"Exactly."

"Shit."

A message popped up on my computer screen announcing Mr Gromov's arrival.

"Sorry Hayley but I've got to go, client meeting."

"Okay," she said. "Keep me updated on Hungary."

"Will do," I answered and hung up.

There was a knock at the door and Lucy introduced a wide-set, dark-haired Russian man.

"Mr Gromov," I said, getting to my feet. I walked round my desk and held out my hand. He shook it firmly.

"You have postponed this meeting more than once. I am not happy." His accent was thick but his English was very good.

"Yes, Mr Gromov, I can only apologise. We've been dealing with a... crisis situation." I walked back to my chair and Mr Gromov seated himself opposite my desk.

"Let me make this perfectly clear, Mr Hunter. I am a very wealthy man, and there are a lot of people who would like to hurt me. I need protection I can rely on."

"That's exactly what we offer. We're a national leader in personal protection. One of the best," I said, hoping to convey confidence.

"That is why I chose you."

I nodded. "So what can we do for you?"

Gromov gave a nod of satisfaction. "I already have a personal team but I need residential protection. Around the clock surveillance."

I nodded and began to make notes. Gromov continued, outlining the number of men he would need, the shift patterns he wanted them working, the screening process he wanted them to undertake and what he needed them to do should there be a breach.

I had to give him credit, the man knew what he was talking about. I mentally tried to calculate the costs – it was going to be expensive. Gromov finished his demands and I wrote down a final few notes before briefly reading through what I'd written so far.

"Are you in a position to disclose the reason for this level of protection?" I glanced at Gromov. His face remained expressionless. "I only ask because an understanding of your situation means we may be able to help, monitor and adjust the protection accordingly."

Mr Gromov was silent for a few seconds. "There is a bounty on my head," he said.

For the first time, a glimmer of emotion flashed across his face. This shit was serious.

Mr Gromov cleared his throat and shuffled in his seat. I had a horrible feeling I was about to find out something I really didn't want to know.

"Perhaps I will disclose more once your services have proven efficient," he said.

Trust, I thought. He didn't trust me. That stung, but I knew it was justified.

"Would you like to discuss payment options now or would you prefer for me to draw up the contract first?"

*** 

I emerged from my office hours later, after painstakingly going through every aspect of Mr Gromov's contract. Talk about being paranoid. He was beginning to give me some serious cause for concern. A man that desperate could only be a liability.

"Lucy," I said, leaning against her desk.

"You look exhausted," she said.

"Cheers. Can you –"

She handed me a thick brown folder before I could even finish my sentence.

"What would I do without you?" I asked.

"Fail miserably?" She smiled sweetly.

I walked back into my office and set up an online radio player on my laptop. I sighed. There was a knock at the door and Lucy appeared with a mug of what I hoped was coffee.

"Hot chocolate," she said. "It even has marshmallows."

"Remind me to give you a pay rise," I said with a grin.

"A long overdue pay rise," she answered.

"Ah, the ulterior motive."

I took a sip of the hot chocolate and felt my stress melt away. Opening the folder, I pulled out Mr Gromov's background check. Lucy had run his name through our background screening service and also pulled up all sorts of information through Google. I wasn't shocked to find out that he was well known.

He'd overtaken, commandeered and brutally manipulated notorious gangs and mobsters to get to the top. He had connections to money laundering, fraud, drugs and murder but, of course, nothing had stuck. He'd evaded judge and jury each time. And now something had gone wrong, which is why he'd come to me.

After leafing through a number of articles, I dropped the folder on top of the contract details and tried to push it out of my mind. The radio tuned in to their latest news bulletin and I wasn't surprised to hear Stacey was still the number one talking point. It was predictable but still worrying. Was this what the stalker wanted? What about the killer?

Again, my mind circled back to whether they were the same person.

I got up out of my chair and wandered over to the window to watch the sun set. Stretching my back and then my arms, I looked down on the streets below.

It was busy, as usual. And the homeless man across the road was begging for change, as usual. It had been a warm and sunny day, and the tourists had abandoned the oversized anoraks, strutting around in shorts and t-shirts. It was easy to spot who was British; the bright red sunburn was a huge giveaway.

My phone started vibrating on my desk, pulling me from my thoughts. I snatched it up to see Stacey's name lit up on the screen. An involuntary smile spread across my face as I answered.

"Well, you're not an easy man to get hold of." I pulled the phone away from my face, glanced down at the screen and saw two missed calls.

"Sorry," I said. "I was with a client. It's been a tough day. What's up?"

"Well, I was hoping you'd invite me in for dinner so we could discuss this romantic weekend getaway but unless you like walking around in the dark, I'm going to guess you're not home," she said. I laughed at her sarcasm, something I liked in a woman.

"I'll be home in about half an hour."

There was an exaggerated sigh. "Fine," she said. "But I can't promise any of this takeaway will still be here when you get home."

I reassured her that I would be there as soon as possible and began gathering up my paperwork.

"I hear Mr Gromov's contract went well?"

I looked up to see Adam leaning against the door frame.

Yes," I said. "He's asked for a high level of protection and I've gone through all the small print. It's for an unspecified amount of time and he's assured me money won't be an issue."

"Good. Is he coming back in?"

"Yes. I'm going to have his contract formally drawn up for him on Monday and he's going to make an advance deposit."

"Good. Don't mess this up, Jason. We could have lost this one."

"Yes, boss," I said.

# Chapter 20

## JASON HUNTER

### HOME

*Thursday 30th July*

By the time I got home, it was raining. Stacey was sitting huddled in her leather jacket, staring out the passenger window of an old Merc. Today's bodyguard, Tony, was sitting in the driver's seat. I ran over and knocked on the glass, startling her. Climbing out the car with the takeaway, we both made a dash to the house.

I fumbled with the keys before the door finally swung open.

I slammed the door behind us and we desperately shrugged out of soaking wet coats. It was useless, the water had managed to seep into my shirt and had reached my skin. I was beginning to shiver.

I followed Stacey into the living room and she disappeared into the kitchen, dropping her duffel bag on the floor by the sofa as she went.

Slipping off my shoes, I left them in the hallway and padded into the kitchen.

Stacey had already rummaged around in the cupboards; I'd caught her with two wine glasses in one hand and an open bottle on the counter.

I dropped the folder of paperwork on the side and carefully peeled away the cover to check everything was relatively dry.

"I'm gonna go change," I said.

"Okay. Do you mind if I unpack some stuff?"

"No, that's fine. You'll be stuck in my room again, that okay?"

She nodded and put down the glasses, poured the wine and handed me one. She picked up the second glass and without saying a word, walked past me, grabbed the duffel bag and headed upstairs. I took a sip of the wine and then followed her.

Stacey was carefully unpacking a laptop from amongst some very expensive-looking clothes. I rummaged through one of my drawers and pulled out some joggers and an old t-shirt.

I changed in the bathroom and when I reappeared five minutes later, Stacey was sitting cross-legged on my bed and studying the laptop screen with a scowl.

"What are you concentrating so hard on?" I asked, dumping the wet clothes in the hamper.

"I'm looking at the latest news from Hungary."

"Anything interesting?"

"No, nothing new." She sat back and reached for her wine. "Very attractive," she said, taking in my outfit for the evening.

"Funny," I said with a smirk. "What do you want to do? Go downstairs or keep the party here?"

"It's warmer here," she said.

"Fair enough. I'll sort food."

Stacey didn't answer me; she'd gone back to her laptop screen. I disappeared downstairs. I reheated a few of the takeaway dishes in the microwave and the smell of Chinese food filled the house. Juggling the disposable containers on a lap tray, I carried them upstairs.

"So what have you got?" I asked, setting the tray down on the bed and removing lids.

"What?"

"You booked flights?"

"No," she said, innocently.

"No?" I repeated.

Stacey started laughing again. "Of course I have," she said, nudging me. "Just because I'm blonde, it doesn't mean I'm an idiot," she said.

"I know, I know."

"Out tomorrow, back on Sunday. That's plenty of time. And Adam won't get his knickers in a twist."

I laughed.

"I'll need your passport info," she said.

"Of course." I rummaged in my bedside table and pulled out my passport, dropping it on the bed.

"Who are we flying with?" I asked.

"I just went with EasyJet. They were the simplest option with the best times."

"A bit low budget for you, isn't it?"

She rolled her eyes at me. I picked up a chicken ball, dipped it in the sweet and sour sauce and then popped it in my mouth.

"All sorted then?" I asked.

"Yep, just looking at hotels now," she said.

# Chapter 21

## JASON HUNTER

### HOME

*Friday 31st July*

I was up early the next morning. Sleep had evaded me most of the night as I ran through everything that needed to be done in my head. I opened my laptop to see an email from Inspector Zsaldos thanking me for making flight arrangements. I'd sent him an email late last night after Stacey had gone to sleep.

"Morning," said a sleepy voice behind me. I turned to see Stacey yawning and stretching in her pyjamas. She padded into the kitchen and poured herself a mug of coffee.

"Morning."

Stacey smiled.

"Captain Zsaldos has sent me an email. I think he's looking forward to seeing us."

"Is he now?"

I smiled and watched Stacey wander into the living room, switch the TV on and make herself comfortable. I followed, taking my laptop with me and settling down in the armchair.

A reporter appeared on the screen, midway through her story.

*"The question all race fans are asking themselves is: will Stacey James be competing in the Belgian Grand Prix? Back to you, Steve."*

I glanced in Stacey's direction, but she was staring intently at the coffee cradled in her lap.

I looked back to the TV and just caught sight of the chaos from Oxford Street on Wednesday before the aforementioned Steve appeared, sitting on his BBC studio sofa.

*"Thanks, Deborah. Yes, that's a question we're all asking ourselves. I have Derwood Andrews here with me. Now Derwood, you have experience in this field, having set your own records. What do you have to say about Stacey's position?"*

Derwood Andrews, sitting next to Steve on the bright red sofa, chuckled.

*"Thanks Steve. Yes, although I've never managed what Stacey is attempting to do. I understand her struggle…"*

Stacey switched the TV off.

"I can't be dealing with their analytical bullshit. They're going to assess every damn decision I've ever made and criticise it."

"I don't think I've ever seen you mad," I said with a smirk.

Stacey looked up at me. She was trying to keep a straight face but she cracked, a smile slowly appearing.

"Well, now you have," she mocked. "Anyway, I'm getting dressed."

She flicked her hair at me and walked out with her coffee, stomping up the stairs. I closed the laptop lid and slipped it into its case.

# Chapter 22

## JASON HUNTER

### PRESTIGE HOTEL, BUDAPEST

*Friday 31st July*

"Look at this place!" I said, dropping my suitcase by the door. "I thought we'd be in a budget hotel."

"I'm world famous, Jason. If I was caught on camera walking into an Ibis, I'd make front page news."

I laughed.

"And I've had enough of that for the moment, thank you," she muttered.

The room wasn't so much a room but a suite. The lounge area had a plush brown sofa and two armchairs made of a soft velvety material and there was a 55-inch flat screen TV mounted on the wall. I took my shoes off and placed them carefully by the door. I almost slipped on the polished wooden floor as I made my way over to the window. Deep green curtains were draped on either side. I peered through the glass at the busy city scene below.

Stacey had disappeared through the double doors into the bedroom. I followed her to see the biggest bed known to man.

"What is that? A super king? It's huge!" I said, unable to contain my amazement.

Stacey laughed. "I think you'll find it's an Emperor bed," she said with a wink.

"Wow," I let out a deep breath. There was an intricately carved pattern on the wall above the bed. I couldn't help but run my finger along the smooth wood. I turned around to see Stacey smelling the fresh flowers on the dressing table.

I walked into the en-suite and let out a low whistle. Everything was made of marble. I'd never seen a room so shiny. The shower was big enough for at least five people and the mirror ran the entire length of the room.

"I could be a trophy husband," I said and sighed wistfully. Stacey laughed.

"I propose dinner," she said.

"Okay, where?" I said, rummaging in my duffel bag. Stacey disappeared into the bathroom. I pulled my tee off, pulled a clean shirt from my bag and slipped it on.

"The restaurant downstairs looks gorgeous," she said through the door. "Let's try there."

"I'm guessing I need to change out of my jeans?"

I heard the sound of the bathroom door opening and Stacey stepped out wearing a short black dress that sparkled in the light. Her heels clicked on the polished wooden floor.

"That was quick," I said.

"How do I look?" she asked, twirling on the spot.

I turned to look at her fully and suddenly felt my jaw slacken a little. "You look amazing," I said, doing the last button on my shirt.

"Thanks," she said with a smile that dazzled me. My legs felt weak.

\*\*\*

We entered the glittering restaurant and at least half of the tables were already occupied. A melodic clinking of wine glasses filled the air.

"You scrub up pretty well, Mr Hunter," whispered Stacey as we waited for the Maître d'.

"You're too kind, Ms James," I whispered back. Her hand was looped through my arm and we both gazed around the room. The tables and chairs were black with white decoration. The floor was a dark, polished wood. An impressive piece of artwork hung on the back wall, although I couldn't quite work out what it was depicting. I was still staring when a smiling waiter came and led us over to a table in the far corner. He held out Stacey's chair and I waited for her to sit before doing the same.

"So, tell me," I said as the waiter handed us a menu each. "How did you get into racing?"

"Oh, you know. I've been racing anything and everything for as long as I can remember. I stole my brother's remote-controlled car when I was about five and would create these amazing, elaborate tracks. The kids on our street loved it. I always won, of course. Even against kids twice my age. My dad once caught me taking bets from the crowd of kids that were watching. Yeah, I got into trouble for that one."

I laughed, imagining a younger Stacey being the boss of her street.

The waiter appeared and asked for our drinks order.

"Shall we have champagne, Mr Hunter?"

"Only the best for the lady," I smiled.

"Champagne it is."

The waiter disappeared.

"What happened after the remote-control racing?" I asked, fascinated by the strong-willed, gorgeous woman in front of me.

"I started racing on bikes. I had this amazing mini mountain bike in black and red, flames all up the side. It was the coolest bike on the block – none of that My Little Pony stuff for me, no way. I was coordinating street races between all the kids, setting up marshals and everything. I think that's when my dad realised he needed to get me in a kart. So I started karting at around the age of 6 and you know, it went on from there."

The waiter reappeared with the champagne in an ice bucket and two glasses. He filled them, placed them on the table and stood poised with his pen, ready to take our food order.

I'd been so engrossed in Stacey's story, I hadn't bothered to look at the menu. I glanced down now and suddenly felt very out of my depth. This wasn't the sort of food I ate. I didn't fancy eating foie gras, and pigeon was definitely not my thing. I glanced up at Stacey and she seemed engrossed in the choices. I ducked down behind mine and looked at my options again. I was feeling cornered. How could I possibly eat any of this?

I looked up at Stacey again. She was giving me a strange look.

"Shall we have some olives to share?" she asked, a half smile tugging at the corner of her mouth.

I swallowed. "If you like," I said, putting on my best smile.

"And then we'll go grab a pizza," she laughed.

\*\*\*

"I can't believe you," I said as I unlocked the door. I was laughing so hard I could barely stand up. Stacey was laughing too.

The door swung open into our room and I almost fell over. There was a fresh peal of laughter as Stacey waltzed in. Even in her half-drunken state, she still looked glamorous.

She dropped the pizza box on the coffee table and collapsed onto the sofa. I flopped down next to her and felt more relaxed than I had done in years.

"You're such a gentleman," said Stacey.

"How do you mean?" I was breathing heavily, trying to catch my breath.

"Taking me out to dinner, providing me with good company. All very gentleman-like actions."

"We had pizza, it wasn't exactly the Ritz," I said with a sigh.

We sat in silence for a while, admiring the décor. Stacey leaned across me and reached for the TV remote. My nostrils filled with her perfume and I had a sudden urge to reach out and touch her.

The moment seemed to last forever before she finally sat back. A news reporter came to life on the screen, interrupting the silence. Stacey flicked through the channels and finally settled on some American sitcom. She curled up on the sofa next to me. I put my arm around her and within minutes, I could hear her gentle breaths become longer and deeper.

"Stacey?" I whispered. "Stacey?" She didn't even stir. I gently untangled myself from her and went into the bedroom. I pulled the duvet back before going and carefully collecting the world-famous Formula One driver from the sofa. I laid her on the bed and pulled the duvet over her, tucking it around her. I stroked her hair and desperately wanted to lean forward and kiss her, but instead, I collected a spare blanket from the cupboard and made my way back to the sofa. I pulled out the book I'd been reading on the plane but within moments I could feel my heavy eyelids close.

# Chapter 23

## JASON HUNTER

### PRESTIGE HOTEL, BUDAPEST

*Saturday 1st August*

I woke up on the sofa with my feet hanging off the end. I stretched, rolled onto my back and looked up at the ceiling. Dinner the night before had been so much fun. I smiled.

"Morning," grumbled Stacey. I looked over to see a disgruntled and dishevelled-looking Stacey emerge from the bedroom.

"How did you know I was awake?"

"Women's intuition," she smiled. I was trying to suppress a laugh. Stacey's hair was literally sticking out in every direction and her make-up was so smeared, the term 'panda eyes' took on a whole new meaning.

"You might want to use the bathroom," I said.

"Why?" she frowned and padded across the room to the mirror. "Oh my God! I'm in the bathroom first."

I laughed.

By the time we were both ready, it was already 10am. Captain Zsaldos was going to be waiting. As I drove to our arranged meeting place, a heavy silence settled between us in the car.

"Are you okay?" I asked as we pulled into the racetrack car park.

Stacey nodded but didn't look at me.

"It'll be fine," I said. I took hold of her hand and gave it a squeeze. We got out of the car and walked across the tarmac towards the handful of police cars parked by the entrance. We were greeted by a square-shouldered man with a terrible handlebar moustache and a thick Hungarian accent.

"Mr Hunter, Miss James, it is good to finally meet you. Captain Zsaldos." He held out a hand.

"It's good to meet you too," I said, shaking his hand. His gruff-looking features softened when he smiled.

"I'm glad you are here." Zsaldos led the way into the stadium. "We have a little problem," he said sombrely.

I felt my stomach sink. Stacey grabbed my hand.

"What do you mean?"

"I told you we had found where the sniper was positioned, but it's proven to be a little more complicated."

"Okay?"

We walked out onto the track, stopping midway between the podium and the stand. Stacey was staring at the blood stain still on the podium, her face pale. Police tape was hanging across the pathway.

"So where was the shooter?"

Zsaldos pointed to the roof of the stadium where two police officers could be seen looking at something on the ground.

"You've got to be kidding me," I breathed. Zsaldos shook his head. He led us over to a ladder propped against the building and we climbed onto the roof.

"What the fuck?" whispered Stacey.

Scuff marks showed where the sniper had been and the officers had carefully drawn the positioning of his body with tape. I frowned. Something didn't look right.

"How did he manage to get up here without being spotted?"

"We don't know."

"Surely the helicopter would have seen something?" Stacey asked. I looked at her. "The camera crew always has a helicopter."

Zsaldos nodded. "We will be taking another look at the raw footage from the day. I will make sure you are given a copy."

"Thanks," I nodded.

"This shows the direct firing line," he said, pointing to a small apparatus holding a laser pointer.

"Do you mind if I...?"

"Go ahead."

I lay down behind the scope and had a perfect view of the podium. The laser showed the exact point the rifle was aimed at. The exact point where Gemma's head had been. I swallowed hard and stood up.

"Bullet casing?"

Zsaldos shook his head. "Forensics have confirmed that the shooter was here. Powder residue," he said at my quizzical look. "They either took the casing with them or it landed on the ground. Officers have looked but found nothing."

"But you have the rifle, right?"

Zsaldos nodded.

"Why did he leave the rifle but take the bullet?" asked Stacey.

"You're thinking rogue military or professional assassin," I stated.

Zsaldos nodded again.

I got to my feet and glanced at Stacey. She had her arms wrapped tightly around her stomach.

"Okay," I said, trying to diffuse some of the tension that seemed to have settled over us. "Are we alright to...?" I gestured towards the podium.

"Of course, of course."

Stacey and I climbed down, leaving Zsaldos on the roof. As soon as I was sure they couldn't see us, I pulled Stacey into a hug. It was more for my benefit than for hers. I felt so helpless but she clung to me with desperation.

Stacey pulled away from me. "I...I'm going to wait in the car." She didn't even look at me as she turned and walked away. I watched her go.

"Okay, Jason?"

I turned to see Zsaldos at the bottom of the ladder.

He indicated the direction Stacey had disappeared. "She is uncomfortable?"

"Yeah." I sighed. I began to walk towards the spot where Gemma had died. "She takes this all very personally."

Zsaldos didn't answer straight away but nodded slowly. "I understand."

I ducked under the tape and placed myself exactly where Gemma had been. I looked out at the stands and tried to imagine what she would have seen. It must have been overwhelming. I looked up at the sniper position and felt a chill run down my spine. The sniper must have been there for hours, perfectly aligned. He would have known Stacey - or rather Gemma - was going to be on the podium. If Gemma had looked up, she would have seen him. She could have done something, moved out of the line of sight.

"For fuck's sake," I said. Anger bubbled inside of me and I felt the urge to shout. Someone *must* have seen a full-grown man lying on the roof in broad daylight.

This was pointless.

I turned around and studied the blood splatter. It was definitely a rifle shot. From what little I knew and had found on Google, even I could see that. The bullet had gone through... Wait, the bullet.

"Where's the bullet?" I looked over my shoulder at Zsaldos. He was talking to one of the other policemen but stopped to look up at me. "The bullet?" I said. "Where is it? Was it found in the body?"

"No," he replied with a solemn shake of his head.

"So it's still here?"

"Possibly," replied Zsaldos. "But my team has found nothing."

I jumped down from the podium and approached the dark stain on the board behind it. I ran my fingers over the blood splatter. Where the hell was the bullet? My fingers grazed over a bump on the surface. I paused and ran my fingers over it again. There was a hole.

"Look at this." I beckoned Zsaldos over and he stood uncomfortably close, his starchy uniform brushing my arm. I pointed to the minute hole in the wall. There was a small scrape to one side.

"It is missing," whispered Zsaldos. "It has been removed."

"How-?"

"We secured the scene," he said, almost disbelieving.

"So he came back? Afterwards."

Zsaldos muttered something in Hungarian before straightening up. He called two of his men forwards and gave them instructions, pointing to the wall as he did so.

I stepped back as the police took over and surveyed the scene once more. It was clear I wasn't going to get anything here. I said my goodbyes to Zsaldos, promising to liaise with him in the morning and walked out into the empty car park.

"Anything?" asked Stacey as I climbed behind the wheel of the rental. She didn't look at me but was fixedly staring out of the window.

"It looks like he might have come back to retrieve bullet fragments," I said quietly.

Her head snapped round to look at me.

"He came back?"

"Looks like it. Let's go back to the hotel."

Stacey nodded. She stared out of the window the whole drive back, not once glancing in my direction. She didn't even speak when she got out of the car and I watched as she walked straight into the lobby.

I slowly followed but instead of heading for the elevator, I walked into the bar. Something told me Stacey needed her space. I ordered a shot of vodka, downed it instantly and then sat nursing a beer. I felt exhausted. Seeing where Gemma had died was like a baseball bat to the stomach. I was winded. The image of her body kept flashing in front of my eyes.

"Another?" asked the bartender.

I shook my head, paid for the two drinks and headed upstairs.

Slipping the hotel key into the door, I let it swing open. The room was empty. I looked around, expecting to see her watching TV on the sofa.

"Stacey?"

"Yeah?" Her head appeared from behind the coffee table. She wasn't looking in my direction, but down on the floor in front of her.

"You okay?"

"Yeah." She disappeared again. I closed the door behind me and walked forwards a few paces until I could see what she was doing.

Stacey had opened my file and spread it out across the floor. My laptop was also open with the emails I'd received from Zsaldos up on the screen.

"What's all this?"

"I couldn't think," said Stacey sheepishly.

"How did you get into my laptop?" I asked, amazed.

"You're not as careful as you think you are," she said with a cheeky grin.

"Note to self," I muttered. "Change all my passwords."

I watched as she moved some photographs about. She'd tacked together four A4 pages and Gemma's photo was in the middle. The rest of the paper was an amalgamation of photos, notes, and questions, all interlinked and criss-crossing all over the place. I'd never seen such organised chaos.

"Okay, so what have you got?" I asked, impressed.

"What if I wasn't the target? What if the sniper wanted Gemma?"

I didn't answer for a moment so I could fully absorb what she was saying.

"Okay," I answered cautiously. "Let's explore that."

"Well, I'm still alive. If the killer went to all that trouble at the race, why am I still here? Surely he would have found another way to do it by now? It doesn't make sense and it doesn't fit. First the threats and now this. It feels like this all escalated really quickly and then nothing. I mean, who does that?"

"I see what you're getting at and maybe it is something worth exploring but have you considered that you're still alive because a) I'm good at my job and b) he wants your death to be public." She flinched. "Whoever is threatening you, whoever killed Gemma, takes all this very personally and maybe he wants the world to know it."

"I guess." She looked back down at her mapping. "Can we at least explore the option? I'm desperate to get the fucker who did this. I don't know how I'll cope if he gets away with it."

"I know. Why don't we get Hayley to look into it whilst we're here?"

"Sure," she nodded. I walked around the sofa and sat down on the floor next to her, studying what she'd put together so far.

"You've missed this guy out." I held up the picture of Captain Cooper.

"I don't think he did it."

"Okay?" I said, drawing the word out into a question.

"If Gemma was the target, then it wasn't him. If I was the target, I still don't think it was him. He would never try to hurt me."

"Stacey, listen to me. Love can very quickly turn to hate, especially if someone is bitter. People always do crazy things and blame it on love. If he's snapped over the breakup then he's a loose cannon and a danger to everyone, especially you. How can you be sure he doesn't blame you?"

"He understood why we had to split up. He didn't want to hold me back as much as... as much as I didn't want to break up with him. It was a long time ago."

"But you did break up with him, Stacey. And that opens you up as a target," I said.

Stacey didn't look at me but shook her head defiantly.

I didn't say anything for a few moments.

"If the killer wants to get you at a public event, then we need to keep you safe," I said slowly.

"Keep me safe?" she asked. "You mean keep me locked up. I'm already going to miss a race because of this. I've had to cancel my whole diary. Ugh, what the *fuck* is wrong with everyone..." She slammed her fist on the ground, got to her feet and walked away.

"Stacey," I said but she'd already disappeared into the bedroom and closed the door. I heard the lock click shut behind her.

*Right*, I thought to myself. I could understand Stacey's frustration but this felt personal. Was *I* in the wrong? I looked over the papers on the floor. She did have a point though. What sort of murderer would disappear after an event like this – unless Gemma really was the target? That would bring about a whole new line of questioning. I wondered if Hayley had considered this possibility.

There was a knock at the door. I dragged myself to my feet, noticing how tired my body felt and peered through the peephole to see one of the hotel attendees standing in the hallway.

"Can I help you?" I asked, pulling the door open.

"This is for you," he said in a thick accent. The young bell-boy awkwardly handed me an envelope with 'Mr Jason Hunter' scrawled across the front.

"Thank you." I took the envelope and closed the door. It was open before I'd even got back to the sofa. A small memory stick slipped out with a business card from Captain Zsaldos. I grabbed my laptop and quickly inserted it into the USB drive. The computer was slow to respond. The cursor changed from a little arrow to the annoying blue circle as the laptop worked out what it was supposed to be doing. I dragged my fingers through my hair, almost pulling some of it out. The screen finally sprang into action and opened a new window before pausing again. I gritted my teeth, got up and decided to get myself a drink from the mini bar.

By the time I got back, the computer seemed to be fully functional again and had opened the memory stick folder. I double clicked the first video file labelled 'Sunday After Race'. The 3-hour footage came entirely from one angle, and pointed towards the stands. I fast-forwarded to moments before Gemma's death and scanned the rooftops. There was no sign of the sniper. Closing the first file, I opened the second titled 'Helicopter Sunday After Race'. It took a while before the chopper gave a clear view of the stands but the moment it did, I hit pause. He was there somewhere. I just had to find him.

It took a good couple of minutes before I was finally able to make out a strange shape on the roof and a faint shadow behind it.

"Got you, you bastard," I muttered. I checked the time stamp and then opened the first file and paused it at the same moment. I looked along the roof again but still struggled to see him. I thought it would have been obvious but the image quality got worse the more I zoomed in. Only when I spotted the barrel of the gun did I realise how clever he'd really been. The particular spot he'd chosen was at a slight angle, keeping his body hidden whilst his gun could still hit the target.

"You son of a bitch," I said.

Zsaldos had sent me three more files, all from different cameras that caught the stands at the time of Gemma's murder. I combed through all of them until I had five pixelated shots of the killer.

Stacey's bedroom door clicked open and she appeared, looking ashamed.

"I - ," she began.

"Come here," I said.

"What?"

I showed her the images.

"Oh my God," she whispered. She peered closer and studied each one. "Have you sent these to Hayley?"

"Not yet. I've only just got them."

"We need to get them printed."

"You don't cope well with computer screens, do you?" I joked.

"Nope, that's why none of my training has ever involved a simulator. Even when I was learning the basics," she boasted.

"Impressive."

Stacey didn't say anything as she continued to flick between the pictures.

# Chapter 24

## Jason Hunter

### Prestige Hotel, Budapest

*Sunday 2nd August*

"Did you get them?" I asked.

"I'm looking at them now," said the voice on the end of the phone.

"Put her on speaker," said Stacey, sitting down next to me.

I hit loudspeaker and laid the phone down on the table.

"You're on speaker, Hayley," I called.

"Hi Stacey, how are you enjoying your spontaneous trip away?"

"It's great," said Stacey, glancing at me with a slight blush on her cheeks. And for a moment I had to wonder if the girls had been talking about me. She saw the look on my face and hastily changed the subject. "What do you think about the photos?"

"Well, they're not great. The amount of zoom you need completely distorts the image. I'm gonna get tech to try and enhance it. I'm hoping we'll be able to pull a face but I doubt it."

"Sure, sure," I said, still aware of Stacey sitting close to me. "We're gonna head down to the station and see Zsaldos again before our flight this evening."

"Okay, give me a ring later."

I hung up the phone and stared at the laptop screen. We were both silent for a few moments.

"When will this all be over?" sighed Stacey, resting her head against my shoulder.

"When we catch him," I answered.

"I thought you'd say that."

I put my arm around her and rested my chin on top of her head. We sat there for at least a minute, both lost in thought until Stacey's exceptionally loud ringtone shattered the quiet. She grabbed her bag and began rummaging inside it.

"Hello?" she said, answering the phone. There was a moment's pause. "What? You've got to be kidding me. How the hell-?"

I sat patiently whilst Stacey listened to whoever was on the other end of the phone. She sat unnaturally straight and her hand clenched into a fist. The look on her face was aggressive and I had a funny feeling I was about to see a side to her that I hadn't come across before.

A minute or two later, Stacey ended the call.

"Some bastard has broken into my flat," she said through gritted teeth.

# Chapter 25

## THE STALKER

### JASON'S HOME

*Sunday 2nd July*

He leaned back in his chair and looked out the window. The sun was shining and the sky was clear, though there was still a chill in the air. He felt relaxed, comfortable, right at home. For the first time in what felt like forever, he was back in control.

Fuck, it felt good!

He took a deep breath and slowly let it out, taking a moment to bask in his success. His own fucking genius. The thought of Stacey finally realising Jason wasn't all that he was cracked up to be was enough to make him feel on top of the world. She'd find his message, realise Jason couldn't protect her, and then she would ditch him.

Which would give him the perfect opportunity to pick up the pieces of poor, broken Stacey.

He studied the living room he was sitting in and admired the tasteful decor. He was impressed with the number of books on the shelves. Standing up, he wandered over to inspect them. Tom Clancy, Andy McDermott and even some Andy McNab. He browsed along the broken spines and was a little shocked to see George R.R. Martin and

Bernard Cornwall amongst them. He didn't know Jason's attention span stretched to stories that long. He really was full of surprises.

He moved across the room to the collection of photographs on the wall. Some were outside, others were special occasions. They were a nice reminder of what he had to lose. One picture in particular caught his eye. It was a boy and a girl, both smiling at the camera, clearly enjoying themselves. The boy had his arm draped around the girl's neck. It looked like it was taken on a family holiday.

"Such a shame," he muttered. "You have beautiful children, Jason." He shook his head and took the picture from the wall, his heart racing in his chest.

"No-one fucks with me," he said.

# Chapter 26

## SAM THORNTON

### STACEY'S APARTMENT

*Sunday 2nd August*

"No, boss. I'll see what I can find. Looks like they were looking for something. Uh huh. Yes, boss."

Sam hung up the phone and surveyed the chaos around him. Not only had someone broken into Stacey's apartment, they'd left complete destruction in their wake. He'd already briefly scanned the apartment for signs the intruder was still there and, satisfied that they'd left, he went back to the living room to start the methodical search before he called the police.

It had been difficult trying to get rid of the concerned neighbour and Sam had reassured the little old lady at least seven times that he would phone the police himself, but not until she'd called Stacey.

Standing in front of the main entrance, he scanned the overturned sofa, the books ripped from the shelves and strewn across the floor, and the smattering of cushion stuffing that lay on top. This had been an aggressive attack.

Taking out his phone, Sam began to photograph the scene from every angle.

He moved through the living room and into the open plan kitchen. Here it was a little more subdued. Drawers and cupboards had been yanked open, but for whatever reason, the intruder hadn't decided to throw the crockery on the floor.

Sam took a few more photos before his eye caught on a crisp white envelope on the marble island in the middle of the room. It was on top of a pile of unopened mail but just had Stacey's name printed across the front. Something about its neat placement made the hairs on the back of Sam's neck stand on end. He rummaged in one of the open drawers for a sandwich bag and carefully manoeuvred the envelope into it using the edge of his sleeve.

Down the hallway in the gym and the bathroom, everything seemed to be in its place, but upstairs in the main bedroom, the chaos ensued. Clothes had been ripped out of the wardrobe, the duvet had been slashed open and the makeup on Stacey's bureau had been trashed.

A gut feeling told him he wasn't going to like what he found in the en-suite and when he pushed the door open with the toe of his boot, he let out a long steady breath.

More of Stacey's makeup lay cluttered in the sink, and wonky pink letters were smeared across the bathroom mirror in what he could only guess was lipstick.

Sam took more photos of the scene before him and then dialled Jason.

"Hey boss, yeah I've taken photos, but you're not going to like what you see."

# Chapter 27

## JASON HUNTER

### BUDAPEST DISTRICT HEADQUARTERS

*Sunday 2nd August*

"Hayley is going to pass the images to their tech department for enhancement," I said.

We were sitting in Zsaldos' cramped office.

The blinds were pulled down so low that the room was steeped in shadow. Stacks of folders were piled everywhere; on the desk, on the floor, on top of the overflowing filing cabinet.

I glanced across at Stacey who sat on the very edge of her seat, looking uncomfortable.

"Good, good," muttered Zsaldos. He was rummaging through the paperwork on his desk. Just seeing the disorganisation of his office made me immediately doubt his policing abilities.

He eventually found what he was looking for and slid Gemma's folder over to us.

"I've already seen the file, Captain," I said, hoping he really wasn't this useless.

He smiled and opened the file himself, slipping out a photograph. I frowned and passed the photo to Stacey. Zsaldos handed me a piece of paper.

"You've identified the bullet?" I said with disbelief.

"Not quite. We have an idea. We're not sure. There's no evidence. But – "

"What?" interrupted Stacey.

"Military."

"Confirmed?"

"For the moment, it's a close guess."

"But it confirms your suspicions?" I asked.

Zsaldos nodded. No-one spoke. It was one thing to speculate but to be able to piece together the evidence and provide an educated guess? This wasn't good. Were we dealing with a hitman? And if yes, who was he after; Stacey or Gemma? Stacey's brainstorming the night before had gotten into my head but no matter how hard I tried, I couldn't discount Cooper as confidently as she could. All sorts of alarm bells were going off, and everything was pointing to Cooper. He was the only one with motive, means and skill.

"Do you have any suspects at the moment?" I asked.

Stacey was studying the floor, refusing to acknowledge anything else.

"No," said Zsaldos.

"Any leads? Any evidence? I mean, do we know when the killer got to the site?"

Zsaldos slowly shook his head. "This is everything."

The fact that we didn't have a clear direction to go frustrated me. We had a killer with a military weapon and what was looking to be military-grade training too, and no leads. Gemma's death pressed down my shoulders like a double-decker bus and for a moment I just couldn't breathe.

"Is there anything else we can help you with?" I asked awkwardly. Zsaldos shook his head. "In that case, we have a plane to catch." I took hold of Stacey's hand and squeezed. She looked up, dazed.

We walked back through the empty corridors of the police station. I caught sight of a lone cleaner wandering between the desks in an open plan office, emptying the bins as she went.

"Cops don't like working at the weekend, it would seem," I muttered.

We climbed back into the rental car and I finally felt like I could breathe again. Stacey pulled out her phone and dialled Hayley's number as I started the engine.

She pressed the speaker button and Hayley's tinny voice filled the space in the car. "I feel like this is going to be bad news."

Stacey brought the phone closer to her face so Hayley's voice wasn't lost in the rumble of the engine.

"No news."

"Nothing at all?"

"They're not a hundred percent sure on anything at the moment. They have an idea on the bullet but it's just guesswork."

"Encouraging."

There was a pause and then Hayley said, "I have some news as well. I'm not sure whether you'll view it as good or bad but it's a step forward."

"Go on," I said.

"We've found Cooper."

Stacey's eyes shot up to mine in a moment of panic.

"What do you mean, you've found him?" I asked, cautiously.

"Don't worry, he's alive. But we can't do anything without justifiable cause. The best I can do is bring him in for questioning but we have no evidence against him, just speculation."

"How about the weapon? Could that not help?"

"Not unless his fingerprints are on it."

No-one spoke.

"I hear there's been an incident at your apartment?" Hayley asked.

"Yeah, someone got in and trashed the place."

"I think there's more to it than that. The sooner you two are back here, the better. I'm going to be taking over your stalker case."

# Chapter 28

## **STACEY JAMES**

### JASON'S HOME

*Sunday 2nd August*

She stepped out of the taxi and breathed in the smoggy London air. Stacey looked up at the beautiful two-storey house that had recently become her home and sighed. She didn't mind staying with Jason, in fact she quite liked it but there was something eating away at her. An ache in her gut. Is this what homesickness felt like?

"You okay?" asked Jason. Stacey nodded. Apprehension was beginning to mount. She knew that the moment the front door closed behind them, everything would be electric. The type of electricity that usually made her feel alive, but her mind and body were too exhausted for it.

She followed Jason through the front door and into the hallway. He disappeared up the stairs and she wandered into the living room. An uncomfortable feeling began to settle on her shoulders and the uneasiness began to work its way into her stomach. Jason appeared moments later.

"You okay? You're really quiet," he asked.

"Something's not right," whispered Stacey, but Jason wasn't looking at her. His eyes were fixed behind her. His body had gone rigid.

Following his line of sight, she turned to see a gap on the wall. A gap where a picture used to be. Stacey went cold. Someone had been here. Someone had been in his house. Someone had broken in without leaving a trace. It was one thing to trash her apartment, but it was another to target Jason.

Jason dashed out of the living room. He raced upstairs, leaving Stacey alone. She crept to the window and peered down the street. It was too dark to see anything. With a shiver, she checked the lock and pulled the curtains closed.

Jason had reappeared with his phone pressed to his ear.

"You need to take the kids and go on holiday," he said. There was a pause. "Please, just do it, Adrianna." Jason sighed. "Everything's fine. I just need you to take them somewhere. Today if you can, or tomorrow." There was another pause. "Be safe," he said and hung up.

"Everyone okay?" I asked.

He nodded and then let out a deep breath.

An iron fist was wrapped around her heart and she felt like she was going to be sick. Jason walked mechanically into the kitchen and then back into the living room. He went and locked the front door, pulled the bolt across and then went upstairs, Stacey following him like a lost puppy.

By the time she made it upstairs, he was already sitting on the edge of his bed with his head in his hands. She sat down next to him and gently rubbed his back.

"Jason," she whispered. He looked up and she could see the fear in his eyes. She struggled to speak. "Jason, I –"

He kissed her. His kiss was filled with longing and she succumbed to it, kissing him back.

Before she knew what was happening, before she could even get her thoughts straight, Jason's hands had buried themselves in her hair and they clung to each other with hungry desperation.

# Chapter 29

## ADRIANNA JACKSON

### HOME

*Sunday 2nd August*

"Who was that mummy?" asked Lily.

"It was Daddy, sweetheart. He was just seeing how you are." Adrianna smiled. "Why don't you go and play with your toys?"

Lily scowled but left the room nonetheless. Adrianna walked into the living room where her husband, Mickey, was sitting in his armchair in the corner with a newspaper open in front of him. His bald head reached past the top of the chair, and his broad shoulders swamped the armrests.

As much as she had her differences with Jason, she knew his instincts were always right, and if he suggested a trip, it was a bloody good idea to go ahead and book one.

Adrianna glanced at her husband. "I'm going to take the kids away for a few days," she said.

"Sure," he answered, without looking up.

Adrianna didn't move. She watched Mickey for a few more seconds but when he still didn't look at her, she sighed and left the room.

Lily had joined Max in his room. She'd pulled his box of old toy cars out from somewhere in the wardrobe whilst Max, completely oblivious to his sister, was playing on his new Xbox.

"Sweetheart, no, no, no." Adrianna dashed forwards and scooped the cars off the floor. "Not on the carpet."

Max turned to see what had happened and began whining at his sister the moment he saw the open wardrobe doors. Lily got to her feet, crossed her arms and stormed out of the room.

Adrianna put the box of cars back into the cupboard. "I need you to pack a suitcase," she said. "We're going away for a few days." She tried to sound excited but even Max could tell it was forced. He frowned.

"Where are we going?" he asked, pausing his game and getting to his feet. "Is Dad okay?" Max hugged her and Adrianna had to fight back the tears.

"Everything's alright, baby. I just thought it would be good if we went away. Where would you like to go?" said Adrianna, stroking her son's hair.

"I don't know, shall we ask Lily?"

"Sure." They walked into Lily's room to find her sulking on her bed.

"We're going on holiday," announced Max.

"What?!" said Lily, instantly forgetting her bad mood and getting excited. "Where are we going?"

"I don't know, sweetheart. Where would you like to go?"

"America! No, Spain! No, Japan!"

"Mmm, how about somewhere a little closer? We're only going away for a few days," said Adrianna.

"How about Southampton?" suggested Max. "We could go on a cruise instead?"

"That sounds like a great idea," she said, nudging him playfully. Max smiled. A quick search on her phone showed there was a ship leaving in two days. She'd book a hotel in the city for tomorrow night and they could board on Tuesday. "Right, pack a bag. We're going tomorrow."

"Yay!" shouted Lily.

Adrianna pulled Lily and Max into a hug. She held her children close and hoped they couldn't feel her heart racing.

# Chapter 30

## JASON HUNTER

### HOME

*Monday 3rd August*

My alarm pierced the air and dragged me from the bliss of sleep. I went to roll over but felt the body curled against me shift. Stacey let out a soft snore as I remembered the night before. I smiled and kissed her gently on the forehead. She gave me a sleepy smile without opening her eyes and I snuggled closer to her.

I lay next to her, holding her close as the sun began to rise and stream in through the curtains. I could still feel the panic bubbling away in my chest as I worried about my kids. The fear from the night before came flooding back in a tidal wave. I didn't have time for cosy morning cuddles, even if it was with one of the most beautiful women I'd ever seen. I looked down at Stacey and felt my heart twinge with guilt. I needed to get up.

I grabbed my phone and slipped out of bed. Less than a minute later, I was in the kitchen. I'd switched the kettle on and was dialling Sam's mobile.

"Hey buddy, sorry it's early. Have you checked Stacey's flat since yesterday?"

"I was gonna head over in an hour."

"Cheers, mate. Give me a ring when you do. And swing by mine when you're done."

"Will do."

With one thing dealt with, I turned my attention to what was really bothering me; Max and Lily.

I glanced at the gap in the pictures on the wall and considered my next move. I finished making my coffee and took it into the living room.

One option was to call Hayley. That was the right thing to do. Hayley was the law, but... something was telling me not to.

There was a noise behind me and I turned to see a sleepy Stacey in the doorway.

"Morning," I smiled.

"Morning." She walked in and curled up on the sofa. "You okay?"

I nodded and took a sip of my coffee.

My face must have given away how I really felt because her expression suddenly changed.

"Hey," she whispered gently. "Hey." She leaned forwards and took hold of my hand. "Everything is going to be just fine, okay?" I looked away, unable to believe her. "Right," she said with more firmness. Stacey stood up and marched into the kitchen.

The clattering of kitchen cupboards told me that she was making a coffee.

She reappeared moments later, mug in hand.

"Where's Sam?" she asked.

"He's going around to your flat in an hour and will call me."

"In the meantime, let's be a bit proactive, shall we? Showered and dressed, please. And then we'll think about what to do next," she said.

I smiled. "Yes, ma'am," I said with a mock salute.

# Chapter 31

## JASON HUNTER

### HOME

*Monday 3rd August*

"Feel better?" asked Stacey as I padded back into the room, wrapped in a towel and dripping water on the wooden floor.

I nodded.

"Have you got to go into the office?" she asked, sitting on the edge of the bed and moisturising her legs.

"Yes. Hopefully Adam doesn't lay into me," I sighed, pulling clothes out of the drawers. I went back into the bathroom and got dressed.

As I buttoned my shirt, the doorbell rang. Knowing it would be Sam, I ran downstairs barefoot. I opened the door and motioned for him to come in. He walked through into the living room and Stacey came down the stairs, dressed in some loungewear and with her hair still wet.

"Coffee?" I offered.

"No thanks." He shifted his weight from one foot to the other. "I took some photos."

"I thought you sent them to me?" I leaned against the counter and my stomach twisted into a knot. Out of the corner of my eye, I saw Stacey fold her arms.

Sam pulled his phone out of his pocket and handed it to me. I flicked through the photos and saw the destruction in the living room, the chaos in the kitchen and the devastation in the bedroom. None of it was new to me. When I came to the photo of the en-suite, my stomach sank.

The word 'whore' had been scribbled in large pink letters across the mirror.

"Why didn't you send this to me before?" I asked.

"Figured you couldn't do anything in Hungary. Best to wait until you were back."

I passed the phone to Stacey and she frowned when she saw the picture. She handed it back to Sam.

"And there was this." He reached into his jacket and pulled out the sandwich bag containing the crisp white envelope. He handed it to Stacey.

She cautiously reached out and took it.

"Where was it?" I asked.

"On the counter. Looked like someone had organised your mail and this was on top," replied Sam.

I watched Stacey as she opened the envelope and pulled out a newspaper clipping. She turned around and placed the article on the counter before pulling out another, and another. In total, there were five articles from different newspapers.

The largest was an account of the car backfire in Oxford Street. Scribbled at the bottom of the article were three words that sent a chill down my spine.

*You need me.*

"What the fuck?"

"We need to give this to Hayley," I said.

"My fingerprints aren't on it, I made sure of that," said Sam.

"Thanks." I clapped him on the shoulder. "I'm gonna need you to stay with Stacey today. And I think it's best if we all go down to the police station," I added.

Sam nodded.

"Call Liam and get him to drive over, he can be your partner for today. Where's the rest of the detail?"

"On stand-by until Stacey is back in the country. I would have sent them over last night but this-"

I waved a hand to dismiss his excuses. "Let's get back up and running as soon as possible."

Sam nodded again and then dialled Liam's mobile.

I pulled out my own phone and dialled the office.

"Lucy, I need you to put me through to Adam." It took just a few minutes to bring Adam up to speed and, as expected, he wasn't all too happy with me. "We need to get down to the police station for a statement, there's not much I can do about it."

"Just get in as soon as you can and make sure Stacey's safe."

"Yes, boss."

# Chapter 32

## Jason Hunter

### Hammersmith Police Station

*Monday 3rd August*

We drove down to the station in silence with Sam and Liam following in a separate car. I felt easier knowing the kids were going to be safe, but I knew it wasn't the end of this.

We pulled up behind the station and climbed out of the car. Sam nodded at me as he parked and turned off the engine.

Pushing through the single swing door, we came to a plain waiting room with a reception desk to one side.

"We're here to see Detective Inspector Irons," I said through the thick pane of glass between myself and the receptionist.

The civil servant behind the reception desk looked up at me. He glanced at Stacey and then went back to his crossword puzzle. "Do you have an appointment?"

"No, but-"

"I can't just let anyone in here, pal," he said, looking up again. "You need to make an appointment. Detective Inspector Irons is very busy, and so am I. If you haven't got an appointment, please leave."

"Look, *pal*," I said, leaning forward. "DI Irons knows we're coming-"

"Take a seat and I'll see if the DI is available," he interrupted, waving towards a row of uncomfortable-looking, plastic blue seats.

Muttering under my breath, we sat down just as a text buzzed through on my phone. It was from Sam letting me know that some paparazzi had shown up looking for Stacey. Great. The last thing I needed right now.

I watched the receptionist behind the desk pick up the phone and dial through. After a few moments of murmuring into the handset, he replaced the phone.

Hayley burst through the double swing doors in less than two minutes. She embraced Stacey and kissed me on the cheek. "Come on up."

We followed Hayley back through the swing doors and up to her office. It was a cramped room with filing cabinets lining one of the dirty white walls. We all sat down, Hayley on one side of the desk, me and Stacey on the other. The chairs were hard and uncomfortable and I fidgeted awkwardly. Hayley's degree in Criminology hung on the wall opposite us, next to a photo of a gangly teen.

"Any news?" asked Hayley, peering over the piles of folders on her desk. I was amazed there was space for her to do anything in here. The computer sat in one corner but there was no way she was able to physically use it.

"That break-in at my apartment. They left something." Stacey said, and carefully pulled the envelope, still stored in the sandwich bag, from her handbag and passed it to Hayley.

"What's this?" she asked as she pulled out a pair of latex gloves.

"News clippings of the car attack and a note."

"We also have some photos," I said and pulled my phone from my pocket. I handed it over and she quickly scrolled through the images.

"I'm going to need you to send them to me." She started scribbling furiously on a notepad close by.

"There's more," I added.

"More?" asked Hayley, looking up.

I nodded. "Someone's been in my house, taken a picture of my kids off the wall."

Hayley frowned. "Who has access to your house?"

"Me, Stacey." I nodded in Stacey's direction. "My ex-wife in case of emergencies."

"And your ex-wife hasn't taken it?"

I shook my head. "I don't think so."

Hayley paused for a moment.

"Okay, I'm gonna need you to make a couple of statements; about this and the letter. Oh, and about your trip to Hungary, too."

"Sure," I nodded.

She took us through the lengthy process of taking a statement before reading back to me everything I'd said so far and then asking me to sign it. To log each incident, she'd separated each account of events in case they were unrelated and needed to be handled separately.

It was then Stacey's turn to do the same. She put forward the theories she'd been experimenting with back in the hotel and I saw Hayley raise an eyebrow in response. Ignoring her, Stacey continued to recount her version of events. Once done, she then signed her own statements.

"Where's Cooper?" I asked, checking my watch.

Hayley finished writing some notes before looking up at me. "He's here in London. Flew in yesterday under the name Elijah Nielson. The same name he'd used to enter Hungary."

"Hungary?" asked Stacey. I glanced over at her.

"When was he in Hungary?" I asked.

Hayley grimaced and then nodded.

"Oh my God. Please tell me you know exactly where he is," I said.

"Not quite."

"Not quite?! Jesus!" I stood up and walked away from Hayley's desk. I turned around and looked at Stacey. She looked as agitated as I felt. But she was convinced Cooper was innocent. I wasn't. Judging by the look on Hayley's face, she was on my side. I took a deep breath and sat back down again.

"Please continue," I said slowly.

Hayley glanced at Stacey and then back at me. "Cooper flew into Gatwick and got straight into a taxi. I only found this out about four hours after it happened. We found the cab driver and where he dropped Cooper. Unfortunately, that's as far as we got. I have a warrant for all the CCTV footage within a mile radius to see if we can determine where he went. All we have at the moment is this photo of what he looks like now."

Hayley passed a photo across the desk. I took it. Cooper certainly did look different. Stacey leaned over my shoulder and studied the picture with me.

"How did you find this guy?" I asked.

"Someone submitted a request for his information in America after a drunken bar fight."

"Hang on," I said. "This man has spent *years* keeping himself off the radar and a stupid bar fight is what trips him up? The guy's special forces, right?"

"Used to be, yeah."

"Why did the American want his information if it was just a bar fight?"

"The guy he beat up is in ICU. It's pretty serious."

My jaw dropped. "And they let him leave the country?"

"Well, they didn't. That's why they requested his info."

"He flew out on a fake ID and yet, they were able to request his info? That means they knew his real identity."

"Correct."

No-one spoke. Something didn't feel right.

"You think he did it on purpose?" asked Hayley with a frown.

"Well, what do you think? He hops around different countries and coincidentally lands in Hungary when Gemma is killed but in a matter of weeks, after knowing full well he'd be the number one suspect, he 'accidentally' slips up and lands back on the radar. And to top it all off, he then arrives in the UK as well. That says planted to me."

Hayley was thoughtful. "Well, we're looking into it, but we need the cooperation of the American police so it could take a while."

"Sure, of course." I glanced over at Stacey. "I need to get to work," I said. Stacey nodded but didn't look at me. I'd obviously overstepped here. "Will you girls keep me posted?"

"Of course," said Hayley. I stood there for a moment, trying to convince myself to leave but not wanting to.

"Right," I muttered, and then left.

# Chapter 33

## JASON HUNTER

### LONDON OFFICE

*Monday 3rd August*

Adam sat with his feet on my desk as he looked through Gemma's file. The official one. I tried to act as calm and as normal as possible. I closed the door, slipped off my suit jacket and took a seat opposite my desk.

"Considering you're spending so much time on this case, your file is pretty light," remarked Adam. I didn't answer. "How's our client, Mr Gromov?"

"Good. We're getting the last bits sorted."

"I'm glad to hear it. Good weekend?"

I paused and then nodded. Warning bells were ringing loudly in my head.

"How did it go with the police?"

"Yeah, fine. Stacey's there now and Sam and Liam are with her. I'm going to sort out the rota for the rest of the week."

Adam nodded absentmindedly and looked out the window at the London skyline. Unsure of what to do, and sensing he had something else on his mind, I didn't move. I became painfully aware of the silence and my ears filled with the thumping of my own pulse mixed with the sound of my breathing. I tried taking a deep breath to regain composure but the whole scenario was putting me on edge. *What did he want?*

"Do you have an estimated start date?"

I frowned.

Adam gestured to one of the other manila envelopes on my desk.

"Gromov. Your client," he said.

"Wednesday, next week."

"Schedule another meeting with him."

"Sure," I said cautiously.

"And I also suggest you go to him."

"Okay."

"Today."

"Will you just tell me what the hell you're trying to get at?" I said through gritted teeth. I could feel my anger rising.

"Gromov's in hospital, Jason. He's been shot. He was transferred to London Bridge this morning." Adam got up from my desk, dropping the file back into place and walking towards the door. He paused. "Sort your shit out, Jason. I won't tell you again." And Adam left.

I dove behind my desk and grappled with the computer mouse. Adam had left the news article up on my screen. I scanned through the specifics and dialled Gromov's number.

"Hello?" A heavily accented voice answered but it wasn't Gromov.

"This is Jason Hunter. I've been employed as residential protection. Please may I speak with Mr Gromov?"

The voice laughed. "And where were you yesterday?"

"Just put him on the phone."

"No can do. Everything you need to say goes through me."

"When can I visit?"

"Whenever you like. Mr Gromov is already expecting you."

"I'm on my way."

# Chapter 34

## DI HAYLEY IRONS

### HAMMERSMITH POLICE STATION

*Monday 3rd August*

"What was all that about?" Hayley asked.

"All what?" Stacey replied.

"The sudden frostiness with Jason?"

"He's trying to pin this all on Bill. It's ridiculous. He's got no proof and I've already told him that Bill didn't do it."

Hayley raised an eyebrow but Stacey didn't reply.

"You think he might have a point?" Hayley asked gently.

"Bill didn't do it," replied Stacey.

"You don't know that. You have to keep an open mind with things like this otherwise you won't get anywhere. It's hard, but I've seen more shocking things happen, believe me."

"I feel like I'm drowning. If it wasn't for me, Gemma would still be alive."

"You can't think like that," said Hayley, suddenly feeling more sympathetic. "You didn't pull the trigger, therefore it's not you who's at fault. Some twisted person out there did, and it's them who will pay the price."

"You're right, you're right."

"Of course I am. This is my job."

"What-"

A knock at the door interrupted them, closely followed by a young policeman popping his head round the door.

"Detective Inspector?"

"Yes?"

"The photo results have come back from analysis. I've emailed them to you."

"Thanks."

Hayley quickly logged into her computer and opened up her emails. There were six waiting to be read. She opened the most recent, labelled 'Image analysis results', and scanned through its contents.

"Interesting," she muttered.

"What?" asked Stacey.

Hayley turned the computer monitor so it was facing Stacey.

The screen was filled with an aerial image of the grand prix track in Hungary. A thin black line had been drawn, outlining the figure lying on the roof.

"That's the shooter?" asked Stacey.

Hayley nodded. She shuffled her chair to the left so she could see the screen again and clicked through the next images. They were all similar but showed the figure from different angles. Some photos were further away and others were a blurry mess.

"A pro," she said.

"How can you tell?" asked Stacey.

"His positioning," she pointed to the figure and traced his outline with her finger. "And the analysis report that came with the photos."

"Can you tell if it's Cooper or not?" asked Stacey.

"Well." Hayley paused and scanned through the accompanying document. "The analysis says the shooter's 5'9 and..." She began to rummage through the paperwork on her desk.

"And?"

She found what she was looking for and handed it over to Stacey.

"And, Cooper is at least 6'2, according to his military records."

Stacey continued to read the fact sheet on Cooper.

"Cooper isn't the shooter."

"Unless the image is wrong?" suggested Stacey, suddenly doubting herself.

Hayley shook her head. "Not likely. It's calculated by a computer."

"I need to call Jason," said Stacey. She pulled her phone out and dialled.

# Chapter 35

## JASON HUNTER

### LONDON BRIDGE HOSPITAL

*Monday 3rd August*

It took what felt like an age to battle the congestion and when I finally did, the nurse at the front desk wouldn't let me through. I glanced to my left as the elevator buzzed open. A huge black man in a suit stepped out.

"This way, Mr Hunter," he said in a deep rumbling voice. I recognised it from the call earlier.

I smiled at the receptionist and followed him. We rode the elevator in the uncomfortable silence associated with professional protection. I smiled. My new friend escorted me past two bodyguards outside a private room on the third floor. The steady beep of machines greeted me, along with the harsh smell of disinfectant.

I was actually surprised; the room was nice, with a private en-suite and views looking out on the River Thames. A large flat-screen TV was mounted on the wall showing the national news whilst on mute.

"Hello, Mr Hunter," said Gromov. He was propped up in bed, the bandage on his shoulder clearly showing. I was expecting him to look weak but he actually looked well, the bandage the only indication that anything was amiss. "I believe we have business to discuss." He waved an arm towards one of the purple leather chairs. I sat down and glanced at the bodyguard.

"Of course. I'll fast-track the paperwork and we'll get your residential team up and running tomorrow."

Gromov nodded.

"I do think we should discuss the reason why you need protection," I said, lowering my voice.

"Only when you have proved yourself," he replied.

I nodded. Fair play. "I take it the surgery went well?"

Gromov nodded again. "No complications. I should be allowed home in the next day or two."

"I'll make sure my team carry out a full perimeter search before taking post to ensure the property is secure before you're released."

"The boss needs to rest now," said my Black friend. I nodded and stood up. With nothing else to say, I let myself be escorted from the room.

# Chapter 36

## **DIANE PARSONS**

### LONDON BRIDGE HOSPITAL

*Monday 3rd August*

The knot in her stomach was twisting like an angry snake. It preoccupied her so much that she didn't see the annoyed look on the receptionist's face. Feeling out of place and uncomfortable, Diane perched on the edge of one of the cream seats in the immaculate reception area.

Her eyes darted around the room, taking in the Arab man in a white tunic, the elderly woman wearing chunky pearls, the young-looking man in casual jeans and a chequered shirt open at the neck, and the Latino woman checking her makeup in a compact mirror.

Diane looked at the receptionist who was now tapping away at the keys on her computer. The room was almost silent except for the clack of her nails on the keys. The rhythm was interrupted by the noise of the elevator doors opening at the end of the corridor and the sound of footsteps.

A tall Black man in an impeccably tailored black suit appeared alongside Jason of all people. Her heart pounded and she quickly looked away, hoping he hadn't seen her. Oblivious to her presence, he exited the building.

Then she heard her name being called and looked up to see the Black man staring in her direction. She glanced around at the others in the waiting room who had all turned to look at her before hurriedly getting to her feet and following the bodyguard down the corridor and into the waiting elevator.

Once they reached the third floor, Diane was led along the corridor and into a room where two bodyguards stood outside.

Inside, Gromov was sitting in bed watching the muted TV. A reporter was standing outside the Houses of Parliament. He looked up as she entered. Moments later, Volkov entered, who purposefully avoided Diane's gaze, and sat in one of the leather seats by Gromov's bedside.

She swallowed hard. This wasn't good.

"I heard about what happened," she said, hoping to diffuse some of the tension building up inside her.

Gromov nodded slowly. "It happens. That's why I'm going to be employing your acquaintance, Mr Hunter."

Diane didn't give herself time to wonder how much Gromov knew, but she could sense that she wouldn't like wherever it was leading.

"Have a seat," he said, waving at the empty chair opposite Volkov.

Dianne did as she was told and tried to exude an air of confidence by dropping her bag on the floor next to the chair and sitting back. As soon as she did it, she felt foolish, and pulled herself upright again, perching on the edge of the seat.

"How is Stacey?" asked Gromov after a few moments of silence.

"Fine." Diane tried to smile but could feel the falseness in her cheeks.

"Good. I'm sorry about our previous misunderstanding. I'm assuming you haven't told her?"

"No, of course not."

"Good." Gromov smiled.

"The... er, the police are still investigating, though."

"What have you told them?" he snapped.

"Nothing, I swear. I just thought you'd like to know." The words tumbled out her mouth in a panic.

There was silence. Diane looked at Volkov, hoping to catch his eye in a small gesture of friendship, but the Russian driver was resolutely looking at the muted news reporter on the TV. She looked back at Gromov to see him watching her.

"I have a favour to ask," he said. "Call it repayment for what you owe."

Diane didn't respond. Thoughts were whirling around in her head, trying to predict what terrible thing he was about to ask her to do. If he was going to ask her to kill someone, she wasn't sure she could do it. In fact, she knew she couldn't.

"Actually, I have two favours."

Volkov's eyes snapped to Gromov. This obviously wasn't part of the agreement.

Under her arms, she was sweating. She thanked her lucky stars she'd had the sense to wear a white shirt.

"Firstly, I need you to provide an alibi for our mutual friend here." Gromov waved a hand in Volkov's direction. "My being shot had nothing to do with him and we need to establish that."

Diane nodded, that wasn't too hard. She just had to tell a small lie... to the police.

"Secondly, I want you to make a deposit."

The words caught her by surprise and she couldn't help but say, "Deposit?"

"Yes. One of my men will deliver the money to you and I need you to deposit it in one of Stacey's accounts."

"Why?"

Gromov's eyes hardened. "I don't think it's wise for you to be asking questions."

"Sorry," she whispered and looked down at her hands, hoping she'd find a way out of this. It didn't seem Dimitri was going to be much help.

"I need you to fabricate a transaction to show the money was a legitimate payment to Stacey. Then, I need you to send it to one of my accounts in five smaller payments over the course of the next two weeks. There is going to be some restriction to my assets whilst this shooting is being investigated so your help will be invaluable."

Diane nodded. The penny had dropped. She was in deep, and she wasn't going to be getting out any time soon.

"Do you have any questions? About what you have to do?" asked Gromov.

Diane shook her head.

"Very good."

There was a pause and he turned to Volkov. "Dimitri, perhaps you would like to show our guest out?"

Volkov nodded and stood up, indicating Diane should do the same.

They left the room, went down in the elevator and exited the building together.

Outside, the sun was shining and there wasn't a cloud in the sky. Diane could already feel the heat rising from the pavement. Her thoughts turned towards the tube journey home and its cloying claustrophobia.

"I'm sorry," said Volkov.

Diane looked up at him but he was looking towards the water. So many angry words fought to break free. He should be sorry. It was all his fault in the first place. If he hadn't gone blabber mouthing to his mob boss patron, none of this would have happened.

But the slump in his shoulders, the ways his hands were thrust into his pockets and the constant refusal to look her in the eye told her this was hitting him hard. It might have been his fault, but it wouldn't solve anything to throw blame around.

"I'll accept that apology once this is all over," she said as calmly as she could, linking her arm through his. "You gonna walk me to the tube?"

"Sure," he shrugged.

They turned right and began the short walk to the underground station.

"Are you going to tell me why you need an alibi?"

"It's something to do with business. Mr Gromov won't say exactly. The shooting, the bullet wound, it's all related and he doesn't want my career to be affected."

"And the money laundering?"

Volkov glanced at her.

"Oh come on, I know when someone is asking me to launder money. Even if they do dress it up to make it sound legitimate."

Volkov smiled and then turned serious. "That I really don't know. It wasn't what we'd discussed."

Diane nodded, pleased her assumption was correct. Maybe that kind of instinct would help get her out of this mess.

"When's your next race?"

"The 23rd, in Belgium. Surely you already know that? What with Stacey, and all."

"Just making conversation."

They stopped outside the entry to London Bridge station and Volkov turned to face her.

"It will all work out. I promise."

She nodded.

"Call me if you need me."

She nodded again.

To hug him, she stood up on her tiptoes and enjoyed the fleeting moment where his arms were wrapped tight around her.

"I mean it," he said, pulling away. "I'm worried about you."

"I'll be fine," she replied. She smiled and hoped it looked reassuring whilst inside she was terrified.

*What the fuck was she going to do?*

# Chapter 37

## JASON HUNTER

### LONDON OFFICE

*Monday 3rd August*

I hadn't moved from my desk since I'd got back from the hospital. I hadn't spoken to anyone. Lucy had taken one look at me and knew that I needed to be left alone.

On my right was Gromov's paperwork. In and amongst that was a printed version of the article Adam had left up on my computer. Someone had broken into Gromov's house and shot him. Luckily, the few bodyguards he already had were able to intercept the intruder, causing the bullet to go through his shoulder instead of his heart.

I sat back in my chair and let my mind wander. Some cynical part of me wondered if it was a setup to get me on side quicker, or to prove my incompetency. Perhaps Gromov had spoken to Adam... I dismissed the idea the moment it popped into my head and chastised myself for being so paranoid.

Although, a missing photo of your kids would do that to you. My heart constricted with anxiety and I picked up my phone to text Adrianna.

Her swift reply calmed my nerves and I looked over to the paperwork on my left; everything I knew about Gemma's murder. The file that I had begun to obsess over. It was in my every waking thought and weighed heavily on me.

I pulled out Gemma's mugshot and remembered the day it was taken. She'd been so nervous. I'd just given her the news that we'd decided to employ her and she was absolutely thrilled. Perhaps downplaying it a little. After all, it wasn't cool to be too keen. I smiled.

Gemma had briefly hugged me before composing herself and then shook my hand. I'd tried not to laugh.

"Shall we do your ID and then you can start tomorrow?" I'd asked.

Gemma went pale. I'd never seen someone look so terrified of having their photo taken. I smiled again, sadly. It seemed a whole lifetime ago. And in some ways, it was.

I pulled out the mind map that Stacey had started to put together and pinned it to the wall next to my smart board. Looking at it, I suddenly had an idea. I projected a world map onto the board and began to circle the cities Cooper had visited since he'd left the army, along with the dates. There were big gaps in the timeline but some we could guess at and a few of the more recent ones we knew, especially now Hayley had one of his aliases.

I stood in front of the board for a minute studying my handiwork.

There was certainly no pattern. It looked like he'd been using a pair of dice to determine his next destination. I frowned. I knew that pattern, or at least the lack of it. He was running away from something or someone.

Why would he need a random flight pattern? Who was he trying to hide from? Someone with the resources to track him. Someone like me.

That gave things a whole new perspective. One that I hadn't anticipated. Cooper couldn't be the killer. He had problems of his own.

# Chapter 38

## Jason Hunter

### London Office

*Monday 3rd August*

The ringing of my mobile quickly cut through my reverie. One glance at the screen and I quickly answered.

"Cooper's-"

"Not the shooter," I finished for her.

"How did you know?" asked Stacey.

"The flight pattern. It's all over the place. He's running away from something. Or maybe someone." I began pacing again. The adrenaline of figuring out a clue, being one step closer to understanding, was making me anxious. I couldn't sit still.

"You think he's in trouble?"

"I think it's worth talking to him. He was still in Hungary on the same dates as the Grand Prix and it could be connected. He might not be Gemma's murderer, but he might still know something."

"I'll see if Hayley can help track him down. Speak to you later."

"Good idea."

I hung up and stood still in the middle of the room.

So, if Cooper wasn't the shooter, who the hell was? I paced across the carpeted floor of my office. First one way and then the other. I paused and looked at the map I'd constructed on the board, but it didn't help. My head felt overcrowded and nothing was making sense.

"Hi Jason," came Lucy's voice on the intercom. "I have your ex-wife on the phone." I picked up the receiver.

"Thanks, Lucy. Put her through."

I heard the familiar rustling of Lucy patching a call and then silence. "Adrianna?"

"Yeah, it's me. The kids want to say hi."

There was more rustling as the phone was handed over.

"Hi Dad!" said Max.

"I want to say hi," came Lily's voice in the background.

"Hey buddy, off on holiday, are you?"

"Just for a few days. We're going on this massive boat tomorrow. I've seen it at the dock. You won't believe how big it is!"

I laughed.

"I want to speak to dad," came Lily's whine again.

"Fine," huffed Max. "Bye Dad, love you."

"Bye buddy."

The phone rustled again and then I had Lily rambling on about all the cool things she would be able to do on the boat. I smiled; what had I been worrying about?

"Let Mummy have the phone, sweetheart," came Adrianna's voice.

"Bye Daddy, I love you."

"I love you, too, sugar."

"They're so excited," said Adrianna and I could hear the smile in her voice.

"Is Mickey with you?"

"No... He had to work."

As much as I hated to admit it, I would have preferred her to have someone there, even if it was Mickey.

"When do you leave?"

"About 6 tomorrow evening. We're going to sail over to Amsterdam for a couple of days and then come back. If you need us to go away again, there's another cruise a few days later that we can hop on when we get back to Southampton. I've checked."

"Okay, I might send one of my guys to keep an eye on you."

"Oh, Jason. That's not necessary." There was a pause. "Or is it? Should I be worried?"

"No, it's fine. I just want to make sure you have someone with you."

"I guess."

"If they're not with you by the end of today, I'll have someone waiting in port for when you're back."

"Okay."

"Try to have fun."

"I will."

"Oh, and Adrianna?"

"Yes?"

"Take care of yourself."

She hung up the phone. I felt my throat tighten. I fought back the tears and tried to breathe as slowly and calmly as I could. My heart was racing and my hands were clammy. I sank into the guest chair in front of my desk as the muscles in my legs became weak. How had it all come to this? The anxiety in my chest tightened, making it difficult to breathe.

There was a gentle knock at the door and Lucy appeared with a cautious smile.

"Richard is about to start the team briefing for Gromov's contract. I thought you might want to at least sit in on it?" Lucy tucked a loose strand of hair behind her ear as she spoke.

I nodded, gathered together Gromov's file and headed down to the main boardroom.

I opened the door to see every chair around the long oval table was taken and all heads turned to look at me. I nodded towards the familiar faces before seating myself at the back in a spare chair.

Richard stood by the projector at the other end of the room and held his hand up in greeting before continuing.

"The surveillance will be 24/7 and you will change every six hours in a 3-3 pattern. We will be running training sessions in between shifts to keep you in top form." He paused. "This is Gromov's house -"

Richard clicked the control in his hand and the screen came to life, showing a photograph of a large property. It had two huge white columns either side of an imposing oak door. Neatly trimmed hedges lined the extensive driveway that finished in a circular gravel court-yard. Richard clicked the control again and the image became a cross section.

"There will be postings here, here and here." The pointer moved over the screen, hovering over different points of interest. The camera moved so we were looking at a two-dimensional, birds-eye view of the house and grounds. One of the guards whistled.

"This is a high-profile case," said Richard.

I noticed one of the younger guys glance nervously around the room. It was Liam. He'd been assigned to Stacey since he'd started, more to get him into a routine than anything else, but he was still a fresh face, and one that had been part of Stacey's team on Oxford Street the week before.

Richard took the whole group through a step-by-step dissection of the house. He then moved on to talk about the main locations they'd be covering and the basic routine of Gromov's life. It was certainly a big job. I counted the number of people sitting around the table. Twelve. I wasn't sure it was enough.

"Jason," said Richard, snapping me from my reverie. I looked up and smiled as all eyes were on me. "Is there anything you want to add?" I paused for a second and then got to my feet.

"Richard is the team lead for this contract and will be reporting to me on a weekly basis. Mr Gromov is a high-profile client. Recent occurrences mean that you will all need to be on high alert. I don't want any injuries. This is one job that we can't afford to go wrong. If anyone has any questions, then please come and find me after this meeting." I paused again before sitting back down. No-one moved for a few seconds.

Richard suddenly nodded his head. "Exactly. Questions?" There was no response. "Great. Ben. Graham. Liam. Tony. You're Team 1 and you start at 1800." Richard turned the screen off and promptly left the room whilst the whirring of the projector slowly came to a halt. I closed my file and followed. Within seconds of appearing in the hallway, Richard was by my side. I tried hard not to sigh.

"I wasn't aware that this was such a high-risk job. I mean, I know we don't want a repeat of Hungary -" He abruptly stopped talking.

"You are perfectly right," I said through gritted teeth. "All I need you to do is keep a close eye on everything."

Richard nodded and then disappeared. I opened my office door and swiftly closed it behind me. I stood there for a moment, breathing slowly.

There was a knock and I jumped. "Come in," I said as I walked over to my desk and sat down. The door was opened by Liam.

"I hope I'm not interrupting anything, Mr Hunter," he said, glancing around my office.

"No, not at all. Have a seat. What can I do for you?"

"Well, about the briefing... Sir, I..."

"You're pretty new to this, right?"

He nodded. He looked like he was about to say something, so I waited. "Have I done something wrong?"

"What makes you say that?"

"Well, I was part of Stacey's protection team. Have been since I started. So I don't know why I've changed assignments?"

"Ah, you were there on Oxford Street, weren't you?"

He nodded.

"And you did a great job."

He nodded again but didn't say anything.

"You haven't done anything wrong. We're reducing Stacey's team to allow her more flexibility when it comes to getting around. The current team is too conspicuous. So it's nothing personal." I smiled, hoping he wasn't taking it too personally.

"And there's nothing I can do to be put back on that assignment?"

"It doesn't—"

"I just feel my skills and experience are better suited to that assignment than this new one," he persisted.

"Sorry, Liam," I said. "The decision's already been made. If we make further changes in the future, I'll be sure to consider you."

Liam didn't look convinced. "Of course."

\*\*\*

On my way home that evening, I visited Gromov again. Partly to reassure him that the teams had been given their briefing, but partly because I wanted to reassure myself.

I signed in at the reception desk and the receptionist flashed me a smile. I gave her a wink, watched her blush, and then disappeared up the lift to Gromov's room.

As I walked in, he smiled.

"Mr Hunter, what a pleasant surprise."

"I hope you're feeling better?"

"Much. I believe I'm going home tomorrow."

"Great news. Your team will be operating as of 6pm. They've just had their briefing."

"Ah, good work," he nodded.

An awkward silence followed. I felt like I'd walked in on something. Glancing around the room, I noticed two other people, both of which looked to be bodyguards. Perhaps Gromov had been issuing instructions. Either way, there was nothing more for me to say and so I went to leave.

Just as I got to the door, I handed my business card to the Black bodyguard who'd taken charge on my previous visit. "This is my emergency number. I want you to call me no matter what. Any problem, big or small." He looked at it dubiously for a second before taking it and tucking it into his top pocket.

"You got it, boss," he said in his deep, rumbling voice.

# Chapter 39

## ADAM EDWARDS

### LONDON OFFICE

*Monday 3rd August*

The office was officially closed and almost everyone had already gone home, but Adam was still at his desk.

Dread sat heavy in the pit of his stomach as he patiently waited for Lucy to leave. He could see the light from her desk faintly illuminating the corridor outside his office.

Finally, the noise of drawers opening and closing followed by the click of the light told him she was leaving. He glanced at his watch to see it was already gone seven.

He quickly arranged himself to be looking at something on his computer screen just as Lucy's head popped round his office door.

"I'm off home," she said and smiled sweetly.

Adam looked up from his Mac.

"Have a lovely evening," he replied, returning the smile.

"Don't work too hard," she sing-songed as she retreated.

Adam pulled a face and waited until he heard the elevator doors close before leaving his own office and half-walked, half-ran down the corridor.

He took one final look around and then tried to open the door to Jason's office. It was locked.

"Fuck."

He stole over to Lucy's desk and began rummaging in her drawers. The top one was locked and the other two held nothing of significance. Hunting around on her desk, he looked under paperwork, moved a photo frame and picked up a grotesque-looking paperweight. Bingo. A small silver key shimmered in the dark.

Trying the key in the locked drawer, it immediately sprang open and there, staring up at him, was exactly what he was looking for. A set of three keys on a tacky *I Love London* keyring were thrown on top of the assortment of junk, paperwork and business cards.

Adam picked up the keys and confidently strode back over to Jason's office. Within seconds, he was inside. Even without Jason's presence, Adam had a sense of the self-righteous attitude that filled Jason's day-to-day life.

Sitting at the desk, he sneered at the photo of his two children and began his search. Unlike Lucy, Jason was less meticulous when it came to security. Whilst the computer was password protected, he'd failed to lock any of his drawers and confidential paperwork was haphazardly strewn across his desk.

Having already seen the Gemma file, Adam wasn't sure what he was looking for.

He needed to establish exactly what Jason knew about everything and how close his affiliation with the police was.

Within a few minutes, it was clear he wasn't going to find what he wanted without access to Jason's emails. The paperwork was fairly standard and didn't reveal anything. Not that he expected it to. He browsed the hastily scrawled notes on the notepad and flicked through the pages.

There were numerous reminders for trivial things, like calling Adrianna, swinging by the shop on his way home, and tasks for Lucy. But he paused when he saw his own name followed by a question mark and Adam's pulse quickened.

A harsh ringtone punctuated the air, making Adam jump.

Fishing his phone from his pocket, he answered the withheld number.

"You ready for your next batch?"

"No, I've already told you I can't."

"You failed to explain why. And you know it better be a fucking good reason otherwise the bossman isn't going to be happy."

"I've got the police sniffing around at the moment, it's too risky," whispered Adam.

"What do they want?"

"It's nothing to do with the money, don't worry."

"Then what is it?"

Adam sighed. "Someone died, okay? It's a murder investigation." There was silence at the other end. "Look. The police are coming in every five minutes at the moment. Give me time to let it settle down and then we can go back to the regular deposits."

Silence.

"Sure." A pause. "I'll call in two weeks."

The connection was cut and Adam slumped in Jason's chair, his heart racing.

He was in serious shit.

# Chapter 40

## DIANE PARSONS

### HAMMERSMITH POLICE STATION

*Monday 3rd August*

Diane was led through the secured door and into the bowels of the police station. She'd spent the day flitting between running errands for Stacey and being completely consumed with guilt and worry.

The therapist she'd been seeing since she'd started working for Stacey had left her a voicemail, concerned as to why Diane had missed their session. She just couldn't trust herself not to give the game away.

Complaining about Stacey and the mental toll it took was one thing, but she knew the moment she felt comfortable on that leather sofa, everything would come tumbling out. And she couldn't let that happen.

Now, as she followed the uniformed police officer down the corridor, she felt sick.

There had been a knock at the door, interrupting her latest fretting session and whilst the officer had been kind about it, Diane's throat had gone dry and she'd been unable to utter even a single word. She'd just nodded when the officer explained he needed to take her to the station, a tight knot of worry clenched in the pit of her stomach.

She hadn't been paying attention to where they were going but now the young officer stopped outside a door, knocked and then opened it, indicating for Diane to go inside.

Expecting to see an interrogation room, Diane relaxed when she saw Detective Inspector Hayley Irons sat on one side of a desk and Stacey on the other. The relief that flooded her upon seeing Stacey was as surprising as it was unfamiliar, and it unsettled her.

"Hi Diane," said Hayley without looking up from her keyboard. Stacey flashed her a quick grin.

"Everything okay?" replied Diane, carefully seating herself in the spare chair. Whilst it wasn't what she expected, she still had a bad feeling about this.

"All good. I understand you know Dimitri Volkov?"

Surprised, Diane nodded slowly.

"I didn't know that," said Stacey.

Diane nodded again. "I- I've known Dima for years."

"How?" asked Hayley, her tone now more formal.

"How?" Diane repeated, confused.

"How do you know him?"

"We grew up together. Lived on the same street. Mr Gromov brought him over from Russia when he was young. Saw potential in him."

"So you know Mr Gromov as well?"

"Not really."

"Not really?"

Diane shook her head.

"Dima lived with a foster family when we were kids. I never really met Mr Gromov, but I knew about him."

"And how often do you see Mr Volkov?"

"Not often. We catch up every few months or so."

"You've never told me any of this," interrupted Stacey.

Hayley cleared her throat and gave Stacey a stern look.

"Where were you Saturday evening, Diane?"

"I...I was with Dima."

"Where?"

"At his place. I went round to see him."

"And what were you doing?"

Diane shrugged. "We watched a movie, talked, the usual."

Hayley jotted something down on her notepad.

"Do you have an intimate relationship with Mr Volkov?"

"No," said Diane more forcefully than she'd intended. "No, it's nothing like that."

"Okay. Why doesn't Stacey know about this... friendship?"

The change in direction momentarily threw her. "What do you mean?"

Hayley waved a hand at Stacey. "It's clear you haven't told her about the relationship between you and Mr Volkov. Why not? He's her rival."

"It would be unprofessional of me," replied Diane defiantly. "We don't ever talk about my personal life, it's not appropriate."

"Yes-" started Stacey.

Hayley threw another stern look at her.

"Thanks for your time, Diane. Could you please leave me your number in case we need to get in touch?"

"Sure." Diane glanced at Stacey and then scribbled her mobile number on a piece of paper and handed it to Hayley.

There was an awkward pause before Diane nodded, stood on shaky legs and left the room.

Once the door had closed behind her, she leaned against the wall, breathing heavily. Tears pricked her eyes.

It took a few moments to compose herself before she could walk down the corridor, retracing her steps from earlier and half-guessing where she was going, before she reappeared in the August sunshine.

Once she'd made it around the corner, she rummaged in her hand-bag for her mobile and then dialled.

"I need to see you."

She felt sick.

"Sure. I have the first deposit for you as well."

Diane could feel the bile rising up her throat.

"Okay," she squeaked. "I'll come to yours."

"See you soon."

Diane ended the call and promptly threw up onto the grass verge next to the path.

# Chapter 41

## JASON HUNTER

### HOME

*Monday 3rd August*

I pulled up outside my house and everything was dark. There were no lights on, no noise, and no sign of Stacey. I dialled her number without getting out of the car. It took her a while to answer but when she did, her voice sounded strange.

"What's wrong?" I asked.

"Nothing. I... I'm still at the station. Just... I can't stop thinking about it all."

"Do you want me to come down?"

"No, it's fine. I'll be back soon, maybe an hour."

Walking into my own home without Stacey for the first time in almost a week felt strange, unnatural. I was surprised by how quickly I'd gotten used to having her around.

I switched the lights on one at a time, moving through each room slowly and methodically. I paused in the living room in front of the missing photo. My heart jolted for the thousandth time at the thought of Max and Lily being in danger.

I took a deep breath and moved on, dumping my files on the kitchen counter and opening the fridge. It was almost empty. I couldn't remember the last time I'd been shopping. Opening the freezer, I was confronted with the same issue. I felt my stomach growl but I didn't feel up to eating anything. I grabbed the last beer from the fridge and headed into the living room.

The can opened with a satisfying fizz as I began flicking through the TV channels. There was nothing on, not that I was surprised. I flicked through once more just to be sure before settling on a rerun of Top Gear.

The next thing I knew was the slam of the front door. I jumped, managing to spill my beer down myself and looked up to see Stacey's stressed face looking down at me. I glanced at the TV to see Jeremy standing centre screen. I couldn't have been asleep for long.

Stacey's worried frown instantly transformed into an entertained grin as she noticed the beer sloshed all over my chest. I self-consciously tried to mop it up but it was far too late for that.

"Rough day, was it?" she asked with a cheeky smile.

"You could say that," I laughed. "What about you?"

"Terrible," she groaned. "I don't know what else to do."

# Chapter 42

## STACEY JAMES

### JASON'S HOME

*Monday 3rd August*

"I found out something today. And I'm not sure if I should be worried about it or not," said Stacey as she disappeared into the kitchen.

She reappeared moments later with a glass of wine.

"Oh yeah?" Jason replied, eyeing the wine curiously. Stacey frowned slightly.

"Apparently Diane knows Dima Volkov."

That got his attention.

"What?"

"Uh huh. Grew up together. They go way back."

"And how have you found this out?"

"Apparently, this guy called Gromov has been shot. It just so happens that he's Volkov's patron and is basically responsible for his career in Formula 1."

Jason had frozen, his beer half way to his lips.

"What?" she asked.

"Nothing," he replied too quickly.

There was a brief silence.

"So how did this lead to Diane?" he asked.

"Hayley wanted to speak to her about being Volkov's alibi when this Gromov character got shot."

"Interesting."

"That's what I thought. And she's never told me this before. First I've heard of her being friendly with another driver." She took a swig of her wine.

"Are they together-together?"

"No, Hayley already thought of that and quizzed her on it."

"And you believed her?"

"I'm not sure. It was definitely strange. And when I asked her why she hadn't told me, she said we don't talk about her personal life." Stacey pouted.

"Do you?"

"Well, no. If I'm honest, I struggle being nice to the poor girl. She just infuriates me like you wouldn't believe."

"How so?"

"I don't know. Whenever she's around, she gets my goat up and then I go into this awful bitch mode."

Jason looked at her across the sofa.

"What?"

"Nothing," he replied.

They lapsed into silence. And all of a sudden she felt guilty. Maybe she was too hard on Diane. Maybe this was her fault.

"When did you find this out?" he asked.

"This afternoon. I was with Hayley in her office."

"Whilst she quizzed Diane?"

Stacey nodded.

"That's a bit unprofessional, isn't it? Shouldn't she have spoken to Diane privately?"

Stacey shrugged. "Maybe."

There was a long pause.

"Shall we watch a movie?" asked Stacey, getting up to find the remote for the TV.

Jason nodded absently but she chose to ignore him. Things had suddenly gotten awkward. Had she said too much?

Flicking through the channels, Stacey settled on *How to Lose a Guy in 10 Days*, one of her favourites.

"We need to find Cooper," said Jason after half an hour of silent movie watching.

"Yes, I'm aware of that," said Stacey.

"If we find him, at least we can get some answers."

Stacey reached for the remote and paused the TV.

"Sorry," said Jason, looking apologetic.

"You just can't switch off for one minute, can you?" she said, irked by the interruption.

He slowly shook his head. "I don't think it's him and I know you don't either. But-"

"But what?" remarked Stacey, starting to get annoyed.

"But no-one can deny he's the main suspect. So what if he's over 6ft? The pictures are so blurry, it might not even be accurate."

"Hayley's already said they're reliable. The calculations are done by a computer from multiple angles and multiple pictures; they all came up with the same height."

There was silence.

"I think finding him is a good idea, too. That way we can a hundred percent eliminate him from suspicions, and we can stop wasting our time with this ridiculous conversation," Stacey added. Jason stared at her, surprised at her blunt response.

"He might know something."

"I know, I know. I'm agreeing with you," she said, the frustration evident in her voice.

"What do you propose we do then?" he asked after a few moments.

"Go and find him. Right now."

Jason took a swig of his beer and slowly lowered the bottle. "What are you talking about?"

"Come on, let's go and look for him. He's somewhere in London, Hayley knows that much. We just have to find out where."

"And how do you propose we do that?"

"I did date the guy for a couple of years," she said with a sly smile before heading upstairs.

She needed to slip into something comfortable but appealing, and already knew the perfect outfit.

For one of her glamour shoots at the beginning of the year, Stacey had been gifted a low-cut top that had quickly become one of her favourites and had landed her towards the top of FHM's World's Sexiest Women list. It was exactly what she needed but it wasn't the kind of top she kept tucked away in her duffel bag.

She swapped her current jeans for a newer pair of tight-fitting Levi's and slipped on her casual heeled boots. They gave her a sexy biker look without looking like she was trying too hard.

One look in the mirror told her that her hair was in no shape to be let down and so she threw it up in a quick, rough-handed messy bun with a few strands left curled around her face.

A dab of lipgloss, a brush of blusher and she was ready.

She walked into the living room to see the TV had been switched off. Jason was in the kitchen leafing through Gemma's file.

"We need to swing by my apartment," said Stacey. "I'm not quite ready."

"But you look great."

"You ain't seen nothing yet," she said with a wink.

Jason laughed.

"Hurry up," she called over her shoulder, already walking toward the door.

"I'm just grabbing that picture of Cooper. We might need it."

# Chapter 43

## DIANE PARSONS

### VOLKOV'S APARTMENT

*Monday 3rd August*

Taking another drag of the spliff, Diane finally felt herself relaxing.

"Oh, it was awful," she said to Volkov.

He took the joint from her and smiled.

"You've done well."

Diane nodded absently. She looked around the room, trying hard not to think about what it was she needed to do next. She didn't want to ask, but it was the only way to get this over with.

"Where's the money?"

With the spliff between his lips, Volkov took a long drag, held the smoke in his lungs for a few seconds before slowly exhaling. Passing the joint back to Diane, he went over to a sideboard, pulled out the bottom drawer and lifted up the false bottom. Reaching inside, he pulled out a thick brown envelope.

He handed the envelope to her with a worried crease between his eyes.

"You know what to do?"

Diane swallowed hard, took another drag to calm her nerves, and nodded.

*Grow a pair,* she told herself. It was her own fault she was in this mess. What the fuck had she been thinking? She just needed to deposit the money. Then an idea struck her.

With all of Stacey's recently cancelled appearances, it would be easy to pretend that was where the money had come from. They occasionally received cash deposits from some of these events. Admittedly, not very often. But that would be fine if it was sprinkled in with the other transactions.

"When does he need the money by?"

"Five deposits in the next two weeks."

She nodded again, feeling the effects of the weed lift and becoming, regrettably, clear-headed. She took another desperate drag on the spliff, hoping it could keep her cocooned in the fog that made her feel like everything was okay.

There was enough money in Stacey's account to make the deposits now and then the cash could be fed in over the next few months. That wouldn't be difficult as there were always payments going out for certain things.

They sat in silence for a while longer as they smoked the rest of the spliff, and the panic that had been following her around for the last week almost disappeared. She was feeling surprisingly mellow and it felt good.

Turning her head to the left to look at Volkov, she smiled.

"God, what a mess."

"It'll be over soon," he replied, grinning inanely. He was obviously enjoying the effects of the drug as much as she was.

Without warning, Volkov leaned forwards and gently placed his lips against hers.

Taken by surprise, Diane didn't respond. Her eyes went wide as she looked at the face of her childhood best friend.

His lips parted, his tongue making its way into her mouth and she found herself kissing him back. Something she'd thought about countless times since she was fourteen. The forbidden fruit tasted sweeter than she could have ever imagined.

He slipped his hand inside her top and was kissing her with a desperation she didn't think was possible.

# Chapter 44

## JASON HUNTER

### STACEY'S APARTMENT BUILDING

*Monday 3rd August*

"Park it in the garage," said Stacey, pointing to a ramp that disappeared underneath the imposing multi-storey apartment complex.

I drove my car down the ramp and into the darkness. The motion-sensor lights sprang into action, illuminating the room in a garish white glow. I took a sharp breath. It was a car-lover's dream.

I pulled up before the barrier and Stacey climbed out. She walked round the car, tapped a code into the keypad and walked underneath the barrier as it lifted. I followed her, driving as slowly as I could. There was a stunning Aston Martin DB9 in silver, a red Ferrari 430 Scuderia, a dark green Rolls Royce Wraith, and even a McLaren 650 Spider in bright orange. My head was as far out the car window as it could get and my mouth was hanging open in pure amazement.

"I thought you'd seen this lot before?" she asked.

"The team would have done the necessary checks but I've never been down here," I said.

She laughed. "I'm just going to run and get changed. Wait here, I'll need to pull out for you to park."

She disappeared through the entrance marked for residents and I spent the next ten minutes unable to take my eyes from the car heaven in front of me.

Stacey reappeared looking undeniably gorgeous. She'd swapped her top for something low-cut and classy. She'd gone for a chic sexy that would make any man drool.

She leaned down at the window and I tried very hard to avert my eyes from her cleavage, even as I noticed her lack of bra. I swallowed.

"I'm just gonna get mine out," she said.

I nodded, mute.

Walking ahead of me, she came to a stop next to a sleek, black Maserati GranCabrio Sport. Before I could do anything, she ducked inside the luxury car.

"Whoa, whoa, whoa," I said, running over to her window. "Do you not think it would be smart if I checked the car first, especially after last time?"

"Sure," she shrugged.

I checked underneath and inside the car, meticulously making my way around every part, taking time to appreciate it as I did so before finally checking the exhaust.

"Can we go now?" she asked as I straightened up.

"All good." I gave her a thumbs up.

The engine roared to life and she revved it a few times, entirely for my benefit. I shook my head at her showing off and climbed back into my car.

We swapped the cars over and I climbed into the passenger seat of the Maserati. Glancing back at my beat-up old BMW made me feel incredibly small and overwhelmed by all of the glamour.

"You kept this one quiet," I said as I turned to face the front.

Stacey shrugged. "I don't like to brag."

"Ha! Yeah right," I muttered.

She drove us toward the exit.

"Stop!" I shouted.

Stacey slammed her foot on the break and we both strained against the seatbelts before snapping back into the seat.

"What the-" said Stacey, but I was already out of the car and admiring the magnificent machine that had caught my eye. I walked once, then twice around it, admiring the iconic black and burgundy body. Stacey leaned across the passenger seat.

"Can you please put it back in your pants so we can go," she shouted out the car window.

"It's amazing," I whispered.

"Come on," she said. "I'll ask the guy who owns it to take you for a spin."

"Really?"

"Will you get back in the car?" she demanded. I turned away and climbed back into the Maserati, glancing over my shoulder at the Veyron as we drove away.

Stacey pulled out onto the main road and into the never-ending congestion of London. I glanced at my watch to see it was almost midnight.

"So, are you going to let me in on the secret yet?" I asked.

"We're going to try some of Bill's old hangouts."

"Ah, I see."

It wasn't long until we were cruising around Camden Town, the streets alive with the music and infectious energy of the London nightlife.

"What exactly is your plan?" I asked.

"I'm gonna pull up and ask someone. Give me that picture of him."

I handed it over. She pulled the Maserati up onto the curb in front of a queue for one of the clubs and everyone turned to stare. I knew we should have stayed in my car. At least it was less conspicuous.

"Do you want me to come with you?" I asked.

"It might be best if you stay here. Actually, hop over to this side and then we can make a quick getaway."

"Sure," I nodded.

The car door swung open and there was a collection of squeals as the queue of celebrity wannabes recognised Stacey. As soon as the door closed, I hopped over into the driver's seat and watched her in the wing mirror. She walked up to her fans, gave some hugs here and there and signed anything that was pushed her way. She slowly made her way to the front of the queue, ensuring that everyone could see that she was spending time with her fans.

*Clever girl*, I thought. The paparazzi that were hanging around, hoping for moments like this, were snapping their cameras like crazy.

She got to the front of the queue, kissed the bouncer on the cheek and then showed him the photo. He nodded and then shook his head before she turned and headed back to the car. This time she climbed into the passenger's seat and the moment the door closed, we were away.

"Any luck?" I asked as we rounded a corner.

"Nope," she shook her head. "But there are other places. Let's try Kensington."

"This guy sure has expensive taste," I said. I knew for a fact that his Army pension couldn't afford this level of class; we had enough ex-military guys on the payroll that complained about it. I had a horrible feeling in the pit of my stomach that if he was a high-rolling gun-for-hire, this wasn't going to end well.

"Yeah, I know. That was my fault."

"Did the bouncer recognise him?"

"Yeah, said he'd seen him recently too."

"How recently?"

"In the past week."

"So he's definitely back in London then," I muttered.

"Oh yeah. This next place was always his favourite."

Half an hour later, we arrived in Kensington. It took all of my self-control to keep my eyes on the road and not gape at the stunning buildings that lined both sides of the road.

"Take a left here," she said. "And then pull over."

I turned the corner and bright lights flooded my vision, momentarily overwhelming me. Thumping music seemed to be coming from every direction. I pulled the car up onto the curb and Stacey climbed out. I wasn't surprised that she had the same greeting as the last place. People were leaning over the red velvet rope to touch her, hug her, shake her hand.

It amazed me how much of an icon she'd become.

I couldn't see the entrance to the club, but it was only a few minutes later when she reappeared, and I realised we'd hit the jackpot. She opened the car door.

"He's here," she said as she climbed in. "Drive."

"What? I thought –"

"Yeah we will, just go around the corner. I don't want to leave the car here. Or go through the main entrance."

"Oh okay." We parked the car on the next street and Stacey led me through a back alley to a door guarded by bouncers.

"Hi boys," she said casually.

"Stacey! It's been a while, how are you doing, hun?" said the one on the left. He wasn't particularly tall, but he was wide. He gave Stacey a brief hug and a quick kiss on the cheek.

"Yeah I'm good. This is my friend, Jason."

The two guys nodded in my direction.

"We're looking for Cooper."

"Oh, he's here alright. Already been given a warning."

"Great," muttered Stacey. "Well, duty calls." The bouncers stepped aside and waved us in.

"Thanks," I said as we passed.

The nightclub was my worst nightmare. The music was far too loud and the strobe lighting made it almost impossible to see where we were going. Stacey reached out and took my hand, guiding me through the crowd. We made it over to the bar and she ordered two drinks. I had no idea what, it was impossible to hear anything other than the thumping bass of the disco tune.

A minute later she pressed a cold beer into my hand and looked around.

It was a big place with at least three dance floors and girls dancing in cages suspended above them. The DJ was on a podium to my right, barely visible above the throng of gyrating bodies. We were in an alcove and the ceiling above us must have been some kind of balcony. I looked around, noticing the edges of this dance floor were lined with small booths where people were sitting, drinking, and chatting, but I couldn't see Cooper.

We stood there for a while, simply watching the commotion around us. The people dancing were grinding up against each other, oblivious to the world around them. I suddenly felt very uncomfortable.

I leaned over to Stacey.

"Where is he?" I shouted.

"Just wait. He'll be here for a drink soon," she shouted back. I nodded in response and swallowed a mouthful of beer.

The music changed and another beat began to take over.

A guy approached and leaned against the bar next to Stacey. He said something to her and she shook her head. He didn't move. He said something else to her and moved closer.

"Hey pal, leave her alone," I said, putting an arm around Stacey and pulling her closer to me.

The guy held up his hands defensively, picked up his drink and walked away.

"How very protective of you," said Stacey before kissing me on the cheek.

I glanced down at my watch, feeling restless. The sooner we found him, the sooner we could go. I downed the rest of my beer and ordered another. Stacey tugged on my sleeve and pointed. I turned around but couldn't see where she was pointing.

"What?"

She didn't answer me straight away but hesitated and then pointed again, this time further along the dancefloor. I saw him. Cooper. He was heading for an exit.

"Let's move."

I slapped a £20 note on the counter for the bartender and we both pushed our way through the crowds. It wasn't until we were outside that I realised he'd used the main entrance and the people queuing erupted in excitement at the sight of Stacey.

I put myself between her and the crowd as we tried to steer clear of them, but Cooper was definitely gone.

"Shit," I said, once we'd escaped the rabble.

"Down here," said Stacey. She turned down a narrow alley between two tall townhouses.

"Looking for me?"

There was a figure leaning against the wall a few metres ahead. I couldn't see his face but it was definitely a man. The voice, the stance, and the wide, muscular shoulders gave him away.

"Yes, actually," said Stacey. She crossed her arms and stared at him defiantly. I wanted to move between them but I held my breath, forcing myself to stand still.

"Come here." The figure stepped out of the shadows and opened his arms. Stacey moved forward and hugged him. I didn't know what to do or say. In the half-light coming from a nearby street lamp, I could see Cooper's well chiselled features clearly enough. His hair was cut close to his skull and there was a thick scar on his left cheek that wasn't in his mugshot.

Cooper turned to me, his grey eyes cold and piercing.

"Hi, Jason," he said and held out a hand as he let go of Stacey.

I tried to hide my surprise as I shook his hand.

"We need to talk to you," said Stacey.

"You mean arrest me, more like," Cooper muttered. "I'm not stupid, Stacey. I know exactly what's going on here."

"I..." she faltered.

"No arrest," I said, trying to regain control. "We just need some answers."

Cooper paused for a moment.

"I'll speak to you, or whoever you like. On one condition." He spoke slowly, ensuring we heard every word. "No police."

I looked at Stacey. That wasn't something we could agree to, and she knew it.

# Chapter 45

## BILL COOPER

### SOMEWHERE IN LONDON

*Monday 3ʳᵈ August*

Stacey looked unsure of herself. She looked over to Jason as if he was going to help.

"Okay," she finally breathed.

"Stacey," said Jason in warning.

"I know a great place," said Cooper. He turned and walked away, not bothering to check if they were following. At the end of the alley he turned left and headed back the way they came. It didn't take long before they were walking along Thurloe Place and then on to Brompton Road.

He stopped outside the brightly lit McDonalds and turned to the others.

"Your great idea was McDonalds?" asked Stacey sceptically.

He gestured for them to enter and when no-one moved, he shrugged and walked in first. At the counter he ordered a coffee, paid cash and went to find a booth in the cosiest corner he could find.

He deliberately chose to face the restaurant. He wanted to be on guard in case he'd been set up. Doubtful, but still not something he wanted to risk.

Jason and Stacey made their way over to the table, juggling coffee and what looked like a McMuffin between them. They sat down opposite him.

Cooper slowly tore open a sugar sachet and proceeded to pour it into his coffee. He stirred once, twice and then again before removing the little wooden stick and taking a sip.

"So?" said Jason, attempting to break the ice.

"So, what? You're the one with the questions," Cooper answered.

Stacey coughed a little, perhaps as a warning to Jason, he wasn't sure.

"Did you kill Gemma?" Jason blurted out.

"Jason," hissed Stacey.

Cooper chuckled. "No, mate. Why would I?"

It was clear from the way Jason shifted uncomfortably that the word 'mate' irritated him. The thought made Cooper smile.

"Why were you in Hungary?" asked Stacey.

Cooper shrugged. "If I'm between jobs, I like to come see you race. Is that a crime?"

"No," said Stacey, warily. "But you're a gun-for-hire?" He didn't deny it. Stacey shook her head disapprovingly and looked away. Something inside of him sank.

"Don't judge me, sweetheart. That's not what I am."

"Then what are you?" spat Jason.

"I'm sensing some hostility here, Jason. I don't have to sit here and answer your questions. Would you prefer that?"

"No," he said through gritted teeth.

"Bill," said Stacey, reaching a hand forwards across the table. "Will you please just tell us what you know?" Her eyes were pleading.

"There's nothing to tell. I saw it happen, just like everyone else there. I honestly thought you were dead." He reached out and took her hand. "I was in bits."

Jason cleared his throat.

"I was," insisted Cooper as he let go of Stacey's hand. "The next day I flew to America. I was feeling sorry for myself. I thought you were gone. I got drunk, got into a bar fight, found myself in a Sheriff's station and knew I'd fucked up.

"I came back to the UK on my own passport - I'm guessing that's what flagged me up on your radar - and here we are."

"Can you prove it wasn't you?" asked Jason.

"Are you fucking kidding me? Prove it was me. Innocent until proven guilty, remember?"

"Can you help us track down who might have done it?" Jason asked.

"Now you're wanting my help? You've got no chance, mate, not with the Bobbies on my back."

No-one spoke.

"There were pictures," said Stacey, quietly.

"Stacey," Jason hissed.

Now they had his full attention.

"What pictures?" asked Cooper. He was sitting straighter and leaning over his long-forgotten coffee.

"My car was sabotaged. Someone blocked the exhaust with those banger things that kids play with. It was a distraction. Next thing I know, there's this envelope full of photos on the seat next to me."

"What kind of photos?"

"Me shopping, me seeing friends, me out and about, me in Hungary."

"Please tell me you're joking," said Cooper, his voice tense.

"Someone broke into my apartment."

"And?" His whole body was rigid.

"They trashed the place. Wrote 'whore' on my bathroom mirror."

"Well, that's cliché."

"It doesn't feel fucking cliché," she snapped.

Cooper raised his eyebrows in surprise.

"What else?" he asked.

"Letters, threats. It's a bloody nightmare."

Cooper didn't reply. He sat frowning.

"Aren't you supposed to prevent this sort of shit?" he asked Jason, waving a hand in Stacey's direction.

Jason clenched his jaw and he could see a small muscle twitch.

"There's only so much I can do," he said.

Cooper looked down at the table between them. Something wasn't adding up.

"Have you made any enemies?" he asked.

Jason snorted. "Do you not think we've been through this?" he almost shouted.

"Sssh," hushed Stacey. She glanced over her shoulder but the place was deserted.

"Honestly," said Jason, exasperated. "We're not fucking idiots."

"Then why are you here asking for my help?" snapped Cooper. Anger flared up in him, just below the surface. He paused and took a deep breath. "The shooting at the Grand Prix, the one that killed... Gemma, was it?" Jason nodded. "That was a professional hit."

Jason and Stacey exchanged loaded glances.

"Are you sure?" asked Jason.

"Pretty sure."

"But how-?"

"It was in broad fucking daylight with thousands of people there. What do you think? It weren't no rookie, that's for sure. It was a professional hit. The other stuff, that's not a professional. You've either got one really pissed off motherfucker who's hired a hitman or-"

"There's two of them," whispered Jason.

Cooper nodded.

"Fuck." Jason ran his hands through his hair.

"This isn't a surprise to you, is it?"

There was a pause.

"Hungarian police confirmed it was a professional. The two-person thing, that was just a theory."

Stacey slowly shook her head. She'd gone white and was staring at the table.

Cooper reached across and took hold of her hand. "Look, you're fine at the moment, right? Jason's doing a good job of looking after you, yes?"

"What do we do?" asked Stacey.

Cooper gave a small smile. "Work out who they are." He paused. "Look, I've got to go. I have a plane to catch."

Stacey hadn't moved.

"Stacey," said Cooper, softly. "Look at me, honey." She looked up, her face expressionless. "Listen. I'll be back in a few days and I'll watch you whenever I can. This other shit, it sounds like a stalker, someone trying to worm their way in and get close to you.".

"A stalker?" she asked.

"It wouldn't be out of the realm of possibility. Have another think through everything, okay? Stay safe until then."

She nodded slowly.

Cooper gave a curt nod to Jason and then walked out.

The sun was just about coming over the tree tops and bathing the city in gorgeous early morning light. He zipped up his jacket and began walking down the street. He didn't look over his shoulder, or even scan the trees around him. He already knew there was someone there.

# Chapter 46

## JASON HUNTER

### LONDON OFFICE

*Tuesday 4th August*

"Morning, Mr Hunter."

"Morning, Lucy. How are you?"

"Very good, thank you."

She swivelled her chair, got up and walked around her desk, following me into my office. She was carrying a clipboard piled high with reports.

"The closing report for Montoya," she said, dropping one of the files onto my desk. I slipped out of my suit jacket and hung it on the coat stand. "Very successful." She dropped another file on my desk, this one thicker. "A new contract for Kendrick." She dropped a third. "A new application for the current job opening." And then a fourth. "And I believe this is from Captain Zsaldos, nothing new." The large pile was overwhelming, and I sucked in a deep breath, fighting the feeling of drowning.

"Do you have any good news for me?" I asked desperately.

"Yes. Adam hasn't asked to see you, and Detective Irons has called. She's running late."

"Right," I muttered, collapsing into my seat. "Remind me how that's meant to be good news?"

"Well, it gives you time to prepare and wipe that awful dazed look off your face."

"Thanks," I mumbled.

"I don't mean to be rude, Jason –"

"Please, Lucy. I couldn't imagine you doing such a thing," I replied sarcastically. She smiled sweetly at me. A fake smile, but it was appreciated just the same.

"You look a little haggard."

"It was a late one."

"Was it now?" she smiled coyly.

"Don't you have work to do?"

Lucy smiled and then left, carefully closing the door behind her.

I sent a text to one of my most experienced boys, Isaac, for an update on the current situation at Gromov's house. He replied almost instantly and it seemed that Gromov's condition had improved significantly; he was almost ready to come home. They were prepping for his return and would keep me in the loop.

Before I knew what had happened, a short brunette woman stormed into my office, stopping opposite me with her hands on her hips. Her expression was unreadable.

"I'm sorry Jason, she just barged right past." Lucy was standing in the doorway, an apologetic look on her face. "Shall I call security?"

"You know, for a security firm, your building isn't very secure," said the brunette.

"No, it's fine," I said and waved a hand in Lucy's direction. She shot a look of contempt towards the other woman and left, closing the door behind her.

"Hi Diane," I said, and then gestured to the seat on the other side of my desk. "What can I do for you?"

"I just needed to drop off Stacey's schedule for the next few weeks. She's decided to start doing some of her appearances again."

"What?"

"I know, but it's a necessary evil unfortunately. I'm sure you can sort something?"

"Sure, sure," I said, slightly distracted by the piece of paper she handed me. I ran my eyes along the calendar, mentally calculating how difficult it would be to protect her at all these events.

"How many are here?"

"We've got 6 over the next three weeks, not including the next Grand Prix in Belgium on the 23rd. She'll be flying over earlier in the week."

I let out a long sigh.

"What happened to freezing her publicity calendar until this all settled down?"

Diane simply shrugged. "I'm just the messenger."

"Sure." I showed her out and flopped into the empty chair next to Lucy's desk.

"Who the hell was she?" she asked.

"Stacey's PA."

"Stacey's PA?" she repeated, incredulous.

I nodded.

"You look even worse than before," she said.

"Cheers Lucy, you look like a glamour model yourself."

"Hey, no need to be nasty."

"Sorry."

"What's wrong?" she asked with what sounded like genuine concern.

"Just the stress of it all. I'm not sure I can cope much longer."

"Jason, you've been doing this job for how long now? I'm sure you've dealt with your fair share of stress."

"I'm getting old, I can't handle it like I used to," I said.

"Oh, give over," she said and playfully shoved me. We went quiet for a minute and I watched her type an email. "How's Stacey?" she asked as she hit send.

"Um..." I wasn't sure what to say, mainly because I didn't actually know. She'd seemed really off this morning, and then Diane's announcement that she was hitting the ground running with the public appearances again worried me.

"What's wrong?" demanded Lucy.

Dammit. She was so good. How the hell did she pick up on everything?

"Nothing."

She looked at me sternly. "What the hell is wrong?"

I let out a laugh but even to my ears it sounded fake. "Nothing's wrong."

She went back to typing on her keyboard. "Then why are you sitting here chatting to me? Hmm?"

"Can't I have a conversation with my staff? Check in on them every now and again?"

"No you can't," said Lucy. She stopped typing, stood up and marched into my office without so much as a backward glance. I sighed. There was no avoiding Lucy when she wanted something. I followed her into my office, albeit a little slower. I closed the door behind me and sat behind my desk. Lucy had already made herself comfortable in one of my guest chairs.

"If you don't tell me, Jason, you aren't going to tell anyone. And then what sort of a pickle would you be in, eh?" She peered at me sternly.

When I still didn't answer, she prompted again. "What's going on?"

# Chapter 47

## JASON HUNTER

### LONDON OFFICE

*Tuesday 4<sup>th</sup> August*

"So you're seriously telling me that Cooper had nothing to do with it?"

I nodded.

Lucy let out a long breath.

"I know."

"And you actually went to see him?"

I nodded.

"How the hell did you find him when even the police can't?"

"Stacey knew where to look."

"And you haven't told Detective Irons?"

"Nope."

Lucy let out another long breath.

"How was he acting when you saw him?" asked Lucy. She was looking out the window, thinking hard.

"I didn't like how he acted with Stacey; he's definitely still got feelings for her." I stretched my neck from left to right but didn't feel any better. The tension was in my bones.

"Hmm."

"What?" I asked.

"Nothing." She paused. "I mean, if he's suffered from PTSD, is there some way that his brain could make him believe he's doing all this to protect Stacey?"

I studied Lucy for a few moments. Her blonde hair was pulled back in a ponytail and a few strands hung down around her face. Her elbows were resting on the arms of the chair and she was holding her chin between the thumb and forefinger of her left hand. She looked up at me now and seemed surprised that I was staring at her.

"What?" she asked.

"How many crime novels have you read?"

"What?"

"How many crime novels have you read?" I repeated, slower this time, trying to hide the smile tugging at the corner of my lips.

"Well, I... Why?"

"How far-fetched can you get? PTSD doesn't send you completely loopy."

"It can do," she said defensively.

"Not in the way you mean," I scoffed.

"Such a smartass," she muttered. "Don't want my help? Fine." She gave me a sarcastic smile, got up and left. I couldn't help but chuckle to myself.

A few minutes later, I was lost in my own thoughts.

It really couldn't be Cooper, I was sure of that. The analysis from Hayley was too conclusive. I looked down at the enhanced picture that she'd emailed me. The main giveaway was the build. The figure on the roof had been slim, hardly any muscle. Cooper was huge. Well, less huge and more... well-muscled. There was no way he could have toned down and then toned back up again in such a short space of time, no matter how many protein shakes he had. It just wasn't possible.

I got up from my desk and wandered over to the window. Everything was so familiar; it was the same scene I'd been looking at for the last seven years. But somehow something didn't feel right. It was like I was seeing everything for the first time.

The traffic came and went; the occasional car horn could be heard a few streets away; a double-decker sightseeing tour passed by and the homeless man, Jim, was still sheltered in the doorway. I made a mental note to buy him a coffee the next time I had two minutes.

Something didn't add up though, something felt out of place. I was thinking about the meeting with Cooper. The way he had talked, the way he'd sat. He was definitely military. And whilst I was sure he hadn't pulled the trigger, it didn't mean that he hadn't organised the hit in the first place.

I jumped, startled by a sudden sound, and turned around.

"Hello."

# Chapter 48

## JASON HUNTER

### LONDON OFFICE

*Tuesday 4th August*

"Jesus Christ, Stacey!"

"I did wonder how long it would take you to realise I was here. Are you aware that I was actually talking to you for like a minute before I realised you were in your own little dreamland?" Stacey was sitting where Lucy had been only fifteen minutes before. Her legs were propped up on the desk and she was looking at something on her mobile.

I realised my hand was still over my pounding heart and dropped it to my side. I let out a deep breath and rolled my shoulders.

"You speak to Hayley?"

Stacey shrugged. "Not yet."

I let out a sigh and sat down.

"What's up?" asked Stacey.

"Why does everyone keep asking me that today? Is there something written on my face?"

"Nope, never said that."

She was scrolling on her phone, calm and relaxed. But I could tell that something wasn't right.

We sat in companionable silence for a few minutes and I went back to gazing out the window. There was something comforting about having her there, despite the fact that things were tense between us. The atmosphere in the office seemed to be all over the place, what with Lucy's interrogation and my frazzled thoughts. It was amazing to finally have some peace. Even if it was only going to be short-lived.

"He didn't do it," said Stacey.

"I know," I admitted quietly.

Stacey looked up from her phone. "I know you know."

I looked across my desk at her.

"I don't want to say 'I told you so'," she said with a smug look. "But, I told you so." She grinned at me, evidently pleased with herself.

"Yes, thanks for that," I muttered, looking away.

"So, where does that leave us now?"

"I'm not a hundred percent sure, if I'm honest."

A silence fell between us. Stacey had stopped playing on her phone and was now focused on me. I could feel her eyes boring into me but no matter how much I tried, I couldn't think of another lead.

"Shouldn't you be training? Haven't you got to keep your stamina up?" I asked, changing the subject.

"And how do you propose I do that?" she asked.

"How do you normally do it?"

"Normally, I'd do six days a week in the gym, alternating between strength and aerobics. Then there's the Technology F1 training machine, complete with steering wheel, for added weight training. Or I might be on the Batak reaction board. Failing all that, I also do some Bikram yoga."

"You do yoga?" I couldn't help the smile that spread across my face at the thought.

"Are you mocking me?"

"No, not really," I answered, still smiling. "It's that you're keeping your fitness up. It's important you're safe the next time you get in a Formula One car."

Stacey didn't reply straight away. "Are you worried about my driving ability?" she asked with a raised eyebrow.

"Er, no," I said quickly.

"You are!" said Stacey. She got up from her chair and made her way around the desk. Before I could escape, she'd placed one hand on each arm rest, trapping me in my seat. "How dare you doubt me," she said quietly, and then pressed her lips against mine. I was so shocked I didn't move.

Stacey laughed. "For someone who claims to be intelligent, you sure can be pretty stupid."

"What?" I said. I could barely think straight, let alone process what she was saying. My pulse was pounding, filling my head with the heavy thumping.

"I've been driving since I was four. Do you honestly think a week or two out of the game will have that much of an impact?" she said. Her breathing was slow and steady. She blinked slowly and her mouth curved into a smile.

I coughed self-consciously and leant forward. She released me and stepped back. I began to shuffle some papers on my desk.

"Don't you have a race in two and a half weeks?"

"At this rate, no. I won't be participating."

We both fell silent. Stacey wandered over to the window and looked down at the busy street below. "I'm not sure I like you interfering, Mr Hunter," she said trying to lighten the atmosphere.

"Sorry," I muttered. I shifted awkwardly in my seat, unsure of what to do with myself.

"Besides," she said, turning around to look at me. "I haven't been completely idle. I've managed to do about 75% of my usual regime. And I'm doing a triathlon this weekend." She added this last sentence with an air of nonchalance, as if this was something she said to me every day.

"I'm sorry, what?" I said, startled.

She flashed me a grin. "I said I've still managed to do my usual routine whilst –"

"No, no, no," I said, holding a hand up in the air. I knew she was playing with me and I couldn't help but fall for it. "The other thing." I said, twirling my finger in the air as if I was asking her to rewind.

"Oh, you mean the triathlon? Yeah, it's on Saturday. Please come, it would be great to have your support." Before I could respond, she'd pecked me on the cheek and was on her way out the door. She paused and turned back to me, "I'll see you later," and then she was gone.

The first thing I did was open my Chrome browser and type 'London triathlon'. She wasn't pulling my leg, it was definitely this weekend. Shit.

I sat back in my chair and let out a slow breath. How the hell were we supposed to keep her safe if she was off gallivanting all over London with thousands of others? More importantly, how had she gotten a place so last minute? This event would have been booked up months ago.

Why hadn't Diane warned me earlier? I picked up the discarded timetable, and there it was, written clearly on the 8th August.

Annoyance surged through me. I felt so off my game it was unreal. Everything was precariously balanced and I couldn't pay enough attention to it all to keep all the plates spinning. Thoughts of Max and Lily flooded my mind, thoughts of Gemma. I felt sick.

I browsed the internet a little longer, made some phone calls and did a little bit of research. I didn't feel comfortable with the situation Stacey had put me in and she knew it. But all I could do was work with it. This was clearly something she needed to do and I wasn't going to stop her.

I dug my mobile out of my pocket and dialled Sam's number. He picked up on the first ring.

"Boss?" he grunted.

"How fit are you?"

"How fit do I need to be?" he asked cautiously.

"You're going to be doing the triathlon this weekend and you've got to keep up with that Formula One driver of ours."

"Sure thing, boss." He hung up.

One task done, a million more to go.

I made my way through my emails, flagging the important stuff as I went and deleting the junk. But I just couldn't focus.

A new email notification appeared telling me I had news from Hayley. Short and sweet.

*Sorry I can't call. Swamped this end. Shooter profile attached.*

I opened the attachment. It was a brief profile of the shooter. It didn't contain anything new, simply reinforced what I already suspected; this person couldn't possibly be Cooper. Too small, too slight, not enough weight.

It was reassuring knowing we were all on the same page, but now I was confident Cooper was innocent, I felt unnerved. It had been over a week since Gemma's murder and we'd failed to achieve anything; we didn't even have a suspect.

What the hell was I supposed to do now?

I read through the rest of the report which included a psych analysis. It didn't really contain anything we didn't already know but then we didn't have much to go on.

I pulled Bill Cooper's profile from the pile on my desk and carefully scanned through it, unable to shake him from my mind. Apart from the PTSD, there wasn't anything here that would raise much concern.

There were a few more images in the file. A couple of grainy CCTV shots where you could barely identify him. One was from America, another from Japan. The other pictures were from his army days.

In one he was grinning at the camera with the rest of his squad. I turned the photo over to see someone had scribbled *Basra 2009* on the back.

So Cooper had been at Basra. Not that it had any particular significance, but it could explain a lot.

This wasn't getting me anywhere. We knew it wasn't him so why was I even bothering? I slowly closed the file and put it to one side. I needed a new tactic.

# Chapter 49

## DIANE PARSONS

### HOME

*Tuesday 4th August*

She sat at the breakfast table in her kitchen with her laptop and a glass of rosé wine. She'd poured the wine over half an hour ago but had yet to take a sip.

She felt sick.

Picking up her phone, she dialled the office of Stacey's accountant.

After three rings, there was an answer, "Wilkinson Chambers, Penny speaking. How may I help you?"

"Hi Penny, it's Diane. I just wanted to let Jacob know that I'm putting together three new invoices. All of them have been paid. One is a cash deposit."

"Sure," replied Penny. Diane could hear her quickly scribbling away on the notepad she always kept on her immaculate desk.

"We also have two outgoing payments for sponsorship that will be leaving the account in the next couple of weeks. £10,000 each." There was a pause whilst Penny continued making notes.

"Uh huh, no problem. Is that everything?"

"Yeah. I'll let you know if there's anything else."

"Sure thing, have a nice day, Diane."

"You too."

Diane hung up, placed her phone on the table and then proceeded to take three large gulps of her wine.

She hit send on the email she'd already drafted with the invoices attached and then switched the tab on her browser to Stacey's bank.

So far she'd been able to deposit just under half the money. And with the cash deposit noted on invoice number 2, she could safely add a few more thousand to Stacey's bank account.

The transfers out of the account were to two different businesses. Diane had already had the forethought to check this. She didn't want any additional ties to Gromov if she could help it.

The difficulty might come around if Jacob Wilkinson reviewed the invoices too closely. Normally their sponsorship gigs were pretty simple and whilst this one wasn't any different, it might be an easy ruse to spot.

She poured herself another glass of wine and then texted Volkov.

# Chapter 50

## JASON HUNTER

### LONDON OFFICE

*Tuesday 4<sup>th</sup> August*

So far I'd succeeded in absolutely nothing. I came to my senses, glanced at the clock and realised I'd been daydreaming for at least twenty minutes.

I grabbed a piece of paper from the printer next to my desk and picked up a pen. The blank, white sheet was oppressive and did nothing to spark ideas. *Think.*

I decided to make a list.

A list of everyone that was connected to Stacey, and to Gemma – I wasn't quite ready to rule out Stacey's theory that Gemma had been the intended target for the hit. As much as everything was definitely pointing in Stacey's direction, we had to explore every avenue to catch this fucker. I would deal with the stalker idea later, first I needed to find Gemma's killer.

Two minutes later I had a list of about 15 names. I'd also noted down Stacey's pit team and her driving team, but I couldn't name any of her friends.

I looked down and considered my options. Everyone in the company had been interviewed the day after and they'd all provided strong

alibis. I crossed out a few names. I could probably rule out the families
as well so I crossed out a few more.

I decided to pull up a list of this seasons' drivers and began there.
With ten teams competing, each with two drivers, it gave me a pretty
broad starting point. But then looking at the drivers, the only ones
with the motivation for murder would be in the top ten. So I made
another list:

    1. *Héctor Sanchez*

I could obviously cross off Stacey.

And I underlined Dima Volkov. Twice.

Morrison was going to be a likely suspect as he had the most to lose,
but then he was her team member, so the outcome was being dictated
by their team anyway. But if he felt he was going to be robbed of the
title... We'd ran checks on all the drivers when Stacey initially came to
us but nothing had been flagged. I dug around in one of the cabinets
until I found the folder with all the information. Sitting back at my
desk, I decided to run the names through Google and compare against
what we already had.

After half an hour of reading through crappy news articles and
Wikipedia pages, I realised this really wasn't getting me anywhere. I
needed to speak to Hayley, and made a mental note to check in with
her. I looked at the clock on my phone and was shocked to see it was
passed 7pm.

I gathered everything I would need, printed out the most interesting stuff and put it all together in Gemma's file. I glanced over to
Lucy's desk. Her lamp was switched on but the desk was empty.

I shut down the computer, stuffed the file into my bag and left,
closing the door behind me. It was eerie in the main office. Everywhere
seemed deserted. I glanced down the corridor towards Adam's office

but even he'd gone home. I weaved between the open-plan desks as I made my way towards the double swing doors.

I wasn't sure where Lucy had gone and it was definitely weird that she wasn't at her desk. She very rarely left it during the day unless it was lunchtime. I made my way down the stairs, passing the night guards as they switched off lights and locked doors.

Just as I entered the lobby, Lucy appeared, walking right into me, scattering Gemma's file everywhere.

"Jesus, Jason," she whispered, as she bent down and began collecting the paperwork.

I took a slow breath. "Don't 'Jesus' me, you scared the life out of me, woman," I said, bending down to pick up the now-empty file.

Lucy straightened up and handed me the papers.

"What are you doing?" I asked.

"Doing my job," she said with a raised eyebrow. "What else would I be doing?"

"I...I don't know," I stammered. "It's just not like you to be away from your desk. Was a bit weird, that's all," I muttered, half ashamed of myself. Fucking idiot. I was getting way too paranoid.

"I was using the photocopier," she said, indicating her own pile of paperwork.

"Oh, sorry."

Lucy chuckled and shook her head. "Go home."

# Chapter 51

## JASON HUNTER

### HOME

*Wednesday 5th August*

I fumbled with my keys for a moment before my front door swung open. Stacey stood in the hallway with a glass of wine and a smirk.

"I wasn't sure you were coming home," she teased.

"Sorry." I slipped in through the door and kicked it shut behind me. I was still feeling paranoid and it was messing with my head. The TV was on in the living room; some Channel 4 show. I walked through and into the kitchen, dropping the disorganised file on the kitchen island as I went. I opened the fridge, pulled out a can of beer and popped it open. I took a long swig, guzzling down the refreshing, cool liquid like there was no tomorrow.

"Rough day?" asked Stacey. She was leaning against the door frame between the living room and the kitchen.

"You could say that," I replied.

Stacey was still smirking at me and I only just realised that I had no idea why.

"What's that look for?" I asked.

"What look?" she asked, suddenly serious.

"You know what I'm talking about."

"Oh, nothing."

She wandered back into the living room and settled herself down on the sofa.

"What did you do today then?" I asked, following her.

"Went to the gym. And before you start asking about my driving skills again, I didn't just go to any old gym. I went to the team gym."

"Yeah?" I sat myself down at the other end of the sofa and took a sip of my beer. "Practise your G-force muscles, did you?"

"That doesn't even make sense," she laughed. "My shoulders are aching from the touch board though."

"Cool. Did Sam go with you?" I asked casually.

"As a matter of fact, he did. Funny that, I didn't realise bodyguards followed you everywhere."

"Alright, enough of the sarcasm," I said and turned my attention to the TV. "What's this?"

"Just some weird robot show."

"They don't look like robots."

"That's the whole point."

"Oh I see."

We sat in silence.

"Did Sam say anything to you today?" I asked.

"You know what, now you mention it, we did have a great conversation about the triathlon this weekend."

"Oh yeah?" I hadn't looked away from the TV screen, but my body was tense, waiting for her answer.

"Yeah, turns out he's doing it as well and he's suggested we do it together, you know, to keep each other's pace and all that."

"That's nice of him." I was still trying to keep a straight face but it was becoming increasingly difficult.

"I know it was you," she said, shoving me with her foot.

"It was me, what?" I looked at her with the most innocent expression I could muster.

"Don't look at me like that," she said, laughing. "You and your big mouth. I don't know how you did it but he's doing it with me."

"I guess that's why you pay me though, isn't it?" I paused. "I couldn't just let you go off traipsing around London with no security. Just be grateful I didn't put my foot down," I said defensively.

"You wouldn't dare," she teased.

I didn't respond, but stared blankly at the TV with the hint of a smile tugging at the corners of my lips. I was feeling comfortable. Content.

"How was your day, Mr Smartarse?" she asked. "Did you spend all day basking in your own glorified intelligence?"

"Not really," I said. "And don't go changing the subject. Do you know how much work it took to get Sam his spot? Hours!"

Stacey chuckled.

"I also got an email from Hayley about those pictures."

"And?"

"A hundred percent wasn't him. The shooter's profile was all different. So I decided to take a different tact."

Stacey didn't answer but she was looking at me and I knew I had her full attention.

I got up from the sofa to retrieve my list of drivers from the file on the kitchen island and then plonked myself down again. I passed it over to her.

"I started looking into the different names but couldn't find anything more than some superficial news stories. Figured Hayley would have any dirt. She'll have already flagged anyone that looks suspicious. Besides, you probably know these guys better than anyone, right?"

"I wouldn't go that far," she laughed. "We don't all sit around in the locker room being best pals after a race," she said. "Sure, we socialise together but we're still competing against each other."

"Okay, but you'll have some idea as to who's dodgy?"

She shrugged. "I'm not sure. I mean, it's hard for me to think of any of them having it in for me. Enough to want to kill me? It seems really unlikely. I've never had any disagreements with any of the other drivers and they've pretty much accepted me as one of their own."

"There must be some rivalry," I pushed.

"Yeah, of course there is. But no more so than between Morrison and Keil. It just seems far-fetched."

"I know," I sighed. "But there is someone out there who's tried to kill you."

"Yes, I'm aware of that," she snapped. I didn't answer and we both took a sip of our drinks. "I'm sorry," she sighed. "I'm stressed out. It's a hard pill for me to swallow; thinking that one of my competitors would want to kill me."

"I know," I said gently.

She nodded and took another sip of wine.

"What about the whole stalker thing?" she asked.

I shrugged my shoulders, unsure what to say.

We sat in silence.

The TV show finished and the credits rolled up the screen.

"Pass me that list again," said Stacey, setting her wine down on the coffee table.

I did as I was told and then flicked the channel over to something a little more light-hearted.

"So, Morrison is on my team. I doubt he feels threatened by me."

I shrugged. There was always the possibility...

"Keil is the quiet one, but I don't think he's malicious. Now I think about it though, he wasn't overly compassionate when Gemma died."

"But that in itself isn't a reason to think he killed her."

"True." She continued scanning down the list of names. "I don't know much about Valencia and get the impression that he thinks he's a bit superior to the rest of us, but then he's always so nice to your face. More infuriating than anything else."

I laughed.

"Volkov was arrested a couple times as a kid. I've never personally trusted him."

"Interesting," I replied, wondering whether it was worth looking into him more.

"Sanchez is harmless and St Pierre is like a brother to me. He's taught me a lot of what I know."

I nodded but didn't reply; I knew it could sometimes be those closest to us that could inflict the most damage.

"Don't," she said.

"Don't what?"

"Just don't. I know what you're thinking. Aldric has had his spot in the limelight; he's looking forward to sharing mine with me. He's not someone who would do something like this."

"I never said he was," I replied defensively.

"No, but you were thinking it."

I opened my mouth to reply but couldn't really argue with her.

Stacey picked up her wine and easily drained the glass before heading into the kitchen for a refill.

I was particularly interested in what Stacey had said about Keil. He might be the loose cannon here. He also had the most to lose really, now that Stacey was storming up through the championship and stealing his points.

I wondered if he had any prejudices.

Stacey came back in and sat down with a full glass.

"Does Keil have anything against you?" I asked.

"What do you mean?"

"Well. Does he like women?"

"How am I supposed to know?" she asked.

"I don't know," I shrugged. "Has he ever said anything sexist? Been disrespectful towards women? Belittled you in any way?"

"Are you trying to find out if he feels threatened by my success?"

"Maybe."

Stacey paused for a moment, thinking.

"Actually, he's always been the perfect gentleman. Overly polite and formal with me," she said.

"Hmmm."

"But then he is German and that's kinda how they are, especially to us lot. They're a bit... stiff."

I laughed. "Please don't ever let any German hear you say that."

# Chapter 52

## DI HAYLEY IRONS

### HAMMERSMITH POLICE STATION

*Wednesday 5<sup>th</sup> August*

Hayley sat at her desk, flicking through the most recent case file that had found its way into her hands. Another murder. Another faceless immigrant with no legal documentation or identification. Racial murders had been on the rise and CCTV footage of a gang of white males had done nothing to help the investigation.

The neighbourhood community was primarily Russian and too tight-knit; most people either knew or had a good idea of who was responsible. But they wouldn't tell the police. If they did, they'd be the next dead body on the street corner.

She looked down at the photograph of the mutilated corpse. Stab wounds covered his torso. The coroner said that it had taken only two strikes to bring the man down and once he was on the floor, he was repeatedly stabbed, even after he was dead.

Hayley shivered.

His cold, lifeless eyes stared at the camera.

She'd seen pictures of him whilst he was alive. His few possessions were located in a house about three streets away from where he was found. The woman living there had rented one of her spare rooms to him and said he was the loveliest lodger she'd ever had. He'd never caused her any trouble, was always polite, and even helped tidy around the place occasionally. His English wasn't good but she didn't mind.

Yet the two officers she'd allocated the task of finding out where he worked were coming up empty-handed. It was likely he was being paid cash, working long hours for very little money. The pictures found in his wallet were of a little girl and a woman, and she guessed they were his family. Hayley didn't doubt that he'd been lured to this country with the promise of safe passage for his wife and child once he paid off his own debt.

What a lie.

She scanned through the details of the case again, looking for some unexplored avenue that would help, but it seemed that all the basics had been covered.

The fax machine in the corner of her office jumped to life and began to noisily feed through a piece of paper. Hayley spun around on her chair and retrieved the first sheet as the fax began to print a second.

Just a glance at the top of the page told her that it wasn't good news.

The phone on her desk rang.

"DI Irons," she answered.

"Ah, hello DI Irons, it's Szàzados Zsaldos here. I'm glad you're still up. Have you received my fax?"

"Yes, it's just coming through now. Inconclusive?"

"Yes, I'm afraid so. The lab has just sent those results to me. No trace on the weapon or the bullet. I'm sorry, I was hoping this would be a solid lead. I've submitted the results to the AFIS. They have a record but no identity."

"Thanks for letting me know," mumbled Hayley. She hung up the phone and began reading through the whole report. She'd never seen anything so vague. The weapon was standard issue, easy to pick up through legitimate gun shops in Hungary, even easier to pick up on the black market, . And the serial number was indecipherable.

She finished reading and then hesitated. She knew she shouldn't, it broke all the rules, could even get her fired or demoted, but she was really stuck. There wasn't much else to go on and it seemed like the Hungarian police were starting to give up hope. The media frenzy had barely died down and if word got out, she'd be in a royal shit storm. But what choice did she have?

She picked up the phone and dialled Jason. He answered on the third ring.

"I've just had the final ballistics report as well as the fingerprint results through from Zsaldos," she said, cutting to the chase.

"And?"

"And, not good. Inconclusive. These guys don't have a fucking clue, Jason."

"Shit," he muttered.

"Just thought I'd let you know. I feel like you're more likely to come up with something than we are at this stage."

There was a pause. "I've been thinking about Stacey's competition. We obviously ran background checks on them all when she came on board as a client, but I feel like we've missed something. I'm assuming your systems will be more detailed and do a thorough job. Is it worth revisiting them?"

"It might be worth you taking a look. With everything we know so far and the info you already have, you'll be quicker at spotting any red flags. Nothing obvious came up the first time round."

"Yeah, of course. Whatever I can do to help," he said.

"Great, come to the station when you get time." She hung up.

Hayley didn't feel confident. In fact, it felt like the whole world was pressing down on her shoulders and she needed to find some answers.

She looked down at the lifeless eye of her murder victim and knew with a heavy heart that his killer would never be found. He simply wasn't important enough.

# Chapter 53

## SAM THORNTON

### THE GYM

*Wednesday 5ᵗʰ August*

"Here again, Sam?" asked the cocky, slick-haired manager behind the counter.

"No, I'm a figment of your imagination," he grunted as he walked past and through the glass swing doors. The manager let out a laugh. It wasn't genuine and Sam was grateful when the door closed behind him, drowning out the awful braying sound.

He shook his head.

After dropping his gym bag in one of the lockers, he made his way over to the cycling machine, giving one or two nods of acknowledgement on the way.

He hoisted his heavy frame onto the bike and increased the difficulty a few notches before peddling at a fast, rhythmic pace. This was his favourite part of his workout. The moment where he felt his muscles loosen from the intensity of his day and he could push any frustration out through his limbs until they were exhausted. He didn't take any notice of his surroundings. Head down, he watched his feet perform one rotation after another. Even the chitter-chatter of the other gym enthusiasts was drowned out.

"That's quite a pace," said a voice next to him, shattering his focus and bringing him back to the present.

Sam looked up to see Stacey leaning against the bike next to him.

"Where –"

"I left those goons in the lobby. They know you're here, so nothing to worry about." She slung her slim purple towel over her shoulder and hopped onto the bike next to him. He couldn't help but notice the tight, figure-hugging lycra of her sports outfit; three-quarter leggings and a crop top exposing her midriff.

He glanced around the room and saw that other people had begun to notice her presence too.

"You shouldn't be here," he said.

"Well, how are we supposed to do the triathlon together if I don't know whether you can keep up?" she asked innocently.

"Fair play," he muttered.

"Set your counter back to zero, and make sure your intensity is the same as mine." She leaned across and looked down at his screen. "You need to pump that up a little," she said, before turning her attention to her own bike. Once it was set, she began cycling. "We've got 40 kilometres to cover. Let me know when you hit the finish."

They cycled in silence. Stacey had her headphones in and was concentrating on the mini screen between the handlebars. She was monitoring her heart rate as well as her speed.

Sam felt nervous. 40km was an easy distance for him but he had a sneaky suspicion that he was about to be beaten by a woman.

After twenty minutes, he was starting to feel the burn. His screen said 15km.

"How far are you?" he asked.

"I'm on 19," answered Stacey without sounding out of breath. Sam could hardly believe it. How was she a whole 4km ahead of him?

He pushed himself as hard as he could and when he finally reached the 40km mark with a time of 49 minutes and 53 seconds, he felt like collapsing onto the floor.

"Very impressive," said Stacey.

Sam reached down for his water bottle in the drinks holder and drained almost half of it.

"How far along are you?" he asked, confident that he'd won.

"Oh, I've just passed 30km."

"Wait, what? How's that possible?"

"I wanted to see how well you would do. And how competitive you are. I lied," she said with a smile.

"Nice move," he said, smiling back at her. "You were never ahead of me, were you?" She shook her head, still smiling. He couldn't help but chuckle. "No wonder you've wormed your way to the top. Do you use tricks like this when you're on the track?"

"I have a few things up my sleeve," she answered. "Do you want to move onto the running machine?"

# Chapter 54

## Jason Hunter

### Hammersmith Police Station

*Wednesday 5th August*

"What's this I hear about you terrorising my staff?" I asked with a chuckle. I stood outside the police station with my phone between my cheek and my shoulder as I bent down to tie my shoelace.

"I don't know what you're talking about," said Stacey sweetly on the other end of the phone.

"Yeah, I bet you don't," I said, straightening up. I couldn't stop smiling.

"Alright," she caved in. "You wanted him to do the triathlon with me and I had to make sure he was up to it, that's all."

"And is he?" I asked.

There was a pause. "I'd say satisfactory. How's everything going?"

"Erm, well. We haven't got much to work with really. I'm just sifting through paperwork at the moment, looking for leads."

"And I take it you haven't got any."

"Nope."

"Have you looked at the photos?"

"What photos?"

"The stalkerish ones of me. I thought Hayley said something about getting them tested or identified or whatever."

"I'd actually forgotten about them," I said. "I'll ask."

I ended the call and looked across the road at the busy hubbub of daily life. I let out a sigh. Another thing to add to my to-do pile.

# Chapter 55

## JASON HUNTER

### HAMMERSMITH POLICE STATION

*Wednesday 5th August*

"So, what have we got?" I asked.

"A very generic answer," said Hayley.

The back of the photographs were printed with the name of the website they were bought from. The good news was that it was a step forward. The bad news was it didn't get us very far.

"Assuming they were from the same batch of printed photographs, we could narrow down the dates in which they were taken based solely on the events in the pictures and the moment when they appeared," said Hayley.

"But that still leaves us with a 3-day window."

"Yes," said Hayley. She was frowning.

"What?" I asked.

"I'm thinking."

We were sitting in one of the meeting rooms within the precinct. Gemma's whole file was spread across the table with the recent stalker photos of Stacey on top. A laptop was open but the keyboard was buried under yet more paperwork. I dug it out and brought it closer.

It didn't take me long to find the printers' website; it was a popular choice and came up within Google's first few results.

I browsed the policy information, looking for their turnaround times.

"I think I've just narrowed down our window," I said, passing the laptop to Hayley. "They couldn't have paid for standard delivery because the time frame isn't wide enough, which means they ordered for either special delivery or tracked."

Hayley's face lit up. "And not everyone will have paid for the extra service. Good thinking!" she said.

"How are you going to work out who placed the order though?"

"I've already put a request in. They might not be as willing as we'd hope but we've got to play it by ear and then get a subpoena," she said.

Whilst members of Hayley's team processed all the right requests to help track down the photos, Hayley pulled up the digital files she had on all the drivers.

As Hayley printed out what we needed, I compiled individual mini-folders for each driver.

She was running their names through her databases one last time to make sure we hadn't missed anything, so I did the obligatory hot drink service and fetched us both coffee. This was going to take a while.

After half an hour, she was finished and I laid out each folder on the table so we had a clear view of the photos stapled to the front.

"What do you think?" I asked.

"I'm not sure what to think," she answered. "How do you want to do this?"

"Erm, how about we do one at a time and then brief each other. It'll be quicker."

"I guess," answered Hayley. She carefully unbuttoned her cuffs and then rolled both her sleeves up. I walked the length of the room once, then twice and then a third time, stretching my legs before choosing the seat I would confine myself to for the next few hours.

I took a sip of my coffee and started with Ottoker Keil. He seemed to be the one that had the most to lose with Stacey's success. Hayley started with the Brazilian, Valencia; a glance at his file had already piqued her interest.

Keil's history was pretty scarce. He'd grown up in Germany with his mum, dad and brother, and he'd done well at school. He was accepted into a local racing club and immediately began to show his potential. Some of the guys who ran the place spotted his talent and passed his name to a scout. He was quickly placed in the Red Bull Junior team where he continued to wow his mentors and win every race he entered.

From there it was onward and upward with little standing in his way and it didn't take long before he was in Formula One and challenging the longstanding champions.

It was the same stuff I'd seen on Google except the one time he was arrested by mistake. A misidentification, apparently.

"You done?" I asked, looking across the table. Hayley was sitting with her head in her hands, Valencia's folder open on the table underneath her and was scan-reading it with a frown on her face.

"Almost," she said.

"Sure." I leaned back and stretched before taking a final swig of my coffee. I dumped it in the small bin against the wall.

"Done," she said. "What have you got?"

"Nothing out of the ordinary unfortunately. He seems to be super focused on his career and the lack of love life only reinforces the idea that he's entirely career-driven. There's no history of violence or cheating, but that doesn't mean it wouldn't happen. His lack of a partner leads me to question his sexuality. Stacey said he didn't show any compassion when Gemma died, and I don't know if that's because he didn't know her or if there's perhaps a deeper issue here."

"Are you trying to suggest he's sexist?"

I shrugged. "Not necessarily, but it's a possibility. I'm not even saying all women, but you have to admit that in a profession that's practically all male, Stacey is at some risk of arousing jealousy and I bet there are a couple of people out there who feel like they've been wronged simply by her femininity, irrelevant of the fact that she's a good driver."

"True," muttered Hayley. "So, what you're saying is, you've got no reason to suspect him but you want to keep him on the radar?" she asked.

"Erm, yeah, I guess."

"Right." She shook her head and smiled. "Why do I get the distinct impression that we're not actually going to narrow down your list because you're gonna want to keep everyone on the radar?" she said, still smiling.

I let out a laugh. "I don't know what you're talking about Detective Inspector."

"Yeah, I bet you don't," she muttered.

"What have you found on Valencia?" I asked.

"To be honest, not much," she began. "Like Keil, he's been in racing since he was young. Only difference is there was a time when he went off the rails. Nothing too serious, a little bit of shoplifting, possession of a firearm, association with drug dealers. To be honest, a lot of this seems circumstantial. It looks like he's been mentored by one of Brazil's greatest legends and that seems to have put him on the straight and narrow. Not even a hint of something dodgy since then."

"Sounds like we'll make an F1 fan out of you yet."

"Maybe."

"So you don't think it's him?"

"Nope," Hayley shook her head. "If I'm completely honest, I don't think he's got anything to do with it, but I wouldn't be surprised if he was acting a little nervous around Stacey simply because he knows he'll be the first person we question.

"A lot of youths in his situation are able to turn their life around. It's often got more to do with who he's hanging out with than what he's doing. I'd even be willing to bet he didn't choose to do any of these things but had to find money from somewhere for his racing. Once he was on the fast-track to fame, he didn't need the dirty money anymore."

"Yeah, I don't think he's the guy," I said. "And I don't think he'd be coordinated enough to pull this off anyway. He has much bigger things to worry about, like the fact he hasn't been on the podium in a while and may be at risk when it comes to signing his next contract."

She nodded. "Agreed. So let's cross him off."

She reached out and picked up Volkov's file. That left me with St Pierre or Sanchez and I definitely knew which one I wanted. I picked up St Pierre's.

# Chapter 56

## JASON HUNTER

### HAMMERSMITH POLICE STATION

*Wednesday 5th August*

"Found much?" asked Hayley.

"Nope," I said. "St Pierre is about as normal as they come."

"You mean 'boring'?"

I laughed. "Stacey says he's like a brother to her. He's had his years in the spotlight and I can't find anything out of the ordinary. He seems to be a mellow character and spends a lot of time with Stacey at public appearances."

"Does that not make him more of a suspect? If he works with Stacey more than the others then he would know where she is all the time?" said Hayley with a frown.

"The best person to ask is going to be Stacey," I said.

"Hmmm. I'd prefer not to."

I gave her a quizzical look.

"Oh come on, she isn't gonna admit St Pierre is a liability, they're far too close for that."

"I think she's starting to realise that this could be anyone."

"Well, why don't you ask her?"

"Sure," I shrugged. "What did you get on Volkov?"

"He had a turbulent childhood. Was taken in by the Babichev family after Gromov brought him to the UK. Alik Gromov had a particular interest in the boy and sponsored his racing tuition. Was arrested for dealing Class A, spent some time behind bars for alleged arms trafficking-"

"Wait, go back a bit. Who brought him to the UK?"

"Alik Gromov."

My mind was feeling muggy. "Fuck."

"What?" she asked, suddenly alert.

"Alik Gromov – if we're talking about the same Russian millionaire – is a client of mine. A recent one."

"Sure he's the same guy?" asked Hayley.

"I'm assuming so. He became my client the same week Gemma died, and now it turns out he has a personal interest in Formula One drivers. Isn't that worrying?"

"A little. What do you know about him?"

"Not much. He's been reluctant to disclose his circumstances." I looked across the table to where Hayley now sat with an incredulous look on her face.

"Do you want me to formally investigate your client?"

"No." I shook my head. "You can't. I'll keep an eye on him."

She watched him for a few more moments before relenting and pulling the final folder towards her. "Okay, you can go get a coffee refill then."

"Sure, same again?"

She nodded.

I dumped her empty cardboard cup in the bin and left the meeting room. I entered the sparsely furnished kitchen with thoughts still whirring through my head. Opting for the supplied vending machine instead of making it myself, I dropped in the required coinage and pressed the start button.

Back in the meeting room, Hayley took her drink without looking up from the last file. But the time away from the claustrophobic room had given me a break and got me thinking.

I pulled the laptop closer and loaded up Facebook. It didn't take me long to find a profile for Volkov, although it didn't look particularly authentic. I browsed the professional looking photography and quickly searched his friend's list for a Gromov. There was nothing.

I tried a different tactic and loaded up Wikipedia. There was a lot of information on Volkov's early life and it seemed the whole world knew he had a criminal record. I wondered if it was a publicity stunt: the born-again racer, the world champion who turned his life around.

I snorted.

"What?" asked Hayley.

"Sorry, nothing," I said, taking a sip of my coffee. "You done with Sanchez yet?"

"Yeah just about. Nothing special, nothing stands out. Sounds like a good lad to be honest."

"So who are we left with?"

Hayley looked at the notepad to her left. "Keil, Volkov, and we've both mentioned keeping tabs on St Pierre."

I nodded. "So what's next?"

"That's down to you," said Hayley. She was looking at me with a smile, her elbows on the table and her head resting on her hands.

"Are you fluttering your eyelashes at me?" I asked, amazed.

"No," she scoffed, suddenly sitting up.

"God, you women are a handful. What do you need?"

"Well, I don't have the resources to keep an eye on these guys," she indicated the names on the notepad.

"So you're expecting me to assign my own guys? How do you propose I pay their wages? They're not gonna do it for free!"

"I'm sure you'll sort something out."

"Yeah, thanks," I said sarcastically. I looked down at my watch and realised it was already early afternoon. *Shit.* "Hayley, sorry, I've got to go. It's important. I'll sort something, okay?"

I grabbed my phone and my keys and ran out to my car.

# Chapter 57

## Jason Hunter

### Mortlake Crematorium

*Wednesday 5th August*

I arrived at the crematorium to see the hearse had already arrived and Gemma's coffin was carefully being unloaded by four men dressed in black. The grounds were beautiful. A neatly manicured lawn led up to the one-storey building and I immediately felt a sense of peace.

I parked as far back as I could so as not to draw attention to myself but the family members gathered around the entrance still threw me disapproving looks.

The procession moved inside and I followed, careful to keep my distance. I caught glimpses of beautiful pond areas and tranquil little hideaways, cleverly designed to allow grieving family members the privacy to mourn. My gut twisted in guilt.

We entered the chapel and the coffin was placed at the front.

I took a seat at the very back, wanting to pay my respects but not get involved. It wasn't my place to mourn with her family and friends. After all, I was her boss, I was responsible for her death.

It took an hour for the relevant family members to say their pieces, share their anecdotes and try to make this into something more cheerful. They didn't succeed.

The atmosphere in the room was cold, anguished, and the guilt weighed heavily on me. I scanned the rows of faces all here to celebrate the life of Gemma and felt responsible for every single one. She was greatly loved. *Is,* I told myself, *is greatly loved.*

I looked up at the large photo of a smiling Gemma, framed in gold, sitting at the front of the room, reminding us all of the lively person she once was.

Something changed in the room, the person at the front finished speaking and the coffin started to move backwards. A curtain fell in place, hiding it from view and a wave of sadness washed over me.

It was over. It was all officially over.

Gemma was now gone.

And I still didn't have the fucker that murdered her.

I stood from my pew at the back and made a hasty retreat to avoid getting cornered by an angry family member.

The crying that echoed through the chapel as I left haunted me all the way home.

# Chapter 58

## DIANE PARSONS

### VOLKOV'S APARTMENT

*Thursday 6th August*

Diane looked furtively over her shoulder as she pressed the buzzer to Volkov's apartment again. It was times like this she cursed the fact that he'd never given her access to the building.

She pressed the buzzer again and held it down. Moments later an annoyed face appeared in the window beside the door, making her jump.

"Go away!" came the muffled shout through the glass.

She was about to ask for his help when the snub-nosed twat gave her a shooing motion.

Shooting him a dirty look, she stepped away from the door and pulled her phone from her pocket. Dialling Volkov, it went straight to voicemail.

"Shit," she muttered under her breath.

It was still a few hours before she needed to make an appearance at Stacey's apartment and a knot formed in her stomach at the thought. Without knowing what else to do, she wandered down the street to a local park and settled herself on a bench.

Four voicemails and half an hour later, Volkov's number flashed up on her phone screen. She answered the call immediately, having long given up on trying to distract herself with the passers-by.

"Dima," she said, almost breathless.

"What's wrong?"

"Where are you?"

"On my way back from the gym, I've been training all morning."

Diane let out an exasperated sound.

"How long will you be?"

"I'll be home in about ten minutes. Where are you?"

"I'll meet you outside your apartment."

She hung up and let out a long deep breath that she didn't know she'd been holding.

Ten minutes later and Diane was once again loitering outside Volkov's building. She kept enough of a distance in case she was spotted again by his angry doorman, but couldn't help pacing up and down the pavement.

A slick black Mercedes with tinted windows pulled up a short distance from the kerb and Volkov climbed out with a gym bag slung over his shoulder, saying goodbye to the driver.

Walking up to the building, the car drove off and Diane rushed up to him.

"What's going on?" Volkov asked with a furrowed brow as he opened the door.

"I'll tell you inside," Diane muttered with a nervous look over her shoulder.

They entered the swanky apartment block and the doorman threw her a suspicious look. Reaching the elevator, they rode it in silence and Diane could feel her impatience grow as Volkov fumbled for his apartment keys.

"If you bought a damn thumb scanner, we wouldn't be having this problem."

Volkov didn't reply as he put the key in the door and shot a sideways glance at Diane. He frowned again, turned the key and opened the door.

Once inside, Diane flopped onto the sofa, letting out a huff and dumping her handbag on the floor next to her.

"Make yourself at home," he muttered, closing the door and disappearing down the hallway with his gym bag.

Volkov reappeared moments later and sat himself on the opposite sofa.

"So, what's all this about?" he asked, waving his hand vaguely.

As if she'd been reminded why she was there, Diane sat up straight and suddenly looked a lot more agitated.

"It's about this money," she whispered.

Volkov frowned. "Is everything okay?"

"Well, I don't... I don't know what the fuck I'm doing. I've transferred the first few amounts. I set up payments for charity sponsors and it seems to have gone okay, but I don't know. I haven't heard back from the accountants. I've deposited the money via some fake invoices and that seems fine but all anyone has to do is dig a little deeper and they'll see it's all a load of rubbish. Then what? I'll go to prison, that's what. And then I'll be royally fucked. I can't go to prison, Dima, I just can't." Diane's rant came to an end and before Volkov could reply, she burst into tears.

"Hey, hey, hey," said Volkov, moving to sit next to her. "Less of that. You're fine. Who's going to look into this, eh? Who? You've got nothing to worry about."

Diane wiped at the tears still streaming down her cheeks and hiccupped.

"But what if-"

"You can't think like that," Volkov said gently, taking her hand.

"But-"

"Don't. What's done is done. I'm sorry I got you into this mess, but I'll do my best to help, okay?"

Diane nodded.

"Now, do you have any of the cash left?"

# Chapter 59

## ALIK GROMOV

### HAMPSTEAD MANSION

*Friday 7th August*

Alik Gromov was wheeled into the study of his seven-bed mansion. Along the back wall were floor to ceiling bookshelves lined with more than a thousand books in a number of languages, including rare and first editions in English, Latin, Russian and French.

On the other side of the room was a flat-screen TV mounted on the wooden-panelled wall and a collection of three sofas in dark grey leather. A slim Russian man was sitting on one of the Chesterfield sofas, dressed in a tight-fitting pin-striped suit. His angular features were accentuated by his dark eyes and sunken eye sockets.

Gromov waved a hand and his bodyguard, Liam, hesitated.

"Leave us," snapped Gromov.

Liam left, closing the study door softly behind him.

"What the fuck are you doing here?" asked Gromov, reverting to his mother-tongue.

The Russian smiled and carefully crossed his legs, placing his hands on top of his knees.

"I've told you, I will pay you," Gromov spat when the other man didn't answer.

"And I've told you many things over the years, dear Uncle. But how many of them were true?"

"You will get your money."

"When?" he asked calmly. Not a single flicker of emotion passed across his face. Gromov manoeuvred his wheelchair towards the desk and powered up his Apple Mac.

"Tomorrow. I have bigger problems to deal with right now."

"You mean the alibi for your precious Dima?" he sneered.

"How do you know about that?"

"I have friends in the right places," he replied, casually inspecting his fingernails.

"Get out of my sight."

"Don't disrespect me, Uncle!" exclaimed the Russian. His words tumbled out in an angry flow of the Cyrillic language. "You've become a weak, old man. Your empire is dwindling. The arms race is over. Why else would you not have my money? You've been taken for a fool by some naïve little bitch. Yes, I know about the mix-up," he added, seeing the surprise on Gromov's face.

Gromov didn't reply.

He logged onto the computer and began typing.

"You will have your money tomorrow. I am making arrangements as we speak."

The Russian nodded, satisfied. "Don't let this happen again." He stood to leave.

"I will be throwing a party. Next week." Gromov said.

"A party? What the hell for?" He threw his hands in the air with exasperation.

"Vanya. Get a hold of yourself," snapped Gromov. "My 'empire' – as you put it – is not dwindling. The party will be a chance to see that, and a way for you to potentially pick up some new clients. Besides,

I have a new business deal on the horizon. The arms race is indeed almost over. There's no point supplying Kyiv anymore, they have what they need. Once the stock runs dry, I'll be moving operations elsewhere."

"Elsewhere? Where elsewhere?"

"All in good time, Vanya."

# Chapter 60

## THE STALKER

### TRAFALGAR SQUARE

*Friday 7th August*

"You still haven't been paid?" he snapped.

The voice on the other end of the phone grumbled a reply. It was a hot day but a light breeze caused him to momentarily shiver.

"Fucking hell, Vanya. I thought you had more sense than that. I need my share of that money." He paused. "Tomorrow isn't good enough, you fucking weasel," he whispered through gritted teeth, aware of people nearby. "Don't fucking cross me."

He snapped the phone shut, feeling his blood beginning to boil. Nothing pissed him off more than smart-arse, fucking rich people who thought they could own him just because they had more money. It was not their God-given right, and some people needed reminding of that.

Standing outside the National Portrait Gallery, he leaned against the wall that overlooked Nelson's column. Tourists were clambering on the base, desperate to get the perfect picture. Kids were scrambling on the backs of the four majestic lions like it was a playground.

He seriously doubted William Railton had planned for his most iconic work of architecture to be a climbing frame. He turned away

from the monument, conscious of the anger rising up inside of him.
He needed to regain control.

Lined up in front of the Gallery were the most pathetic looking
individuals. Dressed as famous characters from some of the most
beloved films of all time, they attempted to convince the crowds they
were levitating. He let out a snort. What idiot would fall for this shit?

A few people shot him dirty looks.

He loved the hustle and bustle of this Trafalgar Square. It was comforting in some ways. He felt anonymous. There were all these people
and yet they didn't have a fucking clue about him, about anything.

His every waking thought was filled with Stacey fucking James and
God, how he hated her. Hated her with every fibre of his being. Hated
what she did to him. Yet it was more than that. He also loved her with
every fibre of his being. Would take a bullet for her.

Why couldn't she see that?

# Chapter 61

## JASON HUNTER

### SOUTHAMPTON DOCK GATE 4

*Saturday 8th August*

Adrianna and the kids had gotten a taxi down to Southampton, so it wasn't like they couldn't get one back. But I just felt like I needed to be there. I wanted to hold my kids, make sure they were okay.

I was sitting in my old BMW alongside at least fifty other pick-up vehicles, waiting for Adrianna and the kids to emerge. And it was taking forever.

I'd already texted Adrianna twice to find out where she was and my impatience was putting me on edge.

The huge ship, Ventura, towered above me and I couldn't even begin to imagine what it was like inside. The dock rang with loud shouts as I watched staff and crew unloading bags, loading supplies and organising what was left to do. It was a mammoth operation, and one I didn't envy.

I took the time to quickly text Stacey an update to keep my mind off the waiting.

I then texted Sam to check in with him and make sure everything was running smoothly.

The beauty of smartphones meant I could also run through a few of my emails whilst I was there.

It took another twenty minutes of waiting before I saw three familiar faces emerge from the crowd. I got out of the car and could hear Max and Lily shouting, "Dad!"

Both of my kids ran over as fast as their little legs could carry them. I bent down with my arms out in anticipation of the greatest hug the world could ever give me. Lily got to me first but she didn't slow down. Instead, she barrelled into me and took me out, followed by Max throwing himself on top of us moments later. The three of us lay on the floor like that, ignoring the strange stares, laughing and giggling. I'm sure Lily was squealing and it was the best sound in the world.

Still laughing, I picked myself up from the floor and turned to where Adrianna was standing, an amused look on her face.

"Adrianna," I said and embraced her. She hugged me back and I liked the fact that we now had this mutual understanding. It would be better than the arguing and would definitely be better for the kids.

"Come on then, you lot," I said to the two small faces looking up at me. "Let's get you home."

# Chapter 62

## THE STALKER

### SOUTHAMPTON DOCK GATE 4

*Saturday 8th August*

He watched as Jason embraced his kids. The fucking idiot had no idea.

It hurt him to leave Stacey for so long, but this was more important. He needed to know who he was dealing with – and now he knew what Jason's slut of an ex-wife looked like, too. They seemed cosy. Too friendly for a divorced couple. How did this guy do it? How did he entrap these women? Mr Perfect Hunter seemed to have it all. What a prick.

He frowned.

Taking the photo of his kids had been a stroke of genius and it had sent the trumped-up twat into such a panic. The warm feeling spreading through his body was satisfaction.

They looked the picture of the perfect family as Jason got to his feet, both of his kids wrapped around his legs as he gave his ex-wife a chaste peck on the cheek. It made him nauseous.

He watched them walk back to the car and fantasised about the different ways he could destroy Jason, right now, in front of everyone. Starting with his ex-wife. Make the kids suffer, then make him suffer.

Goosebumps ran over his arms and he looked away, letting out a small laugh.

Turning back, he watched Jason load the bags into the boot of his BMW and then bundle his kids into the back. His ex-wife climbed into the passenger seat and there was a strange emotion on her face. Relief?

A knock on the window startled him and he turned to see some fucking snooty-nosed dock gate staff motioning for him to roll down the window. He plastered a charming smile on his face and pressed the electric button next to the door handle.

"Sir," she said, her voice nasally and irritating. He tried not to grimace. "Are you waiting for someone? We ask all vehicles here to collect holidaymakers to queue over there." She pointed to the loading bays where Jason had parked.

"Sorry, I'll move," he said, holding up a hand as a sign of passiveness.

She gave him an insincere smile. He wound up the window and turned the engine on.

Now, he didn't believe in fate, but Jason was pulling away from his space and driving away.

Perfect timing.

# Chapter 63

## JASON HUNTER

### THE LONDON TRIATHLON

*Saturday 8ᵗʰ August*

"Are you a hundred percent sure you want to do this?" I asked.

"It's a bit late for me to be changing my mind now, Jason." She indicated her running outfit.

"I'm just conscious you're basically putting yourself in the crosshairs."

"Jason, I refuse to let this asshole interfere with my life anymore. I have a championship to win and I've got to keep fit. Besides, I've already had to cancel a bunch of appearances and I'm sick of all this gossiping."

Sam just looked at me and shrugged. Someone tapped Stacey on the shoulder and she turned around abruptly to see a short lady in a poorly tailored brown suit holding a microphone. Directly behind her was a cameraman.

"Stacey James, can we do a quick interview?" The reporter indicated the man behind her and gave an insincere toothy smile.

"Of course." Stacy turned back to me. "Jason, I'll see you at the finish line. Sam?"

Sam nodded and followed Stacey as she made her way towards the starting point, the reporter and the cameraman carving a way through the crowd for her. I could already see the crowd noticing her and beginning to point and stare.

I inwardly groaned and hoped that Sam was on his toes.

"Not ideal, right?"

I turned to see Hayley in an unusually casual outfit.

"What are you doing here?" I asked.

"I didn't have anything in the schedule so I thought I'd come and show my support. Plus, I had a sneaky suspicion you might need a friend."

"Thanks," I said with a smile.

"I can't believe she's actually going through with it," she said with a shake of her head.

"Oh I can," I said. "She's one of the most stubborn people I've ever met. I've done what I can, so now we just need to hope it's enough."

We wandered towards the starting line as the public address system announced there were fifteen minutes until the start.

"She's gonna be right at the front," I said as I spotted the poorly dressed reporter and her cameraman. A few more reporters had seen her and were starting to drift closer, desperate to get a piece of her in light of everything that had happened so far. But I didn't expect to see the man standing next to her.

Stacey waved in our direction. We waved back.

"Is that who I think it is?" asked Hayley.

"Oh yeah," I said through gritted teeth. Stacey turned away to talk to her new friend. I looked in Sam's direction, flicking my eyes towards them when he looked at me. He nodded.

I saw him whisper something in Stacey's ear and then muscle himself between them. The final countdown began.

Both Stacey and Sam were focusing on what lay ahead but I couldn't take my eyes off the man next to Stacey. 10 seconds to go.

"Still thinking he's not a threat?" I muttered.

"I'm not sure," replied Hayley.

Volkov finally looked in my direction and steadily met my gaze, sending a shiver down my spine.

The foghorn sounded, announcing the start of the race and the thousands of people lined up in front of me set off quickly. I lost sight of Stacey almost immediately.

"Fuck!" I stamped my foot in frustration. In the chaos of noise, Hayley was the only person to hear me swear. I pulled my phone from my pocket and began dialling.

"We have a situation. I need everyone who's not on duty to be out here now. Pace them at every mile and I need them looking for Dima Volkov. Yes, the driver. Take him out of the race if necessary, but don't let him anywhere near Stacey." I hung up the phone but I didn't feel any calmer.

"There's nothing else you can do," said Hayley, attempting to placate me.

"I'm aware of that, Hayley," I said through gritted teeth. The racers were already in the water and taking on the 1.5km swim. At least this part of the race was fairly easy to monitor. I scanned the crowd of spectators, looking for familiar faces, anyone to reassure me that my guys were out there.

There were literally thousands of people cheering and waving banners. All of them pressed as tightly as possible to the railings so they could see the competitors.

Over the noise of the crowd, I heard the whirring of helicopter blades. I looked up to see the sleek black machine hovering above us, a camera sticking out the side.

I couldn't keep still and decided to force my way through the crowds. As long as Sam didn't lose her, it would be fine. I pushed my way to the front to get a clear view but it wasn't helping. People were screaming in my ears, jumping up and down, pushing and shoving me. I was slowly beginning to lose my temper.

"I can't do this," I said to Hayley as I retreated to a safe distance.

"Look, why don't we position ourselves near the cycling and we'll be able to spot her then? I'm not sure the underground will be quick enough to get us to the road race as well," she said.

"I'd prefer to be stationed by the finish line, that way we can get her out of here as quickly as possible."

"Let's do that then," said Hayley.

We left the crowds behind as we made our way towards the finish line. Everything was disorientating and it was almost impossible to move. I found a marshal who pointed us in the right direction and within five minutes, I was enjoying the peace and quiet of the underground train as it rattled through the railway tunnels.

A wave of exhaustion swept over me as the tension left my body.

The train was unusually quiet with a few seats still available. Most of them were next to a man dressed in a sequin dress with a feather boa wrapped around his neck. I didn't even look twice.

"Do you love her?" asked Hayley.

"I'm sorry, what?" I asked, jolted from my minute of tranquillity.

"You heard," she whispered.

"Jesus, Hayley. I'm not sure that we can even have that conversation."

"Why not?" She looked hurt.

"We're colleagues, first and foremost, Stacey's my client and you're investigating who's trying to kill her."

"Exactly, so I'm the best person to have this conversation with. Plus, we're not working right now, are we?"

"I'm always working," I muttered.

She realised I wasn't going to answer and sank back against the bucket shaped seat. "I'll take that as a yes," she said with a smirk.

I glanced over at her and could see the smug expression on her face. I didn't have the energy to argue or even defend myself, so I let it go.

We got off the underground and made our way up the stairs and back into the dazzling sunshine. It always amazed me how stuffy the underground could be and I breathed the fresh air with a sense of relief.

We strolled towards the finish line. The race winners wouldn't be due there for at least another hour so we decided to grab a bite to eat. We spotted a nearby Subway and it wasn't long before we were both tucking into a couple of their toasted subs.

"Have you had any luck with the photos?" I asked, taking another bite.

Hayley shook her head and finished her mouthful. "Not yet. We have a list of the orders. I've got someone combing through them as we speak. He'll call me if he finds anything unusual or once he's finished putting the list together."

"The list?"

"Well, we've got to look at everyone who specifically requested the quicker delivery method, right?"

I nodded.

"It's likely to be someone we don't know, or an alias. It could even have been sent to a PO Box and not a legitimate address."

"How often do you come across PO Boxes?" I asked.

"Quite often, especially if we're dealing with organised crime."

"Is that what you think this is?"

Hayley shrugged.

"Great," I muttered.

"Well, it could actually be a good thing."

"In what way?"

"Most of these places will have some form of CCTV, and some hold identification of their clients."

"Forgive me if I don't get excited," I replied sarcastically.

We finished the sandwiches and headed back outside. The first few runners were in sight now but there was no Stacey.

The crowds were beginning to migrate towards the finish line but we were still able to shuffle our way towards the front. The winner crossed the line in an astonishing 1 hour 48 minutes and 27 seconds. There was a huge cheer for him and he raised his arms in the air, revelling in the moment.

My attention now turned to the racers that followed.

The first female crossed the line 8 minutes later to yet more cheers. I hadn't seen Volkov.

Stacey finally crossed the line an agonising 12 minutes after the first woman with Sam by her side. We both barged our way forward before anyone else could get to her. I'd already seen the camera crews lining up to get a piece of her. But not on my watch.

"Stacey, how do you feel running that race knowing someone is trying to kill you?" shouted one reporter.

"Stacey James, is this your rebellion against the murderer and their attempt on your life?" shouted another.

"Stacey, why do you think someone is trying to kill you?"

"Stacey, is it true that you're now involved with your personal security officer?"

I pushed my way in front of the cameras, shielding Stacey from their prying eyes. Hayley stepped up next to me and addressed them.

"My name is Detective Inspector Hayley Irons, and I'm investigating the death of Gemma Brown and the attempted murder of Stacey James. Unfortunately, Ms James is unable to answer any questions at the moment. She has just completed the London Triathlon as part-"

"Who's the killer?" shouted a voice at the back.

Hayley ignored them and calmly continued. "-of her training. We are doing everything in our power to ensure her safety and wellbeing and to bring the offender to justice."

I saw my chance and I took it. Sam helped me carve a path through the crowd and led Stacey to a nearby car. I bundled her in like some counterfeit merchandise and slammed the door behind her. Sam only had enough time to jump in the other side before I banged the roof of the blacked-out Mercedes and it shot off into the congested streets, horn blaring.

I turned to see Hayley still with the reporters, fighting off their rebuttals. I gave her a frantic wave and it only took half a minute for her to extricate herself and join me. We dodged in and out of the crowd, hoping that none of the pesky journalists followed.

Back on the underground we let out a sigh of relief.

"Did you see Volkov?" I asked.

# Chapter 64

## Jason Hunter

### Stacey's Apartment

*Saturday 8th August*

I was pacing up and down Stacey's living room, beginning to wear a path into the carpet. Well, it was less of a living room and more of a living space.

It was an open plan area with coffee tables in between comfy-looking sofas. But I couldn't sit down. I couldn't think. I stopped suddenly in the middle of the room and it felt like my head was going to explode. I caught sight of myself in one of the mirrors propped up on the bookcase. Floor to ceiling shelves lined the wall in front of me. The wall behind held the same. It was covered in square shaped shelving that had been painted a dusty blue colour. It looked good, really good.

Definitely designer.

The stress and frustration of the afternoon had finally taken its toll and I was exhausted.

I let my eyes roam across the shelves, glancing at the piles of books crammed into every corner. They were stood up neatly next to each other in some places and then piled high on their sides in others. I recognised some of the names but most were authors I'd never heard of.

One square shelf contained nothing but fitness books whilst another was a collection of autobiographies from world famous race drivers. Some from the rally profession and others in Formula One. That brought a smile to my face. It wasn't something I had expected to see. I wasn't entirely convinced the book collection was genuine; she'd never once mentioned reading to me.

I heard footsteps and turned to see Stacey coming down the glass stairs. She was in a pair of torn jeans with nothing on her feet and a loose vest top. Her hair was hanging over one shoulder in a damp tangled mess and she was combing her fingers through it.

She stopped in her tracks at the look on my face.

"Never again are you to pull a stunt like that. I don't care what the hell's going on."

Stacey descended the remaining stairs carefully. "Sorry." She wrapped her arms around me and I buried my head in her hair, inhaling the sweet scent of her shampoo.

My mobile began to ring, interrupting us.

Pulling it from my pocket, it was Gromov.

"Mr Gromov, is everything okay?" I answered.

"Mr Hunter," said the thick Russian voice. "I'm calling to let you know I require extra protection at my estate on the 15th for a party. Guests will arrive in the afternoon and I want to ensure they feel safe."

"Of course, Mr Gromov. I'll make a note of it. Can we meet to discuss this in more detail?"

"Yes. Shall we say over lunch tomorrow? Drop by around 12."

# Chapter 65

## JASON HUNTER

### HAMPSTEAD MANSION

*Sunday 9th August*

I parked my car on the gravel drive out the front and made my way towards the doorway framed by two marble columns. The door itself was imposing enough and before I even knocked, it swung open and I was greeted by the butler.

At least that's who I thought he was.

"Mr Hunter," he said with a Russian accent thicker than Gromov's. "I am Vanya, Alik's nephew." He was tall, thin and had dark features, hollow-looking cheeks and sharp cheekbones. He had an air of seediness about him, and I immediately didn't trust him.

"Ah, nice to meet you." I held out a hand and he eyed it suspiciously before reaching out and shaking it.

"What a pleasure. Please come this way. My uncle is waiting."

He led me through the house and I was amazed by the interior. The floor was marble throughout and the furniture was antique, but it still felt light and airy. The walls were painted white and seemed to allow the rooms to breathe. Large windows occupied every outward facing wall.

We walked past the grand staircase in the lobby and through what I can only guess was one of many reception rooms. This one had been decked out in blue. The walls and floors were still a dazzling white but all the furniture was a cornflower blue. It looked expensive.

We entered another reception room, this one was coordinated in a faded lemon yellow. Everything seemed to be in its perfect position and I doubted anyone ever used it.

I was so focused on taking in my surroundings that I wasn't looking where I was going, and almost walked into a woman.

"I'm so sorry," I said, catching myself just in time.

She was about the same height as me, thanks to her sparkling stiletto heels. Her hair was huge and looked horrendously frazzled but had been tamed and styled in a bun on her head. Her makeup was so thick and heavy it was almost impossible to see her face behind it. She didn't smile, but I wasn't sure if that was because she physically couldn't or because she didn't want to.

She wore skin-tight clothes that were perhaps a little too much for a casual day at home and enough jewellery to fill a bank vault. She reminded me of Adrianna, except Adrianna didn't have the dangerous air that this woman did.

The woman said something to Vanya in a brusque tone before slowly letting her eyes wander up and down my body. I shifted uncomfortably.

"Mr Hunter, this is my Aunt, Miroslava," he said.

I nodded and held out a hand to shake. She looked contemptuously at it before walking away.

I almost expected an apology from the nephew but he simply shrugged his shoulders and continued our journey through the house.

We finally made it out onto the patio through the open plan kitchen and some floor-to-ceiling sliding glass doors.

Gromov was sitting in a wheelchair looking out over the who-knows-how-many acres that were part of his property. It was breath-taking.

"Hello, Mr Hunter!" said Gromov in an overly cheerful manner.

"Good afternoon, Mr Gromov. How are you?" I asked.

He indicated one of the seats near him and I took it.

"I'm recovering," he said simply.

"No complications with your recovery then."

He shook his head.

"And the shooter?"

He eyed me for a moment, weighing up how much he would tell me. "It was a misunderstanding."

"Some misunderstanding," I said and let out a breath.

"Indeed. In my line of work, I find emotional reactions are often extreme," he said carefully.

I frowned. Had someone tried to kill out of sheer desperation?

"We will have lunch on the terrace below," he suddenly announced. I nodded my agreement, still thinking about whoever it was that shot him. "But first, I must compliment your boys," he said, waving an arm in the air. I looked over in the direction he indicated and saw Liam stood stiffly by the entrance to the house. He was dressed in a black suit and I could just about see the flesh coloured wire of his earpiece that connected him to the rest of the team. He gave me a small smile.

"They have been doing very well," he continued. "Very competent. And young Liam here is my favourite." He beckoned Liam forward. "Do you like working for me?" he asked once Liam was in earshot.

"Of course, sir," came the reply.

"He's always so polite," Gromov practically snickered. "You keep doing what you're doing, boy, and I may have to give you a promotion." Liam nodded, gave an insincere smile and returned to his post. I made a mental note to check in on him later.

"I'm glad to hear it," I said, smiling and then turned to look back at the scenery. "I also hear you took a shine to young Volkov, once upon a time," I said, glancing out of the corner of my eye to see if Gromov reacted. He stiffened slightly, but made no other movements.

"He is practically family," he said. "I liked him. Saw his talent straight away. I'm the one who got him into Formula One, did you know that?" he asked casually, but I felt like there was a heavier meaning to his words.

"You must be proud."

"Yes, I am. He is like a son to me. Anyone could see he was talented and I was lucky enough to have the money to support him. To get him to where he is now."

"That's very admirable."

"Thank you."

"How many world titles has he won?" I asked, trying to sound casual and interested but worried I might be sounding suspicious instead.

"I lose count," said Gromov, looking at me. He gave me a cold, hard smile before announcing that we should go down for lunch. "You go down." He waved at one of the two staircases that led from the balcony down to the terrace. "I must use the elevator," he said and began to roll himself towards the doors. Liam sprang into action, took hold of the handles on Gromov's wheelchair and pushed him the rest of the way.

I walked down the stairs and found myself looking at a swimming pool almost half the size of an Olympic one. I couldn't bear to think about how much this place was worth, and something told me it may not have been bought with clean money.

# Chapter 66

## JASON HUNTER

### HAMPSTEAD MANSION

*Sunday 9ᵗʰ August*

A table had been laid out at the edge of the pool with only one chair. I stood awkwardly, waiting for someone to appear.

Miroslava Gromov entered. She'd changed from her earlier outfit and was now wearing a bikini, the smallest she could find. She was young, at least half of Gromov's age. Without so much of a glance in my direction or the table laid for lunch, she dived gracefully into the pool with a delicate little splash.

Seconds later she reappeared on the surface to begin a length of front crawl. I watched, mesmerised by her strong, confident strokes. I made a mental note to check the background information we had on her.

My phone started buzzing in my pocket. I checked the caller ID before answering.

"Hi Hayley," I said.

"I've got some news."

"Okay, make it quick. I'm with a client," I said, turning away from the house and walking to the edge of the grass.

"We've had an address come up from those photos. I was right, it was a PO Box. I'm going to swing by tomorrow. Chances are they won't be able to tell me anything but hopefully they'll have some CCTV footage."

"That's good news. Do you need anything from me?"

"Not at the moment, but I'll let you know what I find."

I hung up.

"I didn't think the police were allowed to confide in a civilian?"

I turned to see Gromov had reappeared from the house and was sitting only a few feet away. It was clear he'd heard at least most of the conversation.

I smiled awkwardly, not quite understanding how he knew it was Hayley that I'd been speaking to. "I'm acting as a consultant."

He gave me that cold smile again as he turned and made his way over to the table. I joined him. Two bowls of steaming soup were already there.

"This is Borsch," said Gromov. "A Russian favourite."

He didn't say any more on the matter, instead picking up a spoon and beginning to eat. I followed suit and was surprised to find it thick and full of flavour. We ate in silence until the bowls were empty.

"My party," said Gromov. I nodded. "I will need at least three times the security guards available to ensure my guests feel safe." I nodded again. "They will need to be here in the morning, until maybe 2am the next day." He paused, waiting for me to respond. I pulled out a small notebook and made some notes.

"Okay, so you want the extra guys to arrive here at say... 11 o'clock?"

"Yes."

"And you want them on duty until 2am?"

"Yes."

I made another note.

"Is that going to be a definite cut off time or do you need them here indefinitely?"

"As my guests start to leave, they can start to 'clock-off', as you English say."

"I see."

"I want to choose my guards," Gromov said.

I took a moment before answering. Anything I said would be taken as a formal contract. "I can provide you with a portfolio of all our available security officers and you can choose the ones that you prefer?"

"Photos?"

"Yes, I can get photos."

"Good. Shall we say on Wednesday?"

"Wednesday at about 11 o'clock would be perfect." I wrote the time and date alongside my notes.

"I would like you and Miss James to come as well."

This took me completely by surprise. And the smile on his face told me he knew it. "That's very kind of you," I said slowly. "I'll have to check if Stacey is available but, of course, I'll be there."

"Great. Send me an invoice for the extra guards and I'll have my accountant pay it."

I nodded, still dumbstruck. I closed my notebook and stood up, sensing it was my cue to leave.

"Past my best onto Volkov, will you? I heard he didn't finish the triathlon on Saturday."

# Chapter 67

## DI HAYLEY IRONS

### REGENT STREET

*Monday 10<sup>th</sup> August*

Hayley pulled up in the car park and turned the ignition off.

Jason had sounded a little strange on the phone. He wasn't his usual talkative self and there were underlying tones of stress. She told herself it was just his job. Meeting with any client was enough to put someone on edge. Jason dealt with millionaires and billionaires, she doubted it ever got any easier.

But something was niggling away at her.

She'd called Stacey. Wanted to make sure nothing had happened that she needed to know about but Stacey had reassured her everything was fine.

So why did she have a bad feeling?

He'd mentioned Alik Gromov was a client. Is that who he'd been meeting with? Maybe she should run some checks on him anyway. Jason had said not to, but she was within her right to and he didn't *need* to know.

Hayley let out a sigh and climbed out of her unmarked car. A standard police car had parked nearby and two uniformed officers were climbing out.

"DI," nodded one of them.

"Afternoon," she replied.

They made their way out of the car park and onto Regent Street, appearing next to Calvin Klein. The hustle and bustle of pedestrians immediately swept them up. This street was never quiet and the afternoons were always the busiest.

They headed down the road, past a number of exclusive designer brands before becoming entangled in the queue outside Hamleys. Children gaped open-mouthed at the two uniformed police who smiled graciously as they tried to carve a path between the crowd.

Continuing down the pavement, Hayley tried not to glance at the shops they passed.

Another minute later they stood outside the nondescript number 207 Regent Street. Nestled between Kipling and Camper was a blank looking door at least twice the size of an average one.

"This it?" asked one of the uniforms. Hayley nodded. She pushed the door open and ascended the stairs.

"Make sure no-one leaves the building whilst we're in here," she said over her shoulder. She didn't hold much hope for this place but she had to give it a try.

She came to the top of the stairs and walked into a bare looking reception room. There was a desk against the far wall with a sleepy looking blonde woman behind it, filing her nails, and three seats set against the wall to her right. She counted three doors leading to separate rooms and a flight of stairs up to the next level.

"Can I help you?" asked the receptionist.

A plaque on the wall stated the businesses in the building; a legal associates, an agency of some kind, a mail delivery service, a photography studio, and a solicitors office.

"No, thank you," answered Hayley.

She headed to the door labelled London Mail, pushed it open without knocking and entered.

The room was surprisingly large but crammed full with envelopes, parcels and a desk. Filing cabinets were lined up against one wall but it would have been impossible to open the drawers. The window was almost blocked by the number of boxes precariously balanced on the sill and the only source of light came from the dingy overhead bulb.

A small, bespectacled man was hammering furiously at his keyboard, a frown etched into his forehead. He glanced up at her and then back at his computer screen without so much as a hesitation in his typing.

"What can I do for you?" he said.

"I'm Detective Inspector Hayley Irons and I'd like to have a little chat."

# Chapter 68

## DI HAYLEY IRONS

### LONDON MAIL, REGENT STREET

*Monday 10th August*

The small bespectacled man had enough courtesy to clear the mail from one of the hidden chairs in the room so Hayley could sit. Her presence didn't seem to make him nervous and she wondered whether the police visited often.

"What would you like to chat about, Detective Inspector?" he asked politely.

Hayley pulled a piece of paper from her pocket. "We have reason to believe that a parcel was delivered here between 28th and 29th of July. I am trying to find out who it belonged to."

"Ah, I see," he said. "And you want my full cooperation?"

"Of course," she said with a smile.

"You are aware that I can't really breach my client's confidentiality?" he said.

"Oh, I think you can," answered Hayley, not letting her smile waver. "You see, this individual has been leaving threats, has broken into someone's apartment, and may also be responsible for murder."

He shifted uncomfortably in his seat. "Let me see what the database can tell us," he said. "What were those dates?" She repeated them and he began typing, albeit much slower than when she'd first entered the room. He hit the enter button and waited to see what the computer would deliver.

"Would you like a drink?" he asked.

"No, thank you."

"There were forty-five items delivered in that bracket," he said, scrolling through the on-screen list. "Are you looking for a package, box, or envelope?" he asked, looking over at her.

"A package, probably brown paper or a jiffy bag. It would have come from..."

He nodded, clicked a few times on the screen, typed a little more and then hit enter. This time the results were quicker.

"Okay. I can't sort by sender, unfortunately, but we have fifteen items belonging to eleven clients that match that description."

"Can I please have a printed list of their names, addresses and payment details?"

The man looked up, shocked. "No, of course you can't."

"Mr...? Sorry I didn't quite catch your name."

"Johnson."

"Right. Well, Mr Johnson, I really don't want to have to come back with a warrant. There are lives on the line as we speak and the sooner I can put this criminal to bed, the sooner we can all go home and enjoy an evening with the family."

"I can give you their names and the part of the payment information, but that's it I'm afraid. Only for cross-checking, nothing identifiable."

Hayley weighed up whether it was worth getting a warrant. Time really was of the essence here.

"Fine," she relented.

He nodded, went back to the computer and moments later the sound of a printer had come to life. It was buried under some more packages in the corner of the room. She rummaged through the mail and collected the list.

"And do you have CCTV?"

She could see him struggle with this question. Torn between frustration and patience. "No," he said.

"Who has control of the cameras in the corridor?"

He looked startled and she felt a little pleased with herself, dealing a card he hadn't seen coming.

"The building, I believe," he said.

"And can you give me the details of who I can contact?" Jesus Christ, it was like pulling teeth.

"I don't think I have them. If you speak to Rhonda at the desk in the foyer, she may be able to help."

It was clearly time for her to leave.

"Okay, Mr Johnson. Thank you very much for your time." She leaned over the desk and offered her hand. He stood up, shook it and then abruptly sat down again. "I'll leave my card in case you want to get in touch." She placed a business card with her number on top of a precarious pile of envelopes on his desk.

Back in the foyer, the two uniforms were still blocking the stairwell and a disgruntled businessman was pacing around the room.

"Will you tell these blockheads to move out of my way?" he practically shouted at her.

"Have you got his details?" she asked one of the uniforms.

"Yes, ma'am."

"Okay, you can go. Sorry for the inconvenience," she said politely. He didn't even respond but stalked haughtily out of the building.

"Rhonda, is it?" asked Hayley as she approached the desk.

The blonde looked up from the nail she was now painting.

"Yeah. What do you want?" Her accent had a rough London edge to it which caught Hayley off guard.

"I'm told you have the contact details for the company who controls the building. Is that right?"

"I might do," she said, returning to painting her index finger a disgusting, luminous yellow.

"Well then, please may I have them?"

"Sure, I guess."

She delicately opened her top drawer to reveal a pile of business cards. Being careful not to smudge the polish, she picked one up and then dropped it on the counter.

"Thanks," said Hayley, deadbeat. Rhonda didn't notice.

# Chapter 69

## JASON HUNTER

### LONDON OFFICE

*Monday 10<sup>th</sup> August*

I looked down the to-do list on my notepad and wasn't feeling very encouraged:

- Check in with Liam

In fact, I didn't feel it was either productive or proactive. Frustration coursed through me and I had to fight the anger that came with it. My mind and body were already exhausted with the exertion and I didn't want to make it worse, yet I didn't want the helplessness to overwhelm me.

I decided adding 'Become Superman' was a little over the top and wouldn't help in my current predicament.

I opened Gemma's file and pulled out the photo of her. It seemed like an age ago that she died. When this all started. I hoped Adrianna and the kids were okay. I'd never forgive myself if they weren't.

*Right, Jason. This is the real deal. Get your shit together and work this out.*

I took a deep breath and hoped to God I could find the answers I needed.

"Lucy?" I called.

Her head popped round the door. "Yes?"

"I'm very busy, can you please hold all calls?"

"Sure thing."

My first port of call was Hayley; at least then I'd be up to date on everything we had.

She answered on the second ring.

"Is there anything new at your end?" I asked.

"Actually, yes." Hayley gave him a rundown of what had happened at Regent Street.

"So you've got a list of names?" I asked.

"Yes. Each name has gone through the database for a criminal record check but everyone's come up blank. It's clearly an alias. I've done some Facebook searches and verified a couple of them so far."

"Some people seriously underestimate the power of Facebook," I muttered.

"It gets better. I've managed to get hold of the company in charge of the building. They put me in touch with the security firm that handles their CCTV and they were able to send over some footage. I'm waiting for the rest of it as we speak but based on a cross reference between the footage and Facebook, we've been able to take some more names off the list."

"How many are you left with?"

"Six."

"Six? Bloody hell. That's more than I expected."

"I had eleven to start with. It's a lot better," said Hayley.

"What's the next step?"

"I've got copies of payment details and payment methods for each customer. That should whittle it down to, hopefully, one suspect."

"And there's no way this could go wrong?"

"Sure there is. They could've used a middleman in all three scenarios, or cloned someone's credit card, but at least we'll be a step closer."

"I don't know about you but I feel like we're wading through quicksand. Do you remember that game stuck-in-the-mud? Everyone used to play it at school," I said.

"Yes, but that's the problem with real life. It's not like the movies, it's not always that simple."

"I guess. Is there anything I can do to help?" I asked.

"Not for the moment," she said.

I ended the call and felt a little better. It was a small step forward but at least it was productive. Everything so far had felt like pushing against a brick wall. For the first time in what felt like forever, I could feel a spark of confidence grow inside me.

I suddenly had an idea, and, remembering what Hayley had said about surveillance, I logged onto my Mac and began checking who we had on the books that wasn't on a shift rota at the moment.

There were a lot of people in our system and quite a few ongoing contracts with clients which meant that most of our regular guys were taken. I turned to the more casual workers on the payroll and began making phone calls.

By the time 6 o'clock came, I had two-man teams watching Volkov, Keil and St Pierre around the clock.

# Chapter 70

## DIANE PARSONS

### HAMPSTEAD MANSION

*Monday 10<sup>th</sup> August*

The black Lincoln town car pulled up out front and Diane couldn't help but be impressed by the towering mansion surreptitiously tucked away.

Once the moment of awe passed, Diane suddenly felt sick. Her stomach had dropped when the car had pulled up outside her flat and the anxiety had been building inside her during the hour-long car ride.

The driver parked up, got out and came round to open her door.

The sudden exposure to the warm summer breeze made her flinch.

Cautiously climbing out of the car, she approached the mansion's imposing front door.

Before she could knock, the door swung open and she saw Volkov standing there with a tentative smile on his face.

"Dima," she breathed in relief and threw her arms around his neck.

"Alik's in his office," he said, gently pulling away.

"Sure," mumbled Diane, unnerved by his behaviour.

Volkov led the way through the ornate house and they entered a wood-panelled study lined with books.

Gromov sat behind an oversized desk and looked up when they entered.

"Ah, Ms Parsons. Welcome." He gestured towards the sofa pushed up against the far wall.

Not needing to be told, Diane went and sat down. She glanced around nervously, noticing two of Jason's officers stood in either corner. She swallowed hard and hoped her visit wouldn't filter its way back to him, and then to Stacey. She shivered at the thought of another grilling from Detective Irons.

Gromov waved his hand over his shoulder and the two bodyguards left, closing the study door behind them.

"I want to start by saying thank you," Gromov said with a serious nod.

Diane looked from Gromov to Volkov who still stood by the door. This was unexpected.

"For what?" she blurted out.

"Your help with those deposits."

"Oh," she said. "Of course." Not that she'd had much choice.

"I believe about 75% of the full amount has been deposited, am I right?"

Diane nodded but didn't say anything. She had a funny feeling she knew what was coming next.

"Excellent. I have the next one for you here." He opened a drawer in his desk and pulled out a thick envelope, thicker than the one Volkov had given her originally, and placed it on his desk. She tried to do the maths, to work out how much was in there. Her best guess was over £20K.

"Er, Mr Gromov, sir... I'm not sure I'm the best person to do this."

He paused with his hand halfway back to close the drawer and looked across the room at her. The amicable smile had suddenly disappeared.

Volkov shifted nervously but didn't intervene.

"And why not?" Gromov asked.

"Well, you see." She struggled to find the right words. "I don't really know what I'm doing and I don't want to get caught."

Gromov finished closing the drawer and didn't reply.

"Alik-" began Volkov, but he was silenced by a wave of Gromov's hand.

There was a long moment whilst Gromov studied Diane across the room and no-one spoke.

She shifted uncomfortably on the leather sofa that now clung to the sticky skin behind her knees.

"You are right," he finally said.

"Really?" asked Diane in disbelief.

"Of course. What do you know about these types of processes? But not to worry, I shall arrange a meeting with my accountant. He will be able to give you direction, and that way we can up the amounts."

"Alik-" Volkov tried again.

Whilst Diane said, "Mr Gromov-"

"Don't forget, young lady," said Gromov with a hand in the air to silence them both. "You have a debt to pay."

The room fell silent.

Gromov waved a hand toward the door. Volkov opened it and beckoned Diane to leave. She didn't need to be told twice, quickly scurrying from the room before she burst into tears.

# Chapter 71

## Jason Hunter

### London Office

*Tuesday 11th August*

"Morning Lucy," I said with a smile. She looked up from her desk, looked at the clock and then back to me with surprise.

"Did someone set your bed on fire?" she asked.

I laughed. "No. I thought I'd tackle the day head on."

"That's a first," she muttered.

"What?"

"Nothing," she said, smiling sweetly.

I slipped the key into the lock and opened my office door with a flourish. "Good. The usual please, and can you ask Liam to come in before he's due at Gromov's?" I disappeared inside, closing the door behind me.

The cheeriness disappeared almost instantly. I dropped my coat onto one of the spare chairs and dumped the files on the desk, closely followed by removing my tie and undoing my top button. When did it get so hot in here?

My house was starting to feel particularly empty now that Stacey had deemed herself safe enough to be back in her own apartment, and Sam was now by her side almost 24/7. The killer was still out there, but the lack of threats had lulled her into a false sense of security. I knew it was only a matter of time. This thing wasn't over. But she wouldn't listen to me.

Everything seemed to be under control, but there was a ball of dread in the pit of my stomach that made me feel sick. We still hadn't found Gemma's killer. We still didn't know who Stacey's stalker was. And a niggling voice in the back of my mind told me that Max and Lily still weren't safe.

I couldn't really remember what happened last night. My memory was fuzzy like the aftermath of a heavy night out, but the alcohol sat untouched in my fridge. I'm not sure I could believe that I just went to bed and fell asleep. However, today was the first day the weight on my shoulders seemed bearable. Strange.

There was a gentle tap on the door, followed by Lucy carefully trying to open it whilst carrying a tray.

She bustled over to my desk, carefully moved the strewn paperwork out of the way and put the tray down.

"What's all this?" I asked, eyeing the tray suspiciously.

"I will not be fooled by false cheeriness first thing in the morning, Jason. I know you far too well for all that," she said. I smiled. "There's a coffee to get you going. Some biscuits and a newspaper."

I raised an eyebrow.

"I always figure reading about other people's troubles makes me feel better," she said with a shrug. I gave a slow nod, and then she left.

I added another item to my to-do list: Give Lucy a pay rise.

I sipped the coffee and looked out over London. It was still early but British Summertime meant that the sun was already most of the way to its highest point and there was a gorgeous glow over London's architectural structures.

I decided to take Lucy's advice and pulled the newspaper closer. The front page gave an update on the situation in Ukraine where the reporter documented the ongoing crisis, protests, and how the unnecessary force being used had escalated.

The report included details of how many were now dead, alongside images of soldiers in Ukrainian cities and along the border. I flicked to page four where the full story continued. The journalist had even made some dangerous comments about Putin and alluded to the rumours that he ordered the hit on the presidential competition.

I was shocked. That was one way to put yourself in the firing line.

Feeling more depressed than before, I turned the page to read about some ridiculous World Bog Snorkelling Competition in Wales. I had to read the headline twice to really understand what was going on and then practically laughed out loud. Bog Snorkelling? World Championships? Surely this was a hoax. I did a quick Google search and found a whole host of articles on the championship outcome.

I went back to the newspaper where there were some other stories about the refugee crisis in Europe, the migrating wildebeest in Africa, and something about a double rainbow. It was amazing what some reporters classified as news. I was more baffled by the fact that the newspaper had published the story anyway.

I decided to jump ahead to the cartoon and puzzle pages, knowing that they'd at least take my mind off things for a little while. I finished my coffee, asked Lucy very nicely for a second and cracked on with the Sudoku.

There was a knock at the door when I was about halfway through. I'd been so absorbed in the numbers, I'd momentarily lost my bearings.

"Come in."

The door opened and Liam appeared.

"Hi, Liam," I said, noticing my coat still strewn across the visitor's chair. I hurriedly collected it and hung it up where it was supposed to be. "Take a seat." I indicated the chair I had just cleared and he came in without a word.

"Everything alright?" I asked. He nodded, still not speaking. He looked so young. "You're not in trouble or anything," I added. The relief on his face was instantaneous and I had to try hard not to chuckle.

"I thought I'd done something wrong," he said.

"No, no, no. I just wanted to catch up and see how you were doing?"

"Yeah, fine."

"Fine? That's all you can tell me?"

There was a pause as I sat back down, the chair creaking in the silence.

"I, er, I did actually want to talk to you about something," he said.

"Yes?"

"I like working for Mr Gromov. It's quite easy really and... and I haven't had to do anything I wouldn't want to do. It's just a lot of standing around really-"

"Liam, let me stop you there."

There was an innocence in his eyes and I wasn't sure it would last.

"Whatever you're about to tell me will have no impact on your placement. Anything you do tell me will be held in the strictest confidence," I said in what I hoped was a reassuring voice.

He nodded and then swallowed.

"Would you like a drink?" I asked. "A glass of water, cup of tea, cup of coffee?"

"A coffee would be great, thank you."

I buzzed through to Lucy and a couple of minutes later she appeared with his drink.

"Where were we?" I muttered, trying to pull my thoughts back on track. "You wanted to tell me something?"

Liam nodded, took a sip of coffee and then looked at me with determination, placing his coffee on the desk.

"So, whilst Mr Gromov's in his wheelchair, I'm having to do a lot of wheeling him around. That includes when he has guests over. Last week, I wheeled him into his study and his nephew was there. I only noticed because I hadn't seen him before and checked his details later. You know, how we're supposed to.

"Well, Gromov was agitated and keen to get rid of me straight away. He wasn't happy. I didn't linger and anything I did overhear was in Russian. But the nephew seems to be hanging around like a bad smell.

"I think something's going on," he finished.

Neither of us spoke for a few minutes. I was trying to process this and work out its significance. Gromov had been unusually cagey about what happened but then many clients had trust issues, especially when they felt threatened. But... This felt like there was something else going on. His connection to Volkov, Volkov's relationship with Diane, and Diane's connection to Stacey. It all felt like too much of a coincidence. And coincidences made me suspicious. There was something I didn't know about and something I was being employed to protect. Gromov had always been adamant about the house. He wanted it to be the main priority.

"Has anything else happened since the nephew arrived?"

Liam shook his head. "Mr Gromov is always very careful what he says around us and most of the time he speaks Russian anyway. His office is soundproofed, so he always goes in there when he doesn't want to be overheard."

I nodded. "Okay." I was thinking through every illegal activity I could think of and trying to see if any of them could be a possibility.

The answer was; I wasn't sure. Prostitution, drugs, money laundering, it could be anything.

My attention came back to Liam who was watching me.

"Thanks, Liam," I said. "I..." I trailed off. How much did I tell him? Did I tell him anything at all? Admitting there may be a serious problem would not only jeopardise Liam's position but make me liable for extracting information if it came to it. "I want to ensure that the entire household and all my staff remain safe. That includes you," I eventually said. He nodded. "So it would be wise to not mention this to anyone and if you hear or see any other suspicious activity, let me know."

He nodded again and stood up to leave. Just as he reached the door, he turned back to me. "Thanks, Mr Hunter."

I smiled and he left.

Something fishy was going on, and I needed to find out what.

# Chapter 72

## STACEY JAMES

### HOME

*Tuesday 11th August*

She was on the treadmill when the doorbell went. Stacey hopped off and headed to the front door, peering through the peephole before opening it.

"Am I early?" asked a breathless Diane, taking in Stacey's running outfit and the fine sheen of sweat on her forehead.

"No, you're fine. Come on in."

Diane walked into the apartment and headed towards the kitchen as Stacey closed the door and then followed.

"This place never fails to amaze me," she said and began helping herself to what she needed for a coffee. "Do you want one?" she asked over her shoulder.

"No thanks. I'll just have a water." Stacey opened the fridge and retrieved a fresh bottle. Excusing herself for two minutes, she walked back into her home gym, turned the machines and music off and threw a tattered hoodie over her workout clothes before reappearing as the kettle boiled. They seated themselves on either side of the kitchen island. Diane opened up the file she'd been carrying and spread the documents out over the surface.

"I've been trying to get you back in on a few of the events we cancelled," said Diane without looking up.

"Mmm-hmm," replied Stacey through a mouthful of water.

"Some stuff's been easy." Diane pulled out a large diary and opened it to the current date. "So you're definitely not racing on the 23rd?"

Stacey shook her head. "Although, things have been quiet recently and the triathlon went well, so maybe. But I need to speak to our Team Manager as I need his approval. It's not just me at risk, but Morrison too and he's at the top of the leaderboard. There's a lot more at stake for him."

"Okay, fine." Diane made a note in her diary. "I've got you back in that photo shoot at Glamour next month. There's an opening event in Soho next week and you've also received an invitation to be a sponsor for The Kennel Club."

"The Kennel Club?"

Diane looked up and nodded warily.

"Isn't that for dogs?"

"Uh-huh."

"Ok-ay," she said slowly, trying to digest this new piece of information. "Can you please explain that one to me?"

"Well," began Diane. She suddenly looked nervous. "I was thinking. If we have you as a brand ambassador for something cutesy – like dogs – it gives this cute and fluffy image about who you are as a person."

"Okay, great. But that's not who I am, is it? I don't want people to think I'm getting soft. The competition will eat me alive." She could feel the frustration rise, an emotion Diane seemed to bring out often.

"Well, that's the beauty of it. You can be a lion with a heart."

There was a moment's silence.

"A lion with a heart?" said Stacey. This was fucking ridiculous. Was she being serious?

Diane nodded slowly.

Stacey's mind jumped back to the conversation between Diane and Hayley. The conversation about working for her. Was she that much of a tyrant? "I guess we can give it a go," she shrugged, inwardly cringing at the thought.

"Oh, good." The relief that passed across Diane's face made her feel instantly guilty. "The Glamour shoot?"

"Yeah, fine."

"How about the event in Soho?"

"What's it for?"

"A charity event," said Diane, scanning back through her notes. "Great Ormond Street Hospital."

"Yeah, sure. That's fine," said Stacey, suddenly feeling drained.

Diane went quiet and looked at Stacey. She could sense that Diane wanted to say something, but was holding back. Was she really that much of a bitch? Her mind flicked back to their trip to Selfridges and Harrods only a week or so before.

She'd behaved like a dick, but why hadn't she realised it before?

The moment passed, and Diane was back to flicking through her notes.

"How about appearing on the Graham Norton Show?"

The doorbell rang.

"Sorry, let me get that," said Stacey, hopping up from the bar, relieved to be interrupted. She peered through the peephole and opened the door to Sam.

He handed her a Tesco carrier bag as he stepped into the apartment.

"Thanks so much," she said, peering into the bag.

"No problem." He caught sight of Diane in the kitchen. "I was only gone for two minutes."

"Sorry. I checked the peephole before opening the door," said Stacey.

"Even so," grumbled Sam.

Diane took a sip of her coffee and went back to her notes whilst Sam returned to the book he'd been reading before he'd left.

Stacey went over to the fridge and emptied the carrier bag of chocolatey goods, leaving a packet of biscuits on the side next to Diane.

Diane glanced at the biscuits but didn't reach for them.

Feeling the sudden and overwhelming need for caffeine, she moved towards the coffee maker.

"Coffee, Sam?" asked Stacey.

"Sure," he replied.

As Stacey busied herself with making them both coffee, Diane continued to go through the upcoming appearances.

"I've also given a list of the confirmed appearances over the next few weeks to Jason, so he knows what's going on."

"Okay." As her hands worked, her mind was elsewhere, assessing and reassessing who she was, who she'd become. Had she finally crossed the line into becoming a diva? Had the adrenaline-like fame from this season changed who she was?

"Diane-" she began, unsure how to continue.

"I've also got your fan mail," she replied, deliberately avoiding Stacey's gaze.

Stacey finished making the coffees, took one over to Sam and returned to the open plan kitchen.

"Anything interesting?"

"The usual." Diane handed over a bundle of what she considered to be worthwhile reads.

"Any hate mail?"

"Nothing of interest."

# Chapter 73

## JASON HUNTER

### LONDON OFFICE

*Tuesday 11ᵗʰ August*

"Jason?" said Lucy, popping her head around the door.

"Yes?" I said looking up.

"There's a call for you."

"Can you take a message?" I went back to the paperwork in front of me.

"He won't take no for an answer," she said.

Intrigued, I nodded. She left and patched the call through.

"I wanted to see how you were getting on," said the voice at the other end.

I sighed. I knew that voice.

"Nothing's changed," I said.

"That's disappointing. Stacey's safe, I hope?" replied Cooper.

"Of course, she is, what do you take me for?"

"Well, I only ask because of that fiasco at the triathlon."

"How do you-"

"Save your breath, Hunter."

I paused and took a moment to compose myself. This jackass was going to have me saying something I'd regret.

"Have you found the killer yet?"

"No," I replied through gritted teeth.

"The stalker?"

"No," I repeated.

"Look, I know you don't like me. Let's face it, I'm not your biggest fan. From what I can see, you're incompetent and you've got your own issues going on. You haven't done all that well in keeping Stacey safe, have you? But she likes you, so let's put this macho bullshit behind us and actually sort this shithole out, deal?"

As much as I hated to admit it, he was right.

"Sure."

"Good."

There was another pause and I knew he was waiting for me to divulge information. I wasn't holding out, or maybe I was, but I just didn't know where to start.

I gave him a rundown of everything that had happened since our meeting in McDonald's.

"You think we need to be worried about this Gromov character?"

"I'm not sure at the moment. It seems unrelated but the connection with Volkov makes me nervous."

"Agreed."

"I've got people watching Volkov around the clock-"

"That's gonna be expensive."

"Let me worry about that."

"Sure, you're the boss."

"Gromov's holding a party this week..."

"And you reckon there's gonna be some shady goings on?"

"Maybe, I don't know what to expect."

"Okay, well, how about I do some digging? I'm likely to find out more than your Google searches."

I ignored the dig, and thought his suggestion over.

Having Cooper on side would definitely be a bonus, and it may even be worth getting him on the rota for the evening, too.

But could I trust him?

What's the saying? Keep your friends close and your enemies closer.

"Hey, Cooper, I've had an idea."

"Yeah?"

"How do you fancy going on our payroll?" I smiled.

# Chapter 74

## JASON HUNTER

### HOME

*Tuesday 11th August*

I unlocked my front door and trudged through into the hallway.

I'd been worn down to the usual frustration and helplessness that I'd become accustomed to over the past few weeks. Nothing was simple anymore, and I still didn't know who had killed Gemma.

The idea that Stacey had a stalker made perfect sense; the threatening letters, the tampering with her car, the photos. But then why kill Gemma? Were they just trying to kill Stacey and were biding their time, or was Gemma the intended target?

I was concerned that if Stacey raced again, something big was going to happen. Whether it would be the killer or the stalker, there was no telling. How could I possibly fight that? Protect her from our half-guesses and suspicions. The simple answer was I couldn't.

I'd tried to get hold of the CCTV from Stacey's apartment building when the break-in occurred, but there seemed to have been an issue with the taping system.

Of course there was. Nothing was ever fucking simple.

But more importantly, what did this mean? Was this stalker trying to get in Stacey's head? Was he simply trying to freak her out? Was he trying to show her that she needed him? By scaring her enough that she'd walk right into his arms. That led to a whole new train of thought...

Was the stalker someone we already knew? Did he know she was with me that weekend? Did he methodically trash the apartment at his leisure because he knew she wouldn't be back any time soon?

I thought of the missing picture of Max and Lily on the wall and felt sick. Was he trying to get to me? Was I the stalker's target? Was he trying to make me feel vulnerable? If he was, my God, he was doing a good job. Or maybe he was trying to draw me away from Stacey so he would have a clear shot? Prove that he's ultimately better than me, better than any of us?

Or maybe he just wanted to show me that he was in control, that he knew who I was. If I can't protect myself, how can I protect Stacey? Was that his message?

I walked into the living room to see someone already sitting there, the flickering of the TV illuminating their face. I flicked the light switch on.

"Jesus Christ, Stacey," I said, letting out a breath.

She looked up at me sheepishly. "Sorry."

"What are you doing here?"

"I got lonely," she said with a cheeky grin. I bent down and gave her a kiss. I lingered there as she pressed her lips firmly against mine, both of us craving that physical contact. I pulled away and went to the kitchen to retrieve a beer.

"Hard day?" she called after me.

I sat down on the sofa and felt her snuggle up against me. "Where's Sam?"

"I sent him home," she shrugged nonchalantly.

"What?"

"Joking, joking," she said, holding her hands up in surrender. "He's outside. Man, you're wound up pretty tight."

I dragged a hand over my face, feeling the despair washing over me. When would it end?

"I think we have a big problem," I said.

She paused the TV and looked at me warily.

I told her about my conversation with Cooper, and my concerns about Gromov.

"Fuck, I'm not sure what to suggest," she finally said, looking back at the TV.

"I'm not looking for you to provide the solution," I said.

"I know. But I want to help. You have so much on your plate, I don't want to be a burden."

"It might be hard to believe, but this isn't about you, Stacey," I snapped.

She turned to look at me, a hard expression on her face. "Actually, Jason, I think you'll find this is. I hired you, remember?"

"Exactly, and correct me if I'm wrong, but that means I do your dirty work for you, right?"

"Are you for real?" she said, disbelief written across her face.

"I haven't got time for your shit, okay?"

"Gemma died because of me, Jason. Whether you like it or not, I'm in as deep as you are."

My shoulders sagged. Of course. This all started and ended with Stacey. But then a thought from earlier crept in; what if Gemma was the intended victim?

"I'm sorry," I sighed.

"You bet your damn ass you are," she said, not looking at me.

"It wasn't your fault, either."

She didn't reply but stared stubbornly at the TV.

"Gemma didn't die because of you," I said, reaching out a hand.

She waved it away, dismissing me and my comment.

"Rather than sitting here moping, shall we try to do something useful?" she asked after a long silence.

"What do you have in mind?"

"The usual."

The usual? I frowned. What the hell was she talking about?

She got up from the sofa and returned with a pen and a notepad.

"Where do we start?" I asked, as she handed them over to me.

"The beginning," she said. I nodded, wrote the number 1, followed by the words *Gemma's murder*.

# Chapter 75

## JASON HUNTER

### HOME

*Tuesday 11th August*

We lay curled up on the sofa, the notepad - long forgotten - sat on the coffee table. I'd finished my beer, had another and finished that too. The empty bottles had also been left on the coffee table.

We were watching some terrible late-night movie, something about a Frankenstein fish. It was safe to say I wouldn't be watching it again. Ever.

Tiny snores came from where Stacey lay with her head on my chest. Her hair had become tangled and was draped over her face. I carefully swept it out of the way. In the dim light of the television screen, she looked angelic and peaceful. I stroked the skin on her cheek and loved how soft it felt. She was so beautiful that for a moment I forgot all our other problems.

The film credits rolled onto the screen and I took that as my cue to go to bed.

It was hard trying to extricate myself from Stacey's grasp, to wriggle out from under her without disturbing her. Every time I moved, I was worried she'd wake. I finally shimmied myself onto the floor before getting up, flicking the TV off and draping a blanket over Stacey's sleeping form.

Upstairs, I undressed and slid between the sheets. There was a lot whirling around in my mind. A million and one things that needed to be done. Hayley was chasing CCTV footage, a team of my guys were watching Volkov, and I was sitting here twiddling my thumbs. I made a mental note to call Diane. I needed to talk to her about Stacey's public appearances. Now she didn't have a body double, it restricted things somewhat, and I wasn't comfortable with everything that had been pencilled in her diary. Sam had already been told to stick to her like glue...

Sam.

Fuck. He was probably still outside.

I picked up my phone and sent him a quick text to tell him to go home. He replied instantly. I hopped out of bed and peeked out the curtains just in time to see his black saloon pull away.

As I climbed back into bed, my thoughts turned to Adrianna and the kids. Ideally, I'd want someone keeping an eye on them too. Everything had been fine since they'd got back but it wasn't worth taking any chances.

I rolled onto my side and hoped sleep would come soon.

# Chapter 76

## JASON HUNTER

### HOME

*Wednesday 12<sup>th</sup> August*

"Morning," said Stacey, kissing me on the nose.

I opened my sleepy eyes and yawned. I hadn't slept very well, had spent most the night tossing and turning and now felt like shit.

Stacey was sitting on the edge of my bed, clearly having only just woken up, her tousled hair cascading down her back. I couldn't help but reach out and touch its softness.

I sat up and shuffled closer to her so I was sitting right behind her with a leg either side. I wrapped my arms around her warm body and held her close. She relaxed into my arms and we stayed there like that without speaking.

"Come on," she finally said, pulling away.

Once showered, dressed and ready for the day, I checked my phone. There was a text from Sam saying that he would drop by Adrianna's today and make sure they were all okay.

The bad feeling I'd had the day before persisted. I was on edge and it was already exhausting. My mind was turning over everything we knew so far, searching for the one thing we'd missed. A killer and a stalker. How did we find both?

"I've set up surveillance on Volkov," I said, as Stacey made herself a coffee in the kitchen.

"Okay."

"I'll be bugging his apartment today," I said, watching her reaction carefully.

"You will?"

"Well not me, one of my guys will."

"Okay," she shrugged, then said, "Is that even legal?"

"Er, not quite."

"Right."

Her reaction seemed strange. I'd expected an outburst or some form of disagreement, not nonchalance.

She didn't say anything else.

"Sam's outside."

She gave me a sharp look. "I don't like being babysat all the time."

"It's better than the alternative," I replied.

She mumbled something under breath as I kissed her on the cheek.

Just as I headed to the door, I remembered something.

"Gromov's invited us to a party this weekend," I said, turning back to Stacey.

She had migrated from the kitchen to the sofa with a fresh cup of coffee.

"Your client?" she asked, surprised.

"Yeah. And he specifically mentioned you."

"That's weird, isn't it?"

"A little. But I'm just saying you may need to find something expensive to wear."

"What are you getting at?" she said with a smirk.

"The guy owns a multimillion-pound mansion. His guests are going to be wealthy."

"Okay." She nodded. "I think I can throw something together." She was smiling. "Tell Sam he can come in for a coffee, and then we'll be going back to mine."

# Chapter 77

## JASON HUNTER

### LONDON OFFICE

*Wednesday 12th August*

"Lucy, have you put those files together?" I was already shrugging out of my coat as I walked past her desk.

"Good morning to you too," she said.

"Sorry, I'm in a rush."

She followed me into my office with an armful of folders.

"Perfect," I said as she set them down on my desk in two piles.

"These are the personnel files," she said, indicating the pile of multicoloured folders. "And these are your updates," she said, indicating the second pile of plain brown folders.

"You're a superstar, thank you. Gromov will be in at 11, can you please bring him a beverage of some kind?" I said as I sat down, pulling the brown folders closer.

"Sure, although I'm not sure I like how you've started treating me like a waitress."

I looked up from my desk. "I promise to make it up to you. Can I also ask you to find someone to check these names?" I handed her a printed version of the email Gromov's assistant had sent over that morning. It was a comprehensive list of all the guests he'd invited. "Just the usual. Find out what we can."

She nodded. "Anything else?"

"Not at the moment."

She left the office and closed the door behind her.

I pulled out my mobile and sent a text to one of my guys.

It vibrated moments later:

*Done. Up and running.*

Excellent.

I logged onto my computer and connected to the live bug that had been planted in Volkov's London apartment.

It wasn't as grand as I thought it would be, considering his connections to Gromov. In fact, it was quite modest. Sparse in comparison to Stacey's flat, and I didn't think hers was overdone.

There was a fifty-five-inch TV mounted on the wall to the right, a sofa to the left and a coffee table in between. The room wasn't overly large and there was a thick plush rug in the centre. A single piece of artwork was hung on each wall in an attempt to make the place look homely. I doubted that it was occupied on a regular basis and I wasn't convinced Volkov was the homely type.

I only had one camera and one listening device in the lounge area. It was all I really needed and could afford. If Adam found out what I was up to, he would definitely sack me on the spot. The connection to Gromov was too close, and ultimately the only thing that mattered; Gromov was a high paying client.

"Hi, Jason. Mr Gromov is here," came Lucy's voice on the intercom.

"Okay, great. Let him in."

I minimised the window to Volkov's life and went back to the folder of paperwork on my desk.

There was a knock at the door and I looked up to see Lucy enter, closely followed by Mr Gromov who was leaning heavily on a walking stick. He waved his hand and the bodyguard I'd met at the hospital stayed outside.

"Mr Gromov, can I get you a drink? Tea? Coffee? Perhaps something stronger?" asked Lucy in her sweet for-business-clients-only voice and flashed him a dazzling smile. He shrugged out of his coat and handed it to her.

"Yes, please. Coffee. Milk, two sugars."

"Of course." She hung his jacket on the coat stand and glanced in my direction.

"Coffee for me as well, please."

She nodded and then left.

Gromov settled himself in one of the seats opposite my desk. I shuffled the folders and put them in a pile to one side in an attempt to look professional.

"How are you? It's good to see you out of that wheelchair." I looked up to see his penetrating gaze hadn't wavered.

"Yes, I'm much better. Thank you."

I nodded, leaned back in my chair and feigned a casualness I didn't feel.

"Great." I gave him a smile. "Do you want to get straight to it or go through the details a little more?"

"Let's get right to it," he said.

"Sure." I reached for the multicoloured files and handed them over in one pile. "Take a look through these. Let me know who you would like at the event."

He nodded, pulled the files onto his lap and began looking through them. He opened the first one and I caught a glimpse of a white man with dark hair and heavy-lidded eyes. Gromov was already nodding his head and muttering under his breath in Russian.

Lucy reappeared carrying a tray of mugs, milk and sugar. I cleared a space on my desk and felt the fresh smell of coffee waft over me as she placed it down. I added the milk, mixed in the sugar and placed one of the mugs in front of Gromov.

Rather than sit patiently and wait for him to finish – there were a lot of files to go through – I decided he would feel less pressured if I left the room, just temporarily.

He was on the third file, looking at a picture of a blonde man with a beard in his late forties.

I locked my computer screen, picked up my mug and left the room. I headed over to Lucy's desk and settled myself in a spare chair.

"Did you lock your computer?" she asked without looking up from her keyboard. I was always amazed at how fast her fingers flew across the letters.

"Yes, of course." I glanced through the glass to where I could see him still hunched over the files.

"But I bet you left the confidential files on your desk, didn't you?"

"Fuck."

I dashed back into my office, desperately trying not to spill my drink at the same time. I must have been a little overly enthusiastic as I burst in because Gromov looked up from where he was sitting and shook his head before returning to the files.

I straightened up, cleared my throat and tried to act like everything was under control. I returned to my desk and sat back down, taking a long sip of my coffee. Logging back onto my computer, I saw the tab for Volkov's bug was still open; he was sitting on the sofa in front of the TV watching some reality show.

"These," said Gromov, catching my attention. I quickly minimised the screen and looked up to see he was handing me a small pile of folders. I reached out and took them, noting that the others had been left on the spare seat next to him.

I quickly flicked through the files. "And you just want them for the day? Do you want the standard residential team to stay on for the afterhours?"

"That is fine. I will dismiss the team around midnight."

"I'll put together a schedule to ensure they're rotated. Do you have any specific places in the house where you want extra surveillance?"

"I will be closing parts of the house to the guests," explained Gromov. "I want someone stationed at every entrance and exit from the house. I will need at least two of them positioned by the front door and I want them to be checking each guest in and out."

"Of course. Will you be using that gorgeous patio area?"

"Yes," he nodded, appreciating my flattery. "The pool and the patio balcony will be the main event. I would like to keep everyone outside as much as possible. My house is very expensive and some of my guests... some of my guests are liable to take from me." He paused. "If you understand."

"Completely," I said, nodding. "We'll ensure that entry to the house is restricted and contained within specific parameters. Any guests that enter will be checked against the entry list." I quickly wrote each point down on my notepad as I spoke. "Do you need us to be checking for weapons?" I asked and then looked up.

"You won't need to concern yourself with that. My men can handle such proceedings."

I didn't like his reply. It told me he was expecting his guests to be carrying. If that was something he was going to deal with on his own then so be it. It was going to be his problem. But that put me in a sticky position. Legally, no-one would be allowed to carry anything unless they were armed police and I highly doubted they would make it onto his precious list. Did I need to tell Hayley? The thought troubled me. Alternatively, I made a note on my pad to give the boys a heads up.

"If we're faced with a situation, how would you like my men to respond?"

Gromov looked thoughtful for a moment. "My children will be with the Nanny in a different part of the house. I will want at least two men with them throughout the evening."

I nodded.

"My son, Ruslan, is a very intelligent individual. He is privately tutored and a year ahead of children the same age. One day he will be admitted to Oxford or Cambridge." Gromov's chest puffed with pride and it was the first time I saw a genuine smile. I almost pitied the child.

"You must be very proud," I said.

Gromov nodded. "He is priority." I noticed the exclusion of his daughter in his instructions, but chose not to bring it up.

"What about you and your wife? Do you have a safe room or an escape route which will be accessible on the day?"

"Of course."

I asked questions and made notes for another hour, fine tuning every detail until I was satisfied. By the time Gromov left my office, I was exhausted and hungry.

A phone call from Hayley didn't cheer me up. She'd managed to track the card details used to pay for the photos but they were a hoax too, registered to someone who'd been threatened into making the purchase. So we were back to square one and I was gradually becoming more concerned that the stalker was backing away, covering his tracks and preparing his next move.

# Chapter 78

## DIANE PARSONS

### STACEY'S APARTMENT

*Wednesday 12th August*

"I think that just about does it," said Diane, gathering together her diary and her notes.

"You sure?" replied Stacey, not moving from her kitchen island.

"Yes, everything for the next six weeks."

"It doesn't seem like much."

"Well, we had to make those cancellations. So it's a little more difficult at short notice." Diane hesitated. "And a few more have voiced concerns about you being at their events."

"What?" asked Stacey, an incredulous look on her face. "What do you mean 'have voiced concerns'? What's there to be concerned about?"

Diane looked pointedly over Stacey's shoulder at Sam casually reading on the sofa. "I think they're more worried about the public threat," she said quietly.

"For fuck's sake!" said Stacey.

Diane saw Sam look up from his book and watch the two women for a moment before returning to the page.

"I'm sorry, Stacey. It's not my fault. I'm trying to persuade some of them, but I'm not having much success," pleaded Diane.

"Well, try harder," snapped Stacey. "This is my career on the line."

"It's just, you know, everything in the news has really scared a few of the sponsors."

There was silence.

Diane looked over Stacey's shoulder at Sam again and although he'd supposedly gone back to reading, his posture was tense and he hadn't turned a page in a while.

"Speaking of sponsors," said Stacey after a while. "I have something to ask you."

Diane placed her diary in her bag and nervously looked up at Stacey who was now staring at her, hard.

"Yes?" she said.

"I had a phone call from Jacob Wilkinson this morning."

"Oh yeah?" Diane said, acting casual as she carefully put away the rest of her papers. "Anything wrong?"

"I wouldn't use the word 'wrong'. He just wanted to check a couple of invoices with me. Some small businesses he hadn't heard of, that's all. You wouldn't happen to know anything about them?"

"I can certainly check the diary. Can he send them over to me and I'll take a look?" said Diane with a slow swallow.

"Sure." Stacey gave her a slow smile. "Be happy to." She got up from the kitchen island and walked through into the living room.

Diane gathered her things.

"I'll see you tomorrow," she said on her way out.

Stacey gave her a dismissive wave over her shoulders as she switched on the large flat screen mounted to the wall.

Letting herself out, Diane hurried down the corridor. She impatiently pressed the button for the elevator three or four times before deciding to take the stairs.

She flew down the never-ending flights until she burst out into the building's lobby and made a beeline for the exit.

"Miss!" came a shout behind. "Miss, you've dropped something."

Turning reluctantly, she saw a middle-aged man with a balding head hold up a sheet from her diary.

"Thank you," she smiled politely and took the sheet from him, hoping her face didn't look as forced as it felt.

Turning, she fled the building and once she was on the streets, dug her phone from her handbag and dialled Volkov.

"We've got a really big problem," she said.

Waving one arm frantically, whilst holding her phone to her ear with the other, she managed to flag down a taxi.

"I'm coming over now. Oh, Dima, what the fuck have we got ourselves into?"

# Chapter 79

## JASON HUNTER

### LONDON OFFICE

*Thursday 13<sup>th</sup> August*

I spent the next day organising everything for the party. I'd already phoned around and let the guys know who would and wouldn't be working that weekend. I gave them a brief rundown of the job and then arranged a meeting for that afternoon.

My next task was to put together the necessary documents detailing what would happen on the day and what Gromov had agreed with me.

I printed off a floorplan of Gromov's house - one that he'd given to us when we first took him on – and began to map out who would be posted along the perimeter and the entrances. The guests were only going to have access to three rooms at the rear of the property. A reception room, a drawing room and the kitchen. Everything else would be out of bounds. The children would be kept upstairs on the second floor in their rooms and it was just a case of keeping it that way.

I'd suggested removing the children from the environment completely to minimise the risk but he insisted that they stay and I had a sneaky suspicion he was planning on showcasing his wonderful son to all of his guests.

I found myself thinking about Lily and Max. Shit. They were supposed to be staying at mine on Saturday but Gromov was having his bloody party. I dropped my head into my hands. For fuck's sake.

I called Adrianna.

"How are you?"

"Tired," she said.

"Still not sleeping?"

"No. The kids seem fine though, which is good."

"That's what I called about."

"What?" she sighed. She sounded exhausted. I was worried she didn't seem like her usual self. If this carried on for much longer, we could be dealing with depression or other mental health issues and that's the last thing I wanted. I considered suggesting a counsellor but knew she wouldn't agree.

"One of my clients is throwing a party on Saturday. I don't want to go," I added quickly, in case she thought I was fobbing her off. "I won't be able to have the kids that night. He's a high paying client and I can't afford not to be there. Plus, I need to keep an eye on the guys."

"You don't need to explain yourself. I know how hard it is."

I didn't know what to say. In fact, I was speechless. I was talking to a completely different woman. This wasn't my bolshy ex-wife.

"Okay," I said cautiously. "Well, why don't I have them on Sunday night? They can stay over. I'll take them to school Monday."

"That's fine. You could have them Monday night too, if you like? Mickey wants to take me out to dinner so it would be doing me a favour."

"Of course," I said. "I'd love to. Bring them over about lunch time on Sunday then. It might be a late one on Saturday."

# Chapter 80

## Jason Hunter

London Office

*Thursday 13th August*

"The meeting is about to start," said Lucy. I looked up to see her head sticking out from behind the door.

"Okay, I'm coming. Have you got those photocopies?"

"Here." She placed a stack of neatly-stapled booklets on my desk.

"Perfect."

She disappeared. I opened the tab on my computer that peeked into Volkov's house for one last look. It had been empty all afternoon but I couldn't help looking in every five or ten minutes just to check. I glanced up to make sure the door was closed before turning on the sound, but it was silent.

I closed the screen and picked up my notepad, a pen and the stack of paperwork. I glanced around my desk, feeling naked; like I'd forgotten something. There was nothing that seemed out of place so I locked my computer screen and left for the boardroom. Eight guys were seated around the table; Gromov's chosen ones. It wasn't lost on me that he hadn't chosen any women. Image, I guess, was everything to him, and a female security officer wasn't good for his street cred.

"Sorry, fellas," I said, dropping my stuff at the head of the table.

I felt my mobile vibrate in my pocket, pulled it out and read a text from Hayley.

*Call me when you can. Gromov involved in some serious shit. Maybe trafficking. H.*

I looked up from my phone to see eight expectant faces and for a second I couldn't concentrate. Trafficking? What the hell? Trafficking what?

"Boss?"

I wasn't sure who had said it but it definitely grounded me. I pocketed my phone. "So." I cleared my throat. "You all know why you're here, right?" Nods around the table.

The door to the conference room opened again and I felt like we were doomed to never start.

The imposing figure of Cooper filled the doorway and threw me a lopsided grin.

"Sorry I'm late," he said, closing the door behind him and waltzing into the room. He sat in the only empty seat at the table whilst giving friendly nods to those around the table.

"Team, this is Bill Cooper, retired military. He'll be assisting with this assignment."

There were welcoming nods and murmurs around the table.

"Now that we're all here, I've put together a plan of the house and included your stations. The current residential team will stay at their posts and you guys will fill in the gaps and strengthen the vulnerabilities." Nods again.

I handed out the photocopies of my plan and let everyone spend a moment trying to find their own name. It didn't take long before the disapproving groans were heard.

"Oh, boss," said one of the older lads. "Babysitting? You've got to be kidding me!"

I gave him a smile. "Not kidding."

"Why have I been assigned the kids?" he persisted. "I'm no rookie."

"Exactly. Gromov has made it clear that the children are a priority."

"What about just removing the kids completely?"

"Don't even go there," I said, holding a hand up. "He won't budge." There was more grumbling. "Anyone else want to raise any concerns?"

A hand went up and I nodded towards Liam.

"Am I the only one to have been taken off the RST? I was assigned to Ms James originally, now this?"

"I know. Sorry about that. We've juggled your assignments a little bit. You're not scheduled to work Saturday and Gromov requested you specifically. It seems he's taken a shine to you. Stacey James will be attending the party as a guest so we have Sam in the house as a precaution." I nodded in Sam's direction towards the back of the room where he sat with his arms folded. He gave me a stiff nod.

Liam nodded, looking unconvinced.

"Any more questions?" Everyone exchanged glances and shook their heads. "Are we all clear on what's happening?" Nods round the table. "You need to be at the manor by 11am. Your shift will end around midnight but could be as late as 2am. The RST already in place have coordinated break times so it will be a case of slotting you in between. You'll get a full schedule by the end of the week. Just a word of warning... I've been made aware that Gromov's own personal team will be checking guests for firearms."

There was more murmuring around the table and I could see some of the younger ones looking uncomfortable.

"I know, I don't like it either. But it means you need to be alert at all times - even if you are only looking after the kids," I added. There were a few chuckles. "Any questions?"

They all shook their heads.

"Great. I need to go. If you do have any questions, you know where to find me." Nods round the table. Sometimes it was like talking to brainwashed monkeys.

I dashed out of the room and practically ran to my office, only to find my way blocked by the un-likeable Richard.

"Jason, I-"

"What is it, Richard? I'm kinda busy. Is it important? Can it wait?"

"I just wanted to ask-"

"Ask what, for Christ's sake?!" I was desperately trying to edge my way around him and reach for the door handle but he wouldn't budge. I looked pleadingly over to where Lucy watched my struggle but she just shrugged her shoulders, looking as helpless as I felt.

"There's no need to be rude, Jason."

I took a deep breath. "Richard, if you need to speak to me, schedule an appointment or send me an email. I need to phone the police as a matter of urgency regarding Gemma's murder. Are you happy now?"

His facial expression shifted ever so slightly but I'd said the magic words to make him move and he reluctantly stepped out of my way.

"Thank God," I muttered, stepping into my office and closing the door. I may have told a little white lie. *It wasn't entirely untrue*, I told myself as I dumped my notepad on my desk and pulled out my mobile.

I was surprised I didn't have Hayley's number on speed dial with the amount of times that I'd called her in recent weeks. I dialled and then waited as patiently as I could, anxious to hear what she had to say. Trafficking? That was a whole new ballpark and if it was true, things were going to start getting messy. It would explain why he'd been shot, and his reluctance to tell me what was going on. But what exactly did Hayley know and how would that affect me?

"Jason?"

"Yeah, it's me. What's happened?"

"I've had a request from the FSB to check on a name. Not Gromov, before you ask. They think they've uncovered plans to traffic weapons over the border into Ukraine. The name they gave me brought up nothing but your concern about the connection between Volkov and Gromov made me think. I did a search on him-"

"Hayley," I said. "I told you not to."

"I know what you said," she shot back. "But you can't dictate to the police, Jason. And I had sufficient reason for concern. I passed him over to the FSB as a potential to look into. I told them it might not bring anything but he has been involved in petty crime before."

"Ah, fuck. What have you done?"

"It was only when I was looking at Gromov on our database that I found out he's being financially investigated."

"Financially investigated? Why?"

"Something to do with incorrect tax declarations. Looks like the old boy's not been declaring all of his income."

"How does this have anything to do with weapons trafficking?"

"Well, technically it doesn't, but there's a lot of unexplained money in his accounts at the moment and I just have a gut feeling."

"A gut feeling isn't concrete evidence though, Hayley." I began to knead the bridge of my nose. We were heading towards a slippery slope and one I'm sure Adam wouldn't like.

"Yes, I know that," she snapped. "I don't need you to tell me how to do my job. Something just doesn't sit right."

"Like what?"

"This unexplained money. His links to petty crime in the past. He's been convicted for fraud and carrying a weapon already. He has no valid income yet he's sitting atop a multimillion pound mansion."

"What do you mean convicted?"

"I've done some digging. He has a criminal record alright and it looks like someone's been trying to hide it."

"How is that possible?"

"I don't know," she said. "I'm waiting for the FSB to come back to me and then we'll need a warrant to search the premises."

I ended the call and sat back, letting out a deep breath. Something didn't sit right with me either. I didn't like to believe in coincidences; the FSB were looking into weapons trafficking and then Hayley found Gromov was being investigated? Getting a warrant might take too long and Hayley definitely didn't have any grounds to go snooping around Gromov's house. But I was about to get unprecedented access.

# Chapter 81

## Jason Hunter

### Stacey's Apartment

*Thursday 13th August*

"Evening," I said as I entered the flat.

"Hey, boss," said Sam without glancing up from his book.

"Good day?" asked Stacey. There was a look of concern on her face which meant that I was definitely giving off the wrong vibe.

"Stressful," I admitted.

"Fancy joining me in a workout? I was just about to jump on the cross trainer."

I looked at her outfit; heeled boots, black tights, mini skirt and an open chequered shirt over a vest top.

"You don't look like it," I remarked.

"That's why I said 'just about to'," she said, pulling a face and closing the apartment door behind me.

"Well, really, the correct phrasing would be 'I was thinking about it'," I said. She pulled another face at me. "I don't have any of my gym gear," I said. The thought of getting on a treadmill and working up a sweat was marginally appealing.

"Overrated. I've seen you naked before. Just strip down to your boxers."

I glanced over to where Sam sat, hoping he wasn't paying attention. As much as I suspected our relationship was common knowledge, I didn't feel comfortable with him being privy to our private lives and making it official. We hadn't discussed that part yet.

Seeing the expression on my face, she raised her hands in surrender. Sam hadn't shown any indication he'd noticed but then, I'm sure he turned a blind eye to a number of clients he'd looked after over the years.

"Come on then," I muttered, desperate to get away before she said anything else.

I followed her down the hall. As we entered her home gym, the lights flicked on automatically and the air conditioning unit kicked in with a loud whirring sound. It wasn't a big gym but it was impressive. There was a running machine, a cross trainer, a rowing machine, and an exercise mat with a gym ball in the middle. A set of weights were neatly stacked on their stand and an iPod docking station was plugged into the wall.

"I was only joking about running in your boxers. I think I have some old kit around here somewhere."

"I'm not sure I'll fit-"

"It's for guys," she tutted. Opening one of those fancy hidden cupboards, she rummaged around on a shelf before pulling out an oversized boxing kit: silk shorts and a vest top. They were a perfect fit and Stacey eyed me approvingly as I straightened up. "Looking good, Mr Hunter," she said with a smile.

I flashed her the cheekiest smile I could muster and just hoped I wasn't wearing one of Cooper's old outfits. The thought made me uncomfortable.

"I'll be back in two minutes." She disappeared from the room.

I looked around myself for a moment, feeling slightly lost but then decided to just get on with it. I pressed play on the iPod and jumped onto the treadmill. I wasn't in the mood for a casual jog, so I cranked the speed up until I was running. It only took maybe a minute or two before my chest began to ache and my legs grew tired. But I pushed through it and found myself running along to the theme song from Footloose.

It was a strange song to have on your workout mix, but it had a good beat.

There were floor to ceiling mirrors on every wall and I watched my reflection as each step helped me feel more relaxed and in control.

Stacey reappeared, gave me a satisfactory nod and jumped onto the cross trainer. I felt the burn in my legs and pushed the speed up on the treadmill. I could slowly feel my energy being sapped but the hypnotic effect of the little man running around the athletics track on the screen in front of me kept my legs moving.

I was starting to feel exhausted; one last burst before I slowed it to a steady jog. I'd done nearly five miles running which wasn't too bad, considering. Ten minutes later I slowed the machine right down and hopped off.

"Please tell me you have a sauna," I asked.

Stacey laughed. "Not a private one but there is one on the floor above us. Give me five minutes."

I stretched out my muscles as Stacey increased the heaviness for her final leg-burner. I felt loose but knew that tomorrow would bring aches and pains. Not one for being rude, I decided to ask Sam if he wanted to join us.

I wandered out of the gym, down the hallway and into the living space where Sam still sat reading his book.

"Good book?"

"Yes, boss," he said without looking up.

"Reckon you could pull yourself away for a quick trip to the sauna?"

That got his attention. "Sure," he grinned.

"Good."

I turned to go back to the gym.

"Erm, boss?"

"Yes?" I stopped.

"Everything alright?" He was wearing a frown.

"Yes," I answered cautiously. "Why?"

"Just asking," he shrugged.

I know what he meant though, something wasn't right, whether it was here, at the office or doing the normal routine. It was like everywhere I turned, something was off. I felt like we were treading water and any second something was going to come and drag us under.

"I'm doing everything I can," I said, although my voice gave away my helplessness. Sam nodded and didn't say anything else.

Stacey appeared, her hands holding the towel she'd draped around her neck and her face flushed. Her chest was heaving up and down as she tried to regain her breath.

"Come on," I said. "Sam's gonna join us."

We headed up a floor and made our way into the sauna. It was empty, which was a relief. I honestly didn't feel like I could cope with any more human interaction.

"Feeling more relaxed?" asked Stacey as we settled ourselves in one of the rooms.

"Yes," I sighed. I closed my eyes and leaned back, letting myself forget about everything.

"And are you gonna tell me what's going on?" asked Stacey, jerking me back to reality. My eyes snapped open to see both her and Sam watching me closely. Fuck.

I leaned forwards and propped an elbow on each knee.

"I got a text from Hayley today about Gromov being a potential trafficker. I called her. She says there's a financial investigation into him at the moment but she thinks he's connected to an inquiry the FSB is conducting into weapons trafficking into the Ukraine."

"Shit."

"That's not good," said Sam. "What are you going to do?"

"There's nothing I can do. I can't terminate his contract. And I won't, not until there's concrete evidence. This is all a hunch, but she thinks that Volkov has been - or still is - involved. She's given his details to the FSB."

"Volkov?" asked Stacey, disbelieving.

I nodded.

"And guess where we're going on Saturday," I said with a grimace.

"Oh shit," said Stacey.

"It gets worse."

"How can it possibly get worse?" she asked.

"Great question," muttered Sam.

I was so focused on the fact that we had a serious problem that I hadn't noticed the room seemed suddenly too hot and I was struggling to breathe.

"Jason? Jason?" Stacey's voice penetrated the fuzzy haze that seemed to have descended around me. "Jason, are you okay?"

There was a firm hand on my arm, too strong to be Stacey's. Sam's perhaps? All I could see was a blurry outline and even then I wasn't too sure if that was my imagination playing tricks on me.

"It's proper hot in here," said one voice.

"Let's get him out of here," replied another. The words were far away. I don't know who said them, whether they acted on them or not but the next thing I knew, I was opening my eyes to a blinding white light.

"What the –"

"Don't move," grumbled Sam. He had one massive hand placed on my shoulder, keeping me firmly in place.

"Where-"

"Just shush." His voice was stern, like he was speaking to a child. I wanted to say something but I didn't really know what was happening.

"Is he awake?" Stacey's face came into view.

"Yeah, just."

"Good, let's get him back to mine."

Rough hands grabbed me and hoisted me from the floor. The world started to spin again and I tried to grab hold of something, anything, to try and steady myself.

I don't know whether I blacked out again or if I simply wasn't focusing on what was around me but the next thing I knew I was in Stacey's flat and I was shivering. There was a blanket wrapped around my shoulders. And I was sitting up.

"What the hell happened?" I finally mumbled.

"I don't know," said Stacey. "When did you last eat something?" she asked, her voice was quiet and close to me. I could feel the heat from her body and smell the scent of her skin. She pushed a glass of water into my hand and I couldn't drink it quickly enough.

"What's going on?" asked Stacey.

"What do you mean?" I asked.

"You were talking about Gromov and you said that things were going to get worse. How, Jason?"

The concern on her face was genuine and I half-smiled.

I felt like there was someone else in the room and looked behind me to see Sam, then remembered it was probably him who had carried me in.

"Thanks Sam," I croaked. He nodded but didn't look at me. He was frowning.

"Gromov?" said Stacey impatiently. I tried to think. To ignore the worried look on her face and to go back to what I was saying.

"We need to find some evidence," I finally said.

"Evidence? What evidence? Jason, what are you talking about?" From the corner of my eye, I saw Sam walk away.

"Saturday, at the party, I'm going to take a look around, see if there's anything in the house."

"You've got to be kidding me, right?" said Stacey. She sank back into the sofa, a look of disbelief on her face.

"No." I shook my head slowly, realising the difficulty of the task I was undergoing. It was one thing to sneak past my own guys, it was another to sneak past Gromov's, and although I had an indication as to how many there were, I a) didn't know how accurate that number was and b) didn't know where they'd be stationed. Gromov might not give them strict positions, instead allowing them to roam. On the other hand, he might have them on a strict patrol regime, one that I'm not privy to. If they caught me snooping, what possible explanation could I offer them? And I couldn't bear to think about the level of force they'd use. They wouldn't be restricted by the same rules as the rest of us.

"Erm, boss." I looked at Sam who'd returned. But he didn't look happy, at all.

"What?"

"I think we have bigger problems."

A knot quickly formed in my stomach and I felt sick.

"What do you mean?"

My mouth suddenly went dry and I knew I wasn't going to like what he was about to tell me.

"We've had a visitor."

# Chapter 82

## Jason Hunter

### Stacey's Apartment

*Thursday 13<sup>th</sup> August*

Sam couldn't quite put his finger on what, but something in the apartment had made him feel odd. Like someone had been in and moved stuff.

Turns out, they had.

He led me into the bedroom where the body of a dead cat lay on the bed, blood splattered everywhere.

I immediately turned and blocked Stacey's entry into the room. There was no way I was going to let her see this. The look on my face must have told her how bad it was and she immediately retreated to the living room.

Moments later I heard her opening and closing cupboards in the kitchen.

"Find the CCTV," I said to Sam. "Try and see if you can pinpoint when they entered the apartment. Start with when we re-entered the apartment and then work backwards. We don't know how long this has been here."

Sam nodded. "Do you want me to call DI Irons?"

The bad feeling in my gut intensified. I shook my head. Sam raised an eyebrow.

"Sam," I said. "What if this has something to do with Gromov?"

"What?"

I looked at him.

"How could it?" he asked.

"I don't know. We need to be careful. I don't want to antagonise whoever did this by telling the police."

"But boss-"

I held up a hand.

"We start thinking Gromov might be trafficking weapons and suddenly there's a dead cat in Stacey's apartment. That seems like an awfully big coincidence to me."

Sam didn't reply.

"It's not quite a horse's head, but I think I get the message," I pushed, wanting a response from him.

Sam frowned. "Boss, I definitely don't think it's Gromov. This is classic escalation."

"Maybe."

I took one more look at the cat and left the room, Sam following closely behind.

In the living room, Stacey was sitting on the sofa. Her face was pale and where I expected her to be cupping a warm mug of coffee, she was clutching a very large glass of wine.

"You okay?" I asked.

She nodded.

"What's he done this time?" she asked.

"He?"

"I'm assuming it's my stalker? The same person who trashed the apartment last time?"

"Possibly," I shrugged. The locks had been changed and the security systems upgraded, so I didn't see how he could have fooled us twice.

"Who do you think it is?" she asked sharply, suddenly looking at me.

"I don't know," I replied. "Whoever it was, they've left a message." She stared down into her wine.

"Sam's going to check the security cameras and see if he can find anything." I looked at Sam and he nodded before leaving. I sat gingerly at the other end of the sofa. Despite our previous intimacies, I felt like a gulf had opened up between us. "I need to take a look around Gromov's house."

"What?" Stacey's eyes flashed with anger. "Is that all you can think about right now?"

"I think the two are connected," I said. "This seems like a warning. We need to find out what's going on."

"Someone has broken into my apartment, again, and all you can think about is your precious client and whether he's mixed up in something dodgy? Do you actually know how to do your job, Jason? Remember what that is? You're supposed to be protecting me. And right now, you're doing a fucking shitty job of it."

"You're alive, aren't you?" I almost shouted back.

"But Gemma isn't, is she?"

I opened my mouth to reply and found that I couldn't.

Everything always came back to Gemma. And she was right.

Stacey's face softened. "I didn't mean that," she said.

"Yes, you did," I replied quietly.

She placed her wine glass on the table and shuffled closer to me.

"I'm sorry," she whispered, putting her arms around me.

I returned the embrace and pulled her close.

"It's okay," I said. "We'll see what Sam finds. We'll find out who did this. But I've still got protection to organise, and you have a party to go to."

She nodded slowly.

"And we should take a look round Gromov's house, if we get the chance."

Sam reappeared wearing the same frown as before.

"What?" I asked.

"The system's been down for two days. Engineers are due tomorrow to fix it."

"What? Why didn't anyone tell us?"

Sam shrugged. "The building's maintenance knew about it and seemed to think it didn't matter that much. Not sure who told them."

"We should tell Hayley," said Stacey.

"I wasn't going to," I admitted.

"Because of Gromov?"

I nodded. "But I think we should," I said.

Sam raised an eyebrow.

"If we're going to go snooping, we're gonna need someone on our side, and that means Hayley needs to know what's been happening."

Both Stacey and Sam nodded.

"We're going to have to be careful. If you cross him and Gromov turns out to be exactly who Hayley says he is, we're all dead," said Sam.

"If Hayley can't find the evidence she needs, she's going to need some less-than-legal help."

Stacey groaned. "Fuck. This could ruin my career," she grumbled.

"Mine too," I said.

"Not so publicly," she pointed out.

"True."

We sat in silence for a few moments, all lost in our own thoughts.

"I'm assuming you have contacts with the Russian guys?" Stacey asked Sam.

"Of course," shrugged Sam.

"Well then," she continued. "You'll be our eyes and ears."

# Chapter 83

## DIANE PARSONS

### VOLKOV'S APARTMENT

*Friday 14th August*

She tried to neaten the crumpled dress she wore before the door swung open, but the chaos roiling inside her was impossible to hide and the look on Dima's face told her he could see it.

"Diane? What the-"

She pushed past him into the apartment and frantically checked every room before collapsing onto the sofa, satisfied that they were alone.

Volkov followed her into the living room but didn't sit down next to her.

Diane tried to ignore the feeling of rejection as he stayed on the other side of the room.

"Diane," he said calmly, arms folded across his chest. "What are you doing?"

"I can't do this, Dima. I've tried, but I can't do it. I've done what I can with the money but I can't do any more. I don't care what Alik says."

Volkov didn't reply. He simply stared at her.

"Why are you really here?" His voice was cold and unfriendly.

"I..." she began but words failed her. "I really need your help," she said and then burst into tears.

Volkov sighed and then left the room. She heard him pad across the kitchen floor and then flick the kettle on before opening and closing cupboards.

The moment she was sure he wasn't going to return for a few minutes, she sprang into action. Guilt ate away at her for deceiving her friend, and she could tell the crying routine was wearing thin but she really was at her wit's end.

Diane rummaged through the drawers in the sideboard but found nothing. She dismissed the bookcase and quickly darted down the corridor as quietly as she could and entered his bedroom.

Her first target was the bedside table, but that came up empty too.

Then an idea struck her. Slipping her hand underneath Volkov's mattress, she felt around blindly until her hand closed around the cold, hard metal of his gun.

With a grim smile, she withdrew the weapon, ran back to the living room and hastily stuffed it into her handbag. Drastic situations called for drastic measures, and she needed to regain control. Not all of her outburst had been a lie; she really couldn't keep doing this.

Volkov reappeared carrying two mugs of tea. He placed one on the glass coffee table in front of her and then seated himself as far away from her as he could.

"When was the last time you slept?" he asked.

"Last night," Diane replied, too quickly.

Volkov raised an eyebrow.

"Well, it's true. I did sleep. Just not very well."

Volkov looked into his tea and nodded. "You need to deal with this better," he eventually said.

Diane didn't reply.

"I know it's hard. But you've done great so far. It's only been three days and when Alik says he'll do something, he'll do it. Once you've spoken to his accountant, it'll all be fine."

Diane nodded but didn't look at him. She needed to leave.

"And Stacey doesn't know anything. We've already been over that."

"I know," she replied quietly. "I guess I find it all overwhelming. You're the only one who seems to be able to calm me when I get into a state."

She looked across the room at him, but he avoided her eyes.

Her heart constricted at this gulf that seemed to have opened up between them.

"Don't worry," she said, suddenly getting to her feet. "I'll be fine." She grabbed her bag and moved toward the door. "Sorry to have bothered you."

Before Volkov could react, she'd made it through the door and out into the hallway.

A few minutes later she was walking swiftly down the street, desperately clutching her bag to her as she went.

# Chapter 84

## Jason Hunter

### Hampstead Mansion

*Saturday 15<sup>th</sup> August*

It was a day I'd been dreading.

I'd woken up with a sense of foreboding. Stacey had done her best to calm me down but no matter what I did, I couldn't shake my anxiety.

We stepped out of my BMW and I handed the keys over to a guy dressed in a terrible valet outfit. I smiled at him and he just scowled back.

A second valet opened my passenger door, and Stacey stepped out elegantly. I heard the scowling valet's intake of breath and grinned. She was wearing a tight-fitting, bright red dress and glossy black high heels. Her long blonde hair provided a stunning contrast. She walked around the car and took my arm, flashing me an irresistible smile. I couldn't help but kiss those bright red lips.

She pulled away and studied me for a moment.

"Shall we?" I asked, indicating the path in front of us, hoping to break the tension.

"Let's," she replied.

We were guided around the front of the house and through a charming archway decorated with climbing plants and flowers.

We emerged into the garden and Stacey gave a little gasp. There were flowers everywhere. Fairy lanterns hung in the air as if they were floating. Petals were scattered across the surface of the pool and soft jazz was coming from the open doors of the house.

It was early, about 3pm. It would be a while before the sun set and so Gromov's magnificent grounds were easy to see. The grass was a luscious green that stood in stark contrast to the clear blue sky.

"Wow," Stacey breathed.

"Stunning, right?"

She nodded.

"And just think, after a couple of championship wins, I could be in a place like this," she said, composing herself.

I raised an eyebrow.

"Okay, maybe not somewhere this extravagant, I prefer to preserve my fortune, but you have to admit that this place is cool."

"I admit it, but I wouldn't want to live here."

"Why not?"

I shrugged. "I guess I prefer cosy."

She nudged me in the ribs. "Who knew you were such a big softy, eh?"

"Plus, this would be a handful to manage. Think of the running costs."

Stacey let out a short high-pitched giggle. I looked at her with an expression of mock horror. She slapped her hand over her mouth and raised her eyebrows in surprise.

"I'm nervous," she said, slowly lowering her hand.

"And that turns you into a screaming ghoul?" I asked.

She nudged me again but this time it was more like a thump as she smiled sweetly at the waiter approaching. He handed us both a glass of champagne and Stacey sipped hers gracefully.

"Mmmm."

"Good?" I asked.

"Yes." She drained the glass and swapped it for a fresh one. The waiter looked surprised.

"Long day," I said and steered Stacey in another direction. We wandered the length of the patio at a leisurely pace, took in the views and watched as more guests arrived.

I caught sight of Liam in the same corner he'd been in when I'd visited for lunch. I nodded at him across the patio and he nodded back.

Sam had only spoken to the people he needed to, and considering Liam was out here, he wouldn't be much use to us.

"Mr Hunter." I turned towards the sound of the Russian voice and came face to face with Gromov's nephew.

"Ahh, Vanya. How are you?" I smiled.

"Very well, thank you," he said, shaking my hand. "And who is this lovely lady that you have with you?"

"This is Stacey James. Stacey, this is Vanya, Mr Gromov's nephew."

"Do you mean *the* Stacey James?" he asked with false enthusiasm and held out a hand.

"I'm not sure what you mean by that," said Stacey.

"Are you not the most famous Formula One racing driver this season? I'm a big fan of the sport," he said as he leaned forward and kissed her on one cheek.

"Are you?" She smiled graciously.

"What an honour," he said and then kissed her other cheek. "And how do you two know each other?"

Stacey glanced at me.

"Professionally. We've been working together for years," she laughed with a wave of her hand.

The lie rolled easily off her tongue but I wish it hadn't. Snooty nephew here would know it immediately and I saw the muscle underneath his left eye twitch as he straightened.

"What a delight. Being able to work with such a charming woman," he said, now directing his remarks towards me. He held an unnatural grimace in place.

"That's one way of putting it," I said with a laugh that even to my ears seemed false.

A waiter appeared at Vanya's side, muttering something in Russian.

"Ah, I must go," he said. "There seems to be a problem in the kitchen. But let's catch up later. I want to hear all about your racing." Piercing Stacey with a cold glaze, I felt her body shiver.

Vanya left.

"Jesus Christ, that man gives me the creeps," she muttered the moment he was out of earshot. "Shit, and I know I shouldn't have lied either. He's gonna know I've lied, isn't he?"

I squeezed her hand. "Well if he calls you out on it, just say it's been about six months but feels like years."

She nodded.

"Hey, relax," I said. She felt rigid next to me. "Just try and calm yourself. Everything's going to be fine."

"Mr Hunter!"

We turned to see Gromov's stocky outline emerging from the crowd that was gathered by the pool.

"How are you?"

I don't think I'd ever seen him this happy. His voice practically boomed across the patio.

"And look at this gorgeous young lady you've brought with you. Stacey, what a pleasure to finally meet you," he said.

"Yes, everyone seems to say that," she muttered.

He leaned forward and kissed her on both cheeks.

"Your boys have been a marvel so far. Very professional," he said, waving an arm towards the edge of the party.

I smiled. "I'm very glad to hear it."

"I wanted to introduce you both to Dima Volkov." He waved his hand in the air, beckoning. Volkov appeared out of nowhere, walking to his side. "I remember you asking about him the last time we met," continued Gromov. "I thought the best thing to do was introduce you two and then you can ask away!"

"Thank you. That was very considerate." I held out my hand and Volkov shook it. Gripping tighter, he pulled me forwards.

"I've heard a lot about you," he said with a smile before releasing my hand and straightening up.

"And, of course, you know Miss Stacey James," said Gromov, turning Volkov's attention to Stacey. "It looks like she's going to beat you this year, Dima, my son." Gromov laughed. "Unless you can get those championship points."

"Not if I can help it," said Stacey with a wink. Gromov roared with laughter.

"Oh my, what a charmer you are. You have a good one here, Mr Hunter."

I smiled and squeezed Stacey's hand.

"Please, call me Jason."

"Very well, Jason. I need to speak to some of my other guests. Make yourselves at home," he gestured around him. "Food will be served in about an hour or so." He disappeared to mingle with his other guests, leaving the three of us standing awkwardly.

It wasn't long before Stacey and Volkov began talking about cars. The conversation was like a foreign language and I soon lost interest, but I knew I couldn't leave her alone with him.

We were on the outskirts of the main gathering, close to the edge of the patio. I looked around for inspiration and saw my guys quietly stood half in shadow at regular intervals around the outdoor space. Who was I kidding? Nothing was going to happen here. There were too many people. If Volkov wanted to try something, it wouldn't be here.

# Chapter 85

## THE STALKER

### HAMPSTEAD MANSION

*Saturday 15th August*

She walked through the decorated archway into the backyard and simply took his breath away. He could feel the tiny hairs all over his body stand on end from just looking at her. She was wearing a bright red dress that clung to every curve of her seductive body and for a moment he allowed himself the indulgence of imagining how it would feel to take it off her.

The growing erection in his trousers quickly brought him back to reality and he blinked twice, desperately trying to dispel the image from his mind.

That fucking harlot ruled his life and he felt the overwhelming sense of being trapped wash over him. Whether at work or at home, she ruled his life and there was nothing he could do about it. She never even looked twice at him and that broke his heart every single day.

The sexual tension in his body quickly turned to anger and frustration. The erection disappeared and once again he was able to focus.

He watched Stacey move through the crowd on Jason's arm.

It had been a surprise to learn he was going to be here. The fucking boss lording it up over everyone else. Rubbing it in the face of his pitiful employees. It made him sick. And angry.

He was clearly fucking her. Why else would they arrive together? And that made him feel pity. Not for Jason, he could go rot in hell. But for himself. He pitied himself. How would he ever compare? She could never love someone like him when she had someone like Jason.

He watched the debonair smile and smug demeanour as Jason shook hands with Gromov.

He needed a plan. Something that would swing things in his favour.

The dead cat had been an act of desperation. And he hadn't had time to really achieve what he'd wanted. How was he to know they'd be back so soon?

The thrill of almost being caught didn't combat his disappointment at himself for being so reckless. He hung his head in shame.

Someone cleared their throat nearby and he looked up to see that fucker Cooper eyeing him like he was a piece of shit.

Did Jason really think he was stupid enough to not realise that this was Stacey's ex? What the fuck was he thinking bringing this guy along anyway?

He watched Stacey talk to Vanya, watched him kiss her on both cheeks and from this distance, he could see him inhale her perfume. His whole body ached to swap places with him. He wanted to be that close to her, to smell her scent, to casually put his hand on the small of her back and laugh without a care in the world.

He gritted his teeth as the two of them flirted outrageously.

Letting his hand brush against the barrel of the gun that was taped to his back, he smiled inwardly. Maybe he would get his moment this evening. His moment to really show Stacey what he was made of. To show her that he could be her hero.

Suddenly, he felt on edge and his body was electric.

This could be it.

But there was someone more important he needed to find. Someone he needed to keep an eye on. He watched as Vanya excused himself and left the group, following a waiter back inside the house.

The little fuckwit hadn't even noticed him. He had a score to settle with Vanya before he could do anything else. He owed him money. And he still hadn't paid.

And he needed to remind the Russian snake exactly who it was he was dealing with.

# Chapter 86

## JASON HUNTER

### HAMPSTEAD MANSION

*Saturday 15ᵗʰ August*

Looking around at the guests, I spotted a few Arabs huddled together in one corner near the house, all dressed in their finest robes and headscarves. I was itching to go and introduce myself. I'd made sure to bring business cards with me in case an opportunity arose and as we had numerous Arab businessmen as clients, I felt like this would be an easy win.

I was still trying to work out how to mingle without leaving Stacey alone with Volkov when my view was blocked by Aldric St Pierre. Tall, slim, and with a childlike face that was framed with day-old stubble, St Pierre casually held out a hand. The figure next to him was dressed in an expensive-looking suit; Armani would be my best guess, or perhaps Hugo Boss.

It took me a moment to realise it was Ottaker Keil. The stony-faced German had a square-shaped head and was considerably smaller than St Pierre. In fact, he was stockier, better built and looked like a bulldozer next to St Pierre's slight frame.

I shook St Pierre's hand and gave him a brief smile.

"I believe we've yet to formally meet, Mr Hunter, although I've heard so much about you. Aldric St Pierre," he said, throwing a smile in Stacey's direction who'd turned the moment she'd heard his voice.

"Aldric," she exclaimed with undisguised delight.

He released my hand and proceeded to kiss Stacey on both cheeks. "My dear," he said. "How have you been?"

Keil stood silently nearby and neither offered his hand nor introduced himself.

"What's been going on then? Have the police caught the person who tried to kill you?" Pierre asked, his voice laced with concern, although I couldn't tell if it was sincere.

"No, not yet," I said, jumping in. "The last time I spoke with them, they had a new lead," I lied.

"So you've been in contact with the police?" asked St Pierre with an almost French lilt to his words.

"Of course," I said. "I've been part of the consultation team throughout the entire investigation." That wasn't strictly true but the almost-lie had tumbled from my mouth before I could stop it. But St Pierre seemed to be won over and I immediately liked him. Keil, on the other hand, was less trusting.

"Why would they consult you?" he asked, but I ignored the intended jibe.

"Because I'm a protection specialist and know a professional hit when I see one." I regretted the words the instant they left my mouth. Both men were looking at me, dumbstruck. Keil's earlier composure seemed to have been replaced with a childlike fear.

"Professional hit? Are you sure?" asked Keil.

"Who would do such a thing?" asked St Pierre.

I shrugged.

"We don't know," added Stacey. "So we're assisting the police as much as we can."

I didn't like the turn this conversation had taken.

# Chapter 87

## Jason Hunter

### Hampstead Mansion

*Saturday 15th August*

I was trying to keep an eye on Gromov but it wasn't working.

Sam had slipped onto the patio and stood partially in the shadows. He gave me a brief nod.

I spotted Gromov across the pool. It was getting dark now. The sun had almost set, the soft jazz had taken on a more nightclub-style beat, and someone had lit floating candles on the water of the pool.

Stacey was still talking to St Pierre but Volkov and Keil had long left our little group to talk to someone more interesting.

"...but I told him it wasn't possible," said St Pierre.

"Well it's not," answered Stacey.

"So what do I do?" he asked.

"You've just got to be honest with him, I guess," she said with a shrug of the shoulders.

I slipped an arm around her waist and stood as physically close as I could without attracting glances. She turned to me with a smile and pecked me on the cheek.

We stood in companionable silence and watched the other guests mingle for a moment.

"Those floating lights are stunning," said Stacey.

St Pierre made an approving noise. "He has certainly made this place look beautiful."

"I never asked you, Aldric. How do you know Mr Gromov?"

"I met him through Dima. Dima decided to have a party. It was Mr Gromov here who provided it. I think he's gotten to know most of us drivers that way over the years. Of course, Stacey, you've never had the pleasure."

She shook her head and took a sip of her champagne. "It looks like I've been missing out."

"It's nice to do something different, really. That's the only reason why I come."

"Not a big fan of Volkov?" I asked, curious.

"Well it's not necessarily that, but he's quite an abrasive character. And these Russians-" he lowered his voice. "-they're not the sort of people I like to associate with, if I'm being completely honest."

I nodded. "I know what you mean."

We stood in silence again. I caught Sam's eye, he nodded towards the house. I saw Gromov walking in with his arm around the back of an impeccably dressed man. He was guiding him into the house and before I could do anything, they passed through the doors that marked the boundaries for guests. Shit. It was time to move.

"Stacey, can I borrow you for a minute?"

"Sure."

"Sorry, Aldric," I said with a smile.

St Pierre smiled back and held his hands up in surrender. "Not a problem."

I pulled Stacey away from the crowd, harder than I'd meant to. "Sorry. We need to be quick," I whispered.

She nodded.

We made our way over to Sam and hid in the shadows of the house.

"What's happening?" I asked.

"They're headed to the study, boss. Ground floor, at the back," said Sam. He didn't move, didn't look at me, and it was hard to tell whether he'd spoken at all or if it was a figment of my imagination.

"Well, we can't get in there," I said, frustrated. "There's only one way in and out. Plan B."

"Go into the house, turn right, into the drawing room. There's a door at the other end, leads into reception room three. Go through another door into reception room two. You need to go upstairs. The two children are in bedroom number two, adjacent to bedroom three. I've set up a listening device." He spoke quickly and in a low tone. I had to strain to hear him. I was thinking back to the floorplan I'd studied weeks ago, but it was a little fuzzy and I couldn't quite picture it correctly.

"Perfect. Cameras?"

Sam shook his head. "I couldn't."

"That's fine." I patted him on the shoulder.

"I'm going to go in and relieve the guy outside the kids' room. Wait a few minutes and then follow. Cooper is going to escort you, make it look less obvious."

I nodded. Sam left.

"Cooper?" said Stacey, surprised. "Don't tell me-"

"Hey beautiful." Cooper materialised from nowhere.

"What are you doing here?" hissed Stacey.

"Protecting you," he replied simply.

"I hired him. Temporarily," I added when Stacey shot me a look.

"I don't want to be rude, but this is a conversation for later," he said and glanced at the people nearby.

Stacey nodded and marched into the house.

"I can't believe you didn't tell her," chuckled Cooper.

I rolled my eyes and followed Stacey into the house.

In the open plan kitchen, Cooper guided us towards the door at the back of the room closed off to guests. There were waiters lined up against each side of the room, all of whom were watching us.

Cooper opened the door with purpose and indicated we should go through. "I'm just taking these guests to see the boss man," he said to the guy standing closest.

The waiter gave an almost imperceptible nod as we disappeared into the next part of the house.

I let out a breath when the door closed behind us.

We walked through one lavishly decorated reception room and then another before we emerged into the grand hallway.

We made it quickly to the top of the elegant centre staircase, passing another one of my guys on the way who gave us a quick hello.

I spotted Sam outside the second bedroom and he opened the door. "They're having a bath."

We walked in and I could just about hear giggles and the Russian dialect behind another sturdy-looking door. There was a splash, a squeal, and then a stern adult voice.

"Remind me why we're in this room?" asked Stacey, looking in the direction of the giggles uneasily.

I took a moment to look around. The room was imposing, daunting for a child. Traditional wallpaper covered each wall and an original-looking chandelier hung from the ceiling. There was only one bed, a four-poster with a plain white duvet neatly made. There were blue silk hangings pulled to one side. No toys on the floor, a chest of drawers that looked Italian with golden inlay and a matching wardrobe. Not a hint that this was a child's room except for the vintage wooden rocking horse in one corner that definitely looked like it had never been ridden.

I hazarded a guess that this was the son's room.

"We need a legitimate reason to be in the house. At least this way, we can pretend we're checking on Sam."

"Right."

"We also haven't got much time," said Cooper, stationing himself on the inside of the door we'd just come through.

I pulled out my phone and logged onto our audio system. I sat on the black chaise lounge in the corner, the leather squeaking slightly as I sat down. Stacey perched next to me and peered over my shoulder. I pulled out a pair of white headphones and plugged them in. Sam carefully pulled the door so it opened a crack, and stood sentry outside.

To anyone exploring this part of the house, it would look like an ordinary detail.

We each took an earphone.

The voices were faint but it didn't take long before we could determine what they were saying. Luckily they were speaking English, or we would have risked ourselves for nothing.

"We're ready to move when you are," said Gromov.

"Well. There seems to be a slight problem with that." The voice that replied was plain, but it held a hint of an accent I couldn't place.

It didn't sound like anyone I knew. And to my dismay, it didn't sound like any of the drivers either. In all honesty, if we were listening in on a weapons trafficking conversation, it was unlikely we would have crossed paths with whoever this mystery man was.

"What's happened?" asked Gromov.

"I've had sixteen men arrested on the border. They're trying to put a stop to our convoys. I need you to guarantee protection."

"Protection? You know I can't do that."

"It's not a case of what you can and can't do. If you want these weapons-"

There was a knock at the door and everything went quiet.

Suddenly Gromov was speaking in quick Russian and I worried that we'd been rumbled.

"Mr Williams, Mr Edwards, this is my nephew, Vanya."

My heart started pounding.

"Nice to meet you," replied the almost-British voice.

"A pleasure," replied another voice, and I felt myself go cold. "Unfortunately, until this matter is sorted, we're unable to proceed any further." I knew that voice.

I could feel Stacey looking at me. She was frowning. But I didn't know if she'd worked it out yet.

There was a soft tap on the door and I looked up to see Cooper springing into action.

"Dude, we've got to go."

I nodded, unplugged the headphones and stuffed my phone back into my pocket.

As we walked out of the room, we came face to face with a waiter carrying a silver tray laden with covered dishes.

"They're currently having a bath," I said.

He nodded but didn't reply and walked into the room.

"I'll escort you back downstairs," said Cooper, purely for the benefit of the waiter.

"I'll catch you later," I whispered to Sam.

He gave me a single nod.

# Chapter 88

## JASON HUNTER

### HAMPSTEAD MANSION

*Saturday 15<sup>th</sup> August*

We made it to the bottom of the stairs without incident.

A thousand thoughts were whirling through my mind. What we had just heard put everything into a new perspective.

Cooper held out an arm, stopping me in my tracks, and shoved me back a few steps. Stacey, only a foot or so away, was frowning. Cooper released me and the look on his face was concerning too.

"What's going on?" I whispered.

Both Cooper and Stacey were looking at something down the corridor towards the kitchen. I peered around and caught a glimpse of someone as they opened Gromov's office door. They stepped through, and swiftly closed it behind them without even knocking.

"Liam?" I asked.

"He's on the team, right?" asked Cooper.

I nodded. That feeling in my gut was back and I didn't like it. There was too much going on here that I didn't understand.

Cooper frowned. "What's he doing?"

I shrugged.

The person to ask would be Sam. He'd know what was going on, what Liam was up to. Unless something else was going on...

"We don't have time for this," whispered Stacey.

Cooper was already making his way over to the study door and carefully pressed his ear against it.

"You won't be able to hear anything," I said. "The study is sound-proofed."

"I could have sworn I heard..." he trailed off.

It only took a few seconds for us to be caught. I felt a hulking presence behind me and Stacey tugged on the sleeve of my jacket.

I turned around and came face to face with Gromov's favourite bodyguard from the hospital. He didn't look too pleased.

I nudged Cooper in the ribs. He turned to snap at me and caught sight of our problem.

"You wanna tell me what the fuck you're doing?" he rumbled.

"Er..."

The bodyguard grabbed me by the scruff of my neck, reached past Cooper for the door handle, pushed the door open and shoved me through. He grabbed hold of Cooper and Stacey, and shoved them in after me. I heard her squeal at being manhandled so roughly.

"Boss, these lot were eavesdropping outside."

It only took one look around the room for me to realise just how much shit we were in.

# Chapter 89

## JASON HUNTER

### HAMPSTEAD MANSION

*Saturday 15ᵗʰ August*

Whilst the room was decadent, with ornate wooden bookshelves lining the room from floor to ceiling, the scene that greeted me was far from what I expected.

Gromov sat behind his huge oak desk, a look of anger on his face.

His nephew, Vanya, was standing in the middle of the room and looking unsure of himself.

Sat on the leather sofa on the other side of the room were two dead bodies, each with a bullet hole in their forehead. One was a man I didn't know. I assumed he was the almost-British voice we'd overheard talking with Gromov.

The other was the owner of the voice I'd recognised; Adam, my boss.

Dominating the centre of the room, and holding the cold barrel of a gun at me, was Liam.

"What the fuck is going on?" said the bodyguard, once he'd recovered from the shock.

None of us spoke.

"Don't fucking move," said Liam through gritted teeth, the gun never once wavering from me.

"Look pal," the bodyguard replied. Holding his hands up, he attempted to step around me.

Before any of us could react, the thwump of muffled shot sounded in the room and the bodyguard dropped like a sack of potatoes next to me. I flinched. The silencer attached to the end of Liam's gun explained why we hadn't heard the shots before.

"How dare you!" roared Gromov. "How dare you disrespect me. You come into my home, threaten me and my guests, then murder my business partners and my staff." Gromov levered himself out of his chair, his fists shaking. "Ебаный Сволочь."

Liam turned the gun on Gromov and adjusted his grip.

The next thing I knew, Stacey was crying.

The sound must have startled Liam from whatever crazed state he'd descended into and he looked at Stacey for the first time.

"Hey," he said softly. "Hey, hey." He walked over and carefully titled her face towards his. "I won't hurt you."

The bolshy, strong-willed woman I knew had been reduced to whimpering tears. Her eyes darted to the two dead bodies on the sofa, then the dead body between us and the blood pooling around his head. A shiver slid down my back. I glanced over at Cooper and could see him desperately assessing the situation, trying to work out an escape route.

Surely, with so many of us here, we could simply overpower him.

"Don't even think about it, Hunter," spat Liam, waving the gun in my direction whilst still looking at Stacey. "Come here, darling." He reached out and took her hand. Then he turned to me. "I know what you're fucking thinking, you pathetic piece of shit."

"Alright, Liam. What the fuck is going on?"

His gun hand grabbed at his hair in frustration.

"I was trying to settle some fucking business, that's what's going on." He waved the gun towards Gromov who's eyes never once left the gun.

Vanya spoke for the first time. "I told you, you'd get your money."

"Yes, Vanya, I know," Liam said, spinning to face him, still holding firmly onto Stacey's hand. "But, you see, I got tired of waiting. You can slither and slide all you like, you snake, but I want my money. And the price has just gone up."

"Mr Perali, you will get your money," said Gromov, his eyes flashing with anger. He waved a hand towards the two dead bodies on the sofa. "But I needed to agree on business with Mr Edwards and Mr Williams in order to do so." He slammed a fist on his desk, making me jump.

The door behind me slammed open and we all spun around. If I thought this was already weird, the dishevelled Diane that burst through took this to a whole other level. And my heart sank at the sight of a gun in *her* hand. Unlike Liam, this one was shaking all over the place.

"Close the door," spat Liam.

Diane did as she was told. She wasn't sure who to point the gun at and so it waved from one person to another.

"Diane," I said, holding out a steady hand. "Put the gun down."

"Ms Parsons," said Gromov, surprising all of us. How did *Diane* know *Gromov*? "I think you should listen to Mr Hunter here," he said, gesturing in my direction. "You don't want to do something else you'll regret."

*Something else?* This was getting more bizarre by the second. What had Diane got herself into?

"Diane?" tried Stacey. I held out my other hand to hold her back from saying anything else.

There were now seven people and three dead bodies in the room and it was starting to feel claustrophobic. Which meant one thing; someone else was going to die.

"Diane," I tried again. "I know you don't want to hurt any of us. Whatever's going on, we can talk about it but I need you to put the gun down."

Diane looked at me. She looked tired. Exhausted actually, like she hadn't slept in a month. Her eyes were unfocused, and I wondered whether she was high.

"Nice try, Hunter," sneered Liam. "But it aint that easy." He marched confidently across the room and snatched the gun from Diane's hand, stuffing it into the back of his waistband. With Liam's back to the rest of the room, I saw Gromov subtly lean down and do something. Considering he was a potential arms dealer, I really hoped he had a gun tucked away somewhere.

I glanced at Cooper and he'd definitely seen Gromov's movement, too.

Liam turned and walked back towards the middle of the room.

"Move again, old man, and I'll shoot you."

"You can't talk-" started Vanya.

A second bullet sounded in the small room and Vanya screamed with pain. He instantly fell to the floor, gripping his leg.

"Consider that a warning," muttered Liam. "Right, where were we before we were so rudely interrupted?" He glared at Diane.

"What's going on?" asked Diane.

Before anyone could answer, Gromov stepped out from behind his desk, gun aimed at Liam.

Liam sighed. "Seriously?"

"I've warned you already Mr Perali. I will not tolerate this kind of disrespect in my house." Gromov pulled the trigger, but Liam moved too quick. He ducked to one side and covered the remaining few feet between them. The bullet meant for Liam shattered a pane of glass as it exited the room and suddenly we could hear the music playing at the party. It felt like a lifetime ago when we were on the patio enjoying the summer evening.

"Nice try," said Liam, as he swiped the gun from Gromov's hand, causing him to wince. "Now if you don't sit down." He pressed the barrel of his gun into Gromov's shoulder and forced him down onto his chair. "I'll be forced to take drastic action." He waved the other gun in the direction of the two dead bodies on the sofa. "I've already had to caution your nephew. And if he can't cough up the money he owes me, you're going to have to take his place. I really can't afford to shoot both of you. This is your last warning."

I could still hear the music from the party and was desperately trying to think of a way for us to pop this bubble. Cooper caught my eye again and gave an imperceptible nod toward the window. What was he planning? Was he going to barrel through it? Did he want me to? Surely if we could smash another pane, or make some kind of noise, we'd attract enough attention to spook Liam and get us out of this sordid mess.

"This psycho thinks he rules the world," said Stacey, gesturing toward Liam. She seemed more composed now. Her tears had smeared mascara down her face, but the Stacey I knew was back. "Don't you? The big I Am with a gun he's not afraid to point at anyone and everyone."

"Don't test me," said Liam through gritted teeth.

"Or what? You'll shoot me too? You think you can solve everything with a bullet?"

"Don't," he warned.

"Or. What?" she repeated.

Liam marched across the room, gun held high and came right at me. The barrel was pressed hard to my temple but I didn't give him the satisfaction of flinching.

Stacey went pale.

"Exactly," he said. "I don't know what you see in him, but I won't hesitate in dispatching him if you push me. I mean, I've tried so hard, so damn hard, to show you how much I care. But you just don't seem to get it, do you? You don't see it, do you?"

"See what?" asked Stacey.

I could see the frustration bubbling under the surface and I worried what Liam would do when he eventually snapped.

"Me, Stacey!" He shouted. "You don't see me. I mean Jesus fucking Christ, Stacey." His exasperation was boiling over. He kneaded the bridge of his nose, gun still in hand and then took a deep breath before grabbing her arm and tugging her closer.

She tried to struggle free but he only gripped her harder. Cooper lunged forwards in an attempt to rescue her but he was too slow. Liam saw it coming and another bullet sounded.

Cooper let out a cry and fell to the ground.

"No!" Stacey screamed.

Cooper was lying on the floor, blood pooling around him.

I instantly stripped my jacket, folded it up and held it against the wound on the right of his stomach.

"What the fuck is wrong with you?" screamed Stacey, turning from Cooper to spit the words at Liam.

"I said not to move," replied Liam calmly. "And you've had more than enough warnings."

"Just what the hell is going on?" I asked.

"Look," said Liam, back to carelessly waving the gun around, not even glancing at Cooper and Vanya on the floor. "These double-crossing Russians owe me money for a tip off. They've been promising me that money for weeks. I've come to collect."

"And they've said they'll give you the money."

Liam looked at me and a smile slowly spread across his face.

"Ah, Jason. There's so much I want to say to you, so much I want to ask you."

I didn't reply.

"Was she good?"

"What?"

"Was she good?" he repeated. "In bed?" He sneered at me and looked over at Stacey.

"I know it was you, Liam," I said as calmly as possible, suddenly slotting all the pieces into place. Why he was so annoyed at being taken off Stacey's detail, how he brought it up whenever I'd see him, how he'd always been close to hand when stuff had gone wrong; the car backfire, the photos. He'd been in Stacey's protection team that entire week, it would have been so easy to get the photos.

*Liam.*

I was still finding it hard to process. One of my own guys. Someone I had personally vetted to join the team. I mean, he was already on the team when this all started. Had that been part of the plan? Terrorise Stacey enough so that she would need protection. It seemed risky. Maybe he hadn't planned it that way. Maybe it was just an obsession that got out of control.

"What?" asked Liam, a small smirk playing across his face.

"You're not as clever as you think." It was so obvious now. Why hadn't I thought of it before? Why hadn't I considered an inside job? I knew each and every one of my guys, that's why. And I trusted them all.

*But still,* said a small voice in my head. I should have considered it as a possibility.

"What are you talking about?" asked Stacey warily.

"It was him," I said, turning to her. "Trashing your apartment, writing threatening letters, leaving messages. It was all him."

Stacey looked at me, speechless. She turned back to the man who had been protecting her, the man she had been trusting to keep her safe as part of her protection team and suddenly saw him in a whole new light. You could see it all play out on her face. How all of a sudden her world looked very different.

"Why?" she whispered.

"Come on, Stacey. You can't be that stupid, surely? I wanted you to *need* me, not him. Even your pathetic secretary here," he waved the gun in Diane's direction, "think she hates you enough to want to kill you."

# Chapter 90

## JASON HUNTER

### HAMPSTEAD MANSION

*Saturday 15<sup>th</sup> August*

We all turned and looked at Diane.

"How are you dealing with the guilt, Diane?" Liam asked.

"What's he talking about?" asked Stacey, suddenly sounding very unsure of herself.

Tears streamed down Diane's cheeks and she wrapped her arms around herself. "It was an accident," she whispered.

"What was?" I asked, unsure I actually wanted to know. There was so much more going on here than I realised. Between Gromov's shady deals and Liam's deranged takeover – where did Diane fit in?

Liam burst out laughing. The rest of the room stayed silent and Liam continued to laugh. He wiped at his eyes as he composed himself.

"Oh, it's a good one."

No-one moved. We all held our breath. Something was about to happen and there would be no going back.

Diane took a deep breath, but Liam beat her to the punch.

"She thinks she killed Gemma," and with that he burst into another fit of giggles.

*What?*

Diane looked shocked.

"What are you talking about?" said Gromov. He'd been suspiciously silent for a while.

"I know all about your little laundering scam, old man, and I know you've got this pathetic runt of a woman doing your dirty work. She didn't order the hit," he laughed. "How could she? She doesn't have a fucking clue! Do you think Dima would really get it that wrong? Of course not, the two of them are too loved up in their own little world."

My head was spinning and I was trying to keep up. Diane ordered a hit? The hit on Gemma?

Diane was staring at Liam, wide-eyed. There was a mixture of relief and pain flitting across her face. She didn't have a clue what was happening. All she cared about was that she'd just been absolved of guilt.

"Do you know how easy it is to swipe a phone in a busy night club?"

Gromov didn't answer. I watched as Liam inched closer towards the huge desk.

"I ordered the hit," he announced triumphantly. "And then gave your guy the tip off. I knew it wasn't Stacey on that podium. I didn't want it to be. I just needed to show her that she needed protection, that's all. And boy did it work." He laughed again. Diane collapsed into a heap on the floor and continued to cry.

I stared in shock. One of my own guys was responsible for Gemma's death. He'd known it wasn't Stacey. He'd never intended to kill Stacey. He'd wanted to kill Gemma.

"You fucker," I whispered.

The room was silent.

"You absolute fucker," I said, unable to voice my anger as it raged through my body.

I needed one of the guns, but getting to either of them was difficult. Liam was still holding his firmly in his right hand, pointing it at each of us in turn whenever he spoke. The other was still tucked into the back of his jeans.

From the layout of the room, Liam was too far away. He would see me coming and shoot me before I could react.

Stacey was still stemming the blood pumping from Cooper, who was now unconscious. Vanya was also lying on the floor, nursing his wound. I didn't know how long we'd been in this room, or whether someone had called for help. I had a whole team of guys on the outside and none of them had heard the gunshots. Wasn't it Liam who'd told me this room was soundproof? The irony wasn't lost on me.

Before I could think of an action plan, I saw Diane move out of the corner of my eye. Liam had his back to her, wanting to keep more of an eye on me and Stacey rather than the pathetically whimpering PA. But now that I looked at her, she seemed to have come to terms with what had happened, that it wasn't her fault. And she looked angry.

I used the distraction.

Diane covered the distance between her and Liam in a few seconds, head down and screaming as she went. She barrelled into him, knocking him to the floor.

I dived forwards at the same time, trying to use Liam's blindside to my advantage.

Yet another gunshot sounded and I held my breath. One of us had been hit, I just knew it. But it wasn't me. I looked at Stacey but she seemed fine.

"No!" shouted Stacey.

She was looking past me at Diane who was sprawled across the floor. For a moment I thought she was dead, but then she coughed and rolled onto her side. Blood spewed from her mouth. I couldn't see where she'd been hit but the wheezing sound she was making didn't sound promising.

My hand felt heavy and, looking down, I realised it was firmly gripping the gun from Liam's waistband.

Liam eyed me from the other side of the room.

I held the gun up, aiming at him.

I moved towards Diane and Liam carefully kept his distance, moving along the other side of the room.

I knelt down next to her and told her to keep pressure on her wound. Blood gurgled in her throat. The next moment, Stacey was at my side, pressing a wad of something to Diane's chest.

I looked back at Liam and something inside me snapped.

"What the fuck, Liam?"

He sneered in reply.

"You planning on shooting everyone? Shooting us one by one until we're dead?"

"What's it to you, Jason? I didn't realise you had a conscience."

He was still moving across the other side of the room. With each step he took, I mirrored. I was edging closer to Gromov and then I suddenly felt a wave of panic. He was after Stacey.

# Chapter 91

## JASON HUNTER

### HAMPSTEAD MANSION

*Saturday 15<sup>th</sup> August*

Liam lunged to his left and grabbed her by the arm. I pulled the trigger but he was too fast and the bullet embedded itself in the bookshelf behind him.

Before I could shoot again, Liam was shielding himself behind Stacey, holding her by the throat and pointing his gun at me.

"I wouldn't if I were you," he snarled and turned the gun on Stacey.

"You wouldn't kill her," I said. This whole thing had been about Stacey, he wasn't likely to give that up now.

"No, perhaps not. But I would enjoy hurting her." His grip on her throat tightened and she looked at me, her eyes wide.

I surrendered, taking my finger off the trigger and pointing the gun up to the ceiling.

"Alright, Liam, you win."

"You're damn fucking right I do."

He was edging towards the door. I could see what was going to happen. He wanted to make a run for it. And I was the only one still standing – Gromov didn't count.

I didn't dare move. Liam's gun was firmly trained on me again, and he'd already demonstrated how good a shot he was. I didn't want to test him again.

He was now only a few steps from the door.

Something made me think this wasn't going to go as smoothly as I hoped.

Stacey was strong and I could see her holding back. She didn't want to struggle until she knew it was safe. But I doubted she could overthrow him. Liam could easily be mistaken for skinny, but he was all lean muscle.

If he was making a run for it out the door, I might, just might, be able to get to Stacey in time. She was only five, maybe six, steps away at most. Could I cover that distance quickly enough?

Liam didn't wait another moment. He fired the gun and I moved. But the searing pain that cut through my side was unlike anything I'd ever felt and for a moment my vision blurred.

By the time I could see clearly, I was on the floor with my hand gripping my side. I pulled my hand away to see a bright smear of blood across it. It was stinging, burning like a bitch. I looked at the door to see it open and Liam was nowhere in sight.

As I got to my feet, Sam appeared.

"Boss-" He stopped dead in his tracks. "What the fuck?" He looked around at the dead bodies. "I'll call Hayley. And an ambulance," he added, looking at me and then Cooper.

"Cooper's still alive. So is Diane. Stem the bleeding," I wheezed.

In the commotion of Liam grabbing Stacey, I'd forgotten that both Cooper and Diane were essentially bleeding to death on the floor. But I considered myself lucky. The bullet intended for me had only grazed my ribs. I hoped they would both pull through, Cooper looked like he would but the grey pallor of Diane's face told me that it was unlikely.

I gingerly moved forwards, testing the pain now wracking my body and determining how much I could move.

I didn't have time for this. And the frustration fuelled me. I was fucking angry.

Once outside the study, it was clear the party was still in full swing out the back and no-one had heard any of the gun shots.

I knew Liam wouldn't have gone out that way; there were too many people and he had Stacey with him. But that meant he could only go out the front. Whilst he would have come to know the house well as part of his job, I doubted he wanted to run the risk of being caught here.

I clenched my teeth as the fire in my side intensified with every movement. I needed to hurry.

I ran through the entrance hall and stood at the bottom of the grand staircase trying to think. But my brain felt hazy and overcrowded. It was then I realised I could hear shouting.

The loud revving of a car engine followed by more shouts was coming from the front door.

I launched myself forward, moving as fast as I could, conscious there was blood seeping into my shirt and sticking it to my side.

I made it out the front to see two valets shouting down the driveway where a set of tail lights disappeared into the dark.

Fuck.

# Chapter 92

## JASON HUNTER

### HAMPSTEAD MANSION

*Saturday 15<sup>th</sup> August*

I didn't have time to think. I ran forwards, shouting for the valet to hand me some keys. The sight of me and the fast getaway of Liam, no doubt with Stacey kicking and screaming, had obviously jarred them into action. One valet threw a set of keys that I caught deftly in my left hand whilst the other was already opening the door on the bright yellow Ferrari that had yet to be parked.

I didn't know what Liam was driving, and I was unsure whether the power of the Ferrari would be enough to catch up.

It was at times like this that I loved modern technology. Without having to faff with turning the engine on, the car roared to life the moment I slipped inside. Throwing the key into the centre console, I put the car in gear and sped away from the house.

The long driveway leading up to the house meant I had time to catch up to the car in front and work out which way he was going to go.

Struggling to put my seatbelt on, I didn't want to let up on my speed. If I didn't get close enough by the end of the driveway, I would be left with two directions to choose from and a potluck guess on which one to take.

I floored the accelerator and felt the car lurch at the increase in power.

With both hands on the steering wheel, and adrenaline pounding in my ears, I tried to think ahead to where he was going. Where would he take her? But I couldn't concentrate.

By some miracle, two tiny lights appeared in the gloom and disappeared to the right. Bingo.

It was still several hundred feet before I'd reach the turning and Liam would know someone would be following, even if he didn't know it was me.

I made it to the end of the driveway and followed Liam right towards Highgate. There were street lamps on this road and I could quite clearly see a green Lamborghini racing ahead, doing a lot more than the 20 miles an hour speed limit. I didn't hesitate. If I was to be arrested, then so be it, as long as I got to Liam first. Better yet, if the police started chasing *us*, they might be able to stop him.

It was late so the roads were thankfully clear. Liam didn't hesitate in cutting a car up on the roundabout at Highgate High Street and the blare of a car horn was barely heard over the sound of our engines. I was slowly gaining on him, but it wasn't going to be enough. And then I realised where he was going.

I could do little more than keep up as we sped past The Whittington Hospital. He ran more than one red light in a desperate attempt to lose me and make it onto the A-road. But it wasn't enough and I kept pace with him the whole way. He was only fifty feet in front of me but I wasn't worried about catching up. Or overtaking.

I just needed to know where he was taking her.

And now we were heading out of London.

He was weaving in and out of the traffic and I was having to slow down in order to be more careful. I'd be no good at catching the fucker if I was dead.

Now we were on the North Circular which meant more lanes, and more traffic.

He was still skipping red lights and weaving dangerously. With every car he overtook, I worried he would clip the bumper. He was cutting in dangerously close and this was only going to end badly. How the fuck was I supposed to get to Stacey?

# Chapter 93

## STACEY JAMES

### THE NORTH CIRCULAR

*Saturday 15th August*

"Liam, will you fucking listen to me?" said Stacey, trying to get his attention. He was furiously weaving in and out of the traffic. She worried about his competence and knew she needed to take control.

"Will you just let me drive? I can go a hell of a lot faster – you know I can."

Liam ignored her.

Slowly, she reached down and unbuckled the straps of her heels.

"What are you doing?" he spat, momentarily distracted and turning his head to look at her. Taking his eyes off the road for even a second was dangerous the way he was driving. She ignored him, and focused on the road ahead, mentally mapping the nuances in the road's direction and the number of cars ahead.

Liam was still frantically trying to look at her. "What are you doing?" he yelled, waving the gun in her direction.

"Taking my damn shoes off, Liam. Chill the fuck out!"

Slipping her shoes off, she relaxed into the seat and glanced over at him. The car had a paddle-shift gearbox but it was clear he had no idea *how* to use it. The engine whined horribly, desperately wanting to shift up.

It was now or never. She wasn't going to let some psycho lunatic control what could be her last minutes on this earth, especially when he couldn't drive for shit.

She launched herself at the gun, using the element of surprise to swipe it from his hand.

"What are you doing?" he shouted at her, both hands gripping the wheel, his knuckles turning white. The Lamborghini swerved violently, throwing her into the passenger window.

She felt her head crack against the glass and winced at the pain.

"Fuck you," she said and reached across the central console for the wheel. "You're going to kill the both of us at this rate, you fucking psycho!"

A swift elbow to the face caused Liam to release his grip on the wheel and scream in pain as blood gushed from his nose. The sudden lack of resistance meant Stacey accidentally jerked the wheel, pulling the car across lanes.

She looked up and out the front of the Lamborghini to see a truck coming up, and fast.

Recovering momentarily from the shock of a broken nose, Liam slammed his hands onto the wheel and jerked the wheel to the left.

"What are you-?!"

Stacey was thrown back onto the passenger side of the supercar as it swerved to the left again, dodging the truck by mere centimetres before mounting the road's side barrier and launching itself into the air.

For a sickening moment, Stacey hung in the air, suspended in the silence.

# Chapter 94

## Jason Hunter

### Wembley

*Saturday 15<sup>th</sup> August*

I slammed on the brakes and yanked the handbrake. The Ferrari gripped hard on the tarmac and I could feel it pushing down into the road.

There was smoke everywhere and a burning wreckage of a Lamborghini only a few hundred feet away.

I climbed out of the Ferrari and was instantly reminded of the wound in my side. I gasped in pain. Someone approached me, an old man from one of the nearby stopped cars, but I waved him away. I needed to get to Stacey.

I could hear sirens in the distance and I hoped they would get here in time. Stacey was inside that mangled lump of garish green metal. And she needed help.

I stumbled forwards as people tried to hold me back.

"I need to get to the car!" I shouted, feeling almost hysterical. Why couldn't these people understand that?

I pushed my way through the fast-growing crowd and approached the passenger side.

I could see her, eyes closed, blood matting her beautiful blonde hair. The seductive red dress now looked gaudy and unnecessary.

She wasn't moving and I wasn't even sure if she was breathing.

I reached in through the smashed window. Thank God she'd been wearing a seatbelt.

That's when I realised I could hear a steady dripping sound. I looked about the car, under the engine and saw it: a petrol leak. Fuck.

I leaned back in through the window, this time frantic with the need to get her out. I fumbled for the seatbelt, trying to release it but it was jammed.

There was a moan from inside the car but it didn't come from Stacey.

Then there was movement.

The driver side door inched open, groaning as it did so.

The fucker was still alive. I watched as Liam slowly came to life, unbuckled his own seatbelt with ease and fell from the car.

I pulled myself out the car window and stood up straight. Liam was limping. There was blood all over his face and he seemed to be cut up badly. But it was his own fault. All this was his fault. Stacey. Cooper. Diane. Even Adam. And Gemma.

Gemma. The thought knocked the wind from me and suddenly I was filled with anger. Who the fuck did he think he was by playing God?

I hadn't taken my eyes off the limping figure struggling to move away from the car. There was quite a crowd but no-one approached him.

I went to move, to go around the car, to go after him, but then I heard another sound. One that brought hope and made my insides squirm. It was a low groan. And I looked down to see Stacey trying to move. She was coming to.

Looking across the A-road, I could still see Liam limping away, but something held me in place. And I was reminded of the dripping again. I looked down at Stacey and felt a pang in my chest. I couldn't leave her.

I took one last look at Liam, committing the murdering fucker to memory before once again reaching into the car for Stacey's seatbelt. I tugged it free.

The pain in my side was intensified by the awkward angle I was at and I doubted whether I'd be able to lift her out, never mind get clear of the car before something exploded.

Before I could do anything else, strong arms reached past me, and more hands gently moved me out of the way.

I looked up into the serious face of a fire officer. The cavalry had arrived.

# Chapter 95

## JASON HUNTER

### LONDON BRIDGE HOSPITAL

*Wednesday 26th August*

I walked into the room that eerily reminded me of when I'd visited Gromov and tried not to think about what had happened since.

Stacey was awake and she smiled when she saw me.

"Hey beautiful," I said and leaned down to kiss her forehead.

"Hey yourself," she replied.

It had been touch and go for a while, with the doctors not sure if she'd make it through. There had been a lot of damage, including broken bones and internal bleeding. But she seemed to be recovering fast.

"They're letting me out today."

I nodded. "I spoke to the doctor on my way in."

She didn't reply.

We'd done all of our talking already.

Obviously, I'd told her about what had happened, and she'd thanked me for saving her life, but there was still a gnawing sense of guilt that was eating me alive.

One of my own guys had killed Gemma.

That was never going to sit well.

Technically, he might not have pulled the trigger. But he was still responsible.

"Hey," said Stacey, reaching for my hand. I wasn't sure she knew how I was feeling but she was damn good at making me feel better. "It'll be fine."

I nodded, unconvinced.

The door opened and Hayley appeared.

She smiled. "Don't you look a million times better?" she said.

Stacey tried to laugh but I could see that it was painful.

"How are you doing?" she asked, turning to me.

"Me? Oh, fine." I gingerly touched the bandage on my side. It wasn't half as bad as it could have been, but it still hurt. I was told it would leave a scar, but Stacey assured me that scars were sexy.

Hayley didn't seem convinced by my answer.

"I thought I'd just drop by and give you an update."

"Have you found him?" I asked.

"No," she admitted. "But we have a good number of leads we're currently following up."

"Right," I said, feeling disappointed. If Liam got away, I had no idea what the repercussion of that would be and the thought scared me.

"We haven't got enough on Gromov to charge him. And before you say it," she added as I opened my mouth. "No, we can't use illegally obtained recordings."

I closed my mouth.

We'd already been down that road. Considering my fingerprints were all over gun number two, I'd spent the best part of a day explaining my story and trying to prove my innocence in all this.

I'd been let off with a warning and the potential of being charged with attempted GBH – turns out firing a gun to save someone's life is still illegal. But Hayley had reassured me it was unlikely to happen.

They had bigger things to worry about and the Crown Prosecution Service would likely dismiss it anyway.

Diane had been rushed to hospital and into emergency surgery thanks to Sam calling for help. She was still in intensive care and I knew Stacey felt guilty for a whole number of reasons. Dima Volkov had visited once but was trying to distance himself from the sordid mess as much as possible – he had a racing career to protect.

"What about Cooper?" asked Stacey anxiously. Cooper had also ended up in intensive care before being moved to an ordinary ward after two days. 24 hours later and he discharged himself. Since then, the guy had been impossible to find. A complete ghost. And I suspected he was trying very hard to keep it that way, but I knew we'd hear from him eventually. When things calmed down.

He wouldn't leave Stacey, that much I knew.

"Nothing," said Hayley. "I think he's long gone."

# Chapter 96

## Jason Hunter

### London Office

*Friday 9th October*

I switched on the TV in the corner of the room and flicked to the Formula One. The camera followed the drivers as they underwent their practice sessions and the commentator's voices discussed the current events.

*"It was announced officially this morning that Stacey James will be pulling out of this year's Championship. She's already taken leave of the last four races in order to recover after the crash in August – not on the track, I may add.*

*"And the decision has been made to withdraw from the team for the remaining five races, so we will not be seeing her on the track today."*

*"Yes, it's such a shame, David,"* replied the second commentator. *"But after all she's been through, it's important that she rests well and then tackles the new season next year."*

The Mercedes team had graciously told her to take time out. She was in no fit state to drive anyway, and it would take too long for her to get back into shape. Instead, they'd set up a rigorous training regime back home so she could come back in the New Year and tackle the Championship all over again.

I casually looked around the office, Adam's office, and made a mental list of what still needed to be done. Who knew taking over would be so hard?

*"Some are wondering whether James will be able to take on the pressures of the Championship next year and if it was this that caused the incident in August."*

*"I know what you mean, Eddie. The poor girl's been through a lot in the last few months and that can do a lot of damage to someone psychologically. I wouldn't be surprised if she doesn't come back at all-"*

I switched the TV off and turned back to my desk.

# Jason Hunter

## Hyde Park

*A year later*

There was a chilly breeze in the air. I zipped my coat up a little higher and admired the orange leaves littering the ground. The air was fresh and I was starting to lose the feeling in my nose.

"Daddy!" yelled Lily. I looked over to where Max was chasing her in between the playground obstacles. She was giggling and he was making some funny dinosaur noise. I waved and smiled. It was good to see them happy.

I thought back to the previous year. I thought of Gemma and the life she would never live. I thought of Diane and the dark path she'd taken because of someone else's dirty trick. I thought of Adam, hiding under our noses the whole time, profiting from the misery of others. And then I thought of Cooper, and wondered where he was.

Stacey looped her arm through mine and squeezed me. I looked at her and smiled. At least one good thing had come from all this. She'd come first in her last race and my chest swelled with pride even now. She was quickly climbing the leaderboard all over again, making it a season no-one would forget in a hurry.

She gave me a kiss and I felt her cold nose on my cheek. She giggled and I could just make out the corners of her smile underneath her furry hat.

"Daddy!" screamed Lily again. "Protect me," she squealed. The other kids were starting to stare. I laughed.

"I'll get the dinosaur," I said to Stacey.

"I'll rescue the damsel in distress," she replied.

We dashed forwards and within minutes had caught them both. I held Max in a bear hug he couldn't break and Stacey was spinning around with a squealing Lily in her arms.

I loved that. It was a memory that was going to stay with me forever. Stacey's blonde hair fanning out in the air, the perfect backdrop of autumn colours, and Lily's gorgeous, smiling face. They even looked like mother and daughter.

My phone rang in my pocket. I set Max down and fished it out.

"It's me," said Hayley, breathlessly. "Someone's broken into Adrianna's penthouse." There was a pause. "Jason, there's a dead body."

# About the Author

I'm a book-loving, writing enthusiast. I love to travel, drink tea and pet every animal I meet. When I'm not elbow-deep in the writing world, you can usually find me helping other authors through my editing services.

I live in Hampshire, UK with my husband and young son.

Instagram: @writernatashaorme
Website: https://writer.natashaorme.com/